Abbeychurch

Charlotte M. Yonge

Contents

ABBEYCHURCH

BY

Charlotte M. Yonge

'Never think yourself safe because you do your duty in ninety-nine points; it is the hundredth which is to be the ground of your self-denial, which must evidence, or rather instance and realize, your faith.'

Newman's Sermons

PREFACE.

Rechauffes are proverbially dangerous, but everyone runs into them sooner or later, and the world has done me the kindness so often to inquire after my first crude attempt, that after it has lain for many years 'out of print,' I have ventured to launch it once more--imperfections and all--though it is guilty of the error of pointing rather to a transient phase of difficulty than to a general principle. The wheels of this world go so quickly round, that I have lived to see that it would have been wiser in the clergyman to have directed rather than obstructed the so-called 'march of intellect.' I have lived also to be somewhat ashamed of the exuberant outpouring of historical allusions, which, however, were perfectly natural among the set of girls from whom my experience was taken: but these defects, as well as the more serious one of tyrannical aversion to vulgarity, are too inherent in this tale to be removed, and the real lesson intended to be conveyed, of obedience and sincerity, of course remains unchanged.

The later story was a rather hasty attempt to parody the modern sensation novel, as Northanger Abbey did the Radclyffe school, but it makes the mistake of having too real a mystery. However, such as they are, the two stories go forth in company, trusting that they may not prove too utterly wearisome to be brought forward this second time.

May 9th, 1872.

CHAPTER I.

One summer afternoon, Helen Woodbourne returned from her daily walk with her sisters, and immediately repaired to the school-room, in order to put the finishing touches to a drawing, with which she had been engaged during the greater part of the morning. She had not been long established there, before her sister Katherine came in, and, taking her favourite station, leaning against the window shutter so as to command a good view of the street, she began, 'Helen, do you know that the Consecration is to be on Thursday the twenty-eighth, instead of the Tuesday after?'

'I know Lizzie wished that it could be so,' said Helen, 'because the twenty-eighth is St. Augustine's day; but I thought that the Bishop had appointed Tuesday.'

'But Papa wrote to him, and he has altered the day as Papa wished; I heard Mamma and Mr. Somerville talking about it just now when I went into the drawing-room,' answered Katherine.

'Will everything be ready in time?' said Helen.

'Dear me!' cried Katherine, 'I wonder if it will. What is to be done if that tiresome Miss Dighten does not send home our dresses in time? We must go and hurry her to-morrow. And I must get Mamma to go to Baysmouth this week to get our ribbons. I looked over all Mr. Green's on Monday, and he has not one bit of pink satin ribbon wide enough, or fit to be seen.'

'Oh! but I meant the things in the church--the cushions and the carving on the Font,' said Helen.

'Oh dear! yes, the Font is very nearly done, we saw to-day, you know; and as to the cushions, Mrs. Webbe may have Sarah to help her, and then they will certainly be finished. I wonder whether there will be any fun!' said Katherine.

'Is a Consecration an occasion for fun?' asked Helen very gravely.

'Why, no, I do not exactly mean that,' replied Katherine, 'but there will be a great many people, and the Mertons staying here, and Rupert is always so full of fun.'

'Hm--m,' said Helen, 'I do not suppose he will be come back from Scotland.'

'And Mrs. Turner says,' continued Katherine, 'that of course as the Bishop is coming to luncheon after Church, Mamma must give an elegant dejeuner a la fourchette to everybody. Next time I go to St. Martin's Street, Mrs. Turner is going to give me a receipt for making blanc-manger with some cheap stuff which looks quite as well as isinglass. It is made on chemical principles, she says, for she heard it all explained at the Mechanics' Institute. And Aunt Anne will be sure to bring us some of their grand fruit from Merton Hall. What a set-out it will be! The old Vicarage will not know itself; how delightful it will be!'

'So you think the happiness of the Consecration day depends upon the party and the luncheon,' said Helen.

'No, no, of course I do not,' said Katherine; 'but we must think about that too, or we should not do what is proper.'

'Someone must,' said Helen, 'but it is happy for us that we are not called upon to do so yet.'

'Why, we must help Mamma,' said Katherine; 'I am sure that is our duty.'

'Certainly,' said Helen; 'but we need not dwell upon such thoughts for our own pleasure.'

'No, I do not, I am sure,' said Katherine; 'I do not care about the grand dejeuner, I am sure I think a great deal more about the Church and the Bishop--I wonder whether he will come by the railroad.'

At this moment, the door was thrown back hastily, and Elizabeth, the elder sister of Katherine and Helen, darted in, looking full of indignation, which she only wanted to pour forth, without much caring whether it was listened to with sympathy or not.

'So have you heard,' she began, 'these Hazlebys are coming. Did you ever hear of such a nuisance? Anything so preposterous? Mrs. Hazleby at a Consecration--I should as soon think of asking Gillespie Grumach.'

'It is for the Major's sake, of course,' said Helen; 'he will like to come.'

'Ay, but he is not coming, he cannot get leave,' said Elizabeth; 'if he was, I should not mind it so much, but it is only Mrs. Hazleby and the girls, for she has the grace to bring Lucy, on Mamma's special invitation. But only think of Mrs. Hazleby, scolding and snapping for ever; and Harriet, with her finery and folly and vulgarity. And that at a time which ought to be full of peace, and glorious feelings. Oh! they will spoil all the pleasure!'

'All?' said Helen.

'All that they can touch, all that depends upon sympathy,' said Elizabeth.

'Well, but I do not see--' said Katherine.

'No, no,' said Elizabeth, 'we all know that you will be happy enough, with your beloved Harriet. How frivolous and silly you will be, by the end of the first evening she has been here!'

'I am sure I think Harriet is very silly indeed,' said Katherine; 'I cannot bear her vulgar ways, bouncing about as she does, and such dress I never did see. Last time she was here, she had a great large artificial rose upon her bonnet; I wonder what Papa would say if he saw me in such a thing!'

'Pray keep the same opinion of her all the time she is here, Kate,' said Elizabeth; 'but I know you too well to trust you. I only know they will keep me in a perpetual state of irritation all the time, and I hope that will not quite spoil my mind for the Service.'

'How can you talk of Mamma's relations in that way, Lizzie?' said Helen.

'I do not care whose relations they are,' said Elizabeth; 'if people will be disagreeable, I must say so.'

'Mrs. Staunton used to say,' replied Helen, 'that people always ought to keep up their connexion with their relations, whether they like them or not. There were some very stupid people, relations of Mr. Staunton's, near Dykelands, whom Fanny and Jane could not endure, but she used to ask them to dinner very often, and always made a point--'

'Well, if I had any disagreeable relations,' said Elizabeth, 'I would make a point of cutting them. I do not see why relations have a right to be disagreeable.'

'I do not see how you could,' said Helen. 'For instance, would you prevent Mamma from ever seeing the Major, her own brother?'

'He cannot be half so well worth seeing since he chose to marry such a horrid wife,' said Elizabeth.

'Would you never see Horace again, if he did such a thing?' said Katherine; 'I am sure I would not give him up. Would you?'

'I could trust Horace, I think,' said Elizabeth; 'I will give him fair warning, and I give you and Helen warning, that if you marry odious people, I will have done with you.'

'When I was at Dykelands,' said Helen, 'everybody was talking about a man who had married--'

'Never mind Dykelands now, Helen,' said Elizabeth, 'and do put down your pencil. That drawing was tolerable before luncheon, but you have been making your tree more like Mr. Dillon's Sunday periwig, every minute since I have been here. And such a shadow! But do not stop to mend it. You will not do any good now, and here is some better work. Mamma wants us to help to finish the cushions. We must do something to earn the pleasure of having St. Austin's Church consecrated on St. Austin's day.'

'What, do you mean that I am to work on that hard velvet?' said Helen, who was a little mortified by the unsparing criticism on her drawing.

'Yes, I undertook that we three should make up the two cushions for the desk and eagle; Mrs. Webbe's hands are full of business already, but she has explained it all to me, and Kate will understand it better than I can.'

'I thought Sarah Webbe was to help,' said Helen.

'She is doing the carpet,' said Elizabeth. 'Oh! if you look so lamentable about it, Helen, we do not want your help. Dora will sew the seams very nicely, and enjoy the work too. I thought you might be glad to turn your handiwork to some account.'

'Really, Lizzie,' said Helen, 'I shall be very glad to be useful, if you want me. What shall I do?'

This was said in no gracious tone, and Elizabeth would not accept such an offer of assistance. 'No, no; never mind,' said she, putting a skein of crimson sewing-silk over Katherine's outstretched hands, and standing with her back to Helen, who took up her pencil again in silence, and made her black shadows much darker.

Elizabeth, who had not been of the walking party, and had thus heard of all the arrangements which had been made that afternoon, went on talking to Katherine. 'As soon as Church is over, the Bishop is coming to luncheon here, and then to settle some business with Papa; then is to be the school-children's feast--in the quadrangle, of course. Oh, how delightful that will be! And Mamma and I have been settling that we will have a little table for the smallest creatures, because the elder sisters get no time to eat if they are attending to them, and if the little ones are all together, everyone will come and help them.'

'The old women in the Alms-houses will,' said Katherine.

'Yes; and Dora will manage that nicely too, the table will not be too high for her to reach, and she will be very happy to be able to wait on her little class. And they are to have tea and cake, instead of dinner, for we do not want to have more cook-ing than can be helped, that people may not be prevented from going to church, and the children will be thirsty after being in church all the morning.'

'But we have a dinner-party, do not we?' said Katherine.

'Yes, but our youth and innocence will save us from being much plagued by it,' said Elizabeth.

'Oh! I thought you and Anne at least would dine with the company,' said Katherine.

'So Mamma thought,' said Elizabeth; 'but then she recollected that if we did, and not Harriet, Mrs. Hazleby would be mortally offended; and when we came to reckon, it appeared that there would be thirteen without us, and then Papa and I persuaded her, that it would be much less uncivil to leave out all the Misses, than to take one and leave the rest. You know Anne and I are both under seventeen yet, so that nobody will expect to see us.'

'Only thirteen people?' said Katherine; 'I thought the Bishop was to dine and sleep here.'

'Oh no, that was settled long ago; Papa found he had engaged to go to Marlowe Court,' said Elizabeth, 'and so there was room for the Hazlebys; I hoped he would have guarded us from them.'

'But will there be room?' said Katherine; 'I cannot fancy it.'

'Oh! half the rooms can be made Knight's Templar's horses and carry dou-ble,' said Elizabeth; 'Mrs. Hazleby and both the girls may very well be in the blue room.'

'And there is the best room for the Mertons, and Horace's for Rupert,' said

Katherine.

'Poor Horace! it is a shame that he, who laid the first stone, should not be at the Consecration,' said Elizabeth.

'Well, but where is Anne to be?' said Katherine; 'if we take Dora into our room, and Winifred goes to the nursery, there is their room; but Aunt Anne's maid must have that.'

'Anne shall come to my room--if Aunt Anne will let her, that is to say,' said Elizabeth; 'I wonder I never thought of that before, it will counteract some of the horrors of the Hazlebys. I shall have the comfort of talking things over with the only person who knows what to feel. Yes, I will go and speak to Mamma, and shew her that it is the only way of lodging the world conveniently. Oh, how happy we shall be!'

As soon as Elizabeth had finished winding her skein, she hastened to Mrs. Woodbourne, and found no great difficulty in gaining her consent to the plan; and she then sat down to write to Miss Merton to inform her of the change of day, and invite her to share her room.

Elizabeth Woodbourne and Anne Merton were first cousins, and nearly of the same age. They had spent much of their time together in their childhood, and their early attachment to each other, strengthening as they grew older, was now becoming something more than girlish affection. Anne was an only daughter; and Elizabeth, though the eldest of a large family, had not hitherto found any of her sisters able to enter into her feelings as fully as her cousin; and perhaps there was no one who had so just an appreciation of Elizabeth's character as Anne; who, though hers was of a very different order, had perhaps more influence over her mind than anyone excepting Mr. Woodbourne.

Sir Edward Merton was brother to Mr. Woodbourne's first wife, the mother of Elizabeth, Katherine, and Helen; he had been Mr. Woodbourne's principal assistant in the erection of the new church, and indeed had added all the decorations which the Vicar's limited means, aided by a subscription, could not achieve; and his wife and daughter had taken nearly as much interest in its progress as the ardent Elizabeth herself. Anne eagerly read Elizabeth's note to her mother, and waited her consent to the scheme which it proposed.

'Well, Mamma,' said Anne, 'can you consent to this arrangement, or are you afraid that Lizzie and I should chatter all night?'

'I hope you have outgrown your old habits of gossipping and idling,' said Lady Merton; 'I believe I may trust you; and it may be inconvenient to Mrs. Woodbourne to find room for you elsewhere.'

'I am very much obliged to you, Mamma,' said Anne, at first gravely, then laughing, 'I mean that I shall enjoy it very much. But pray, Mamma, do not trust too much to our age and experience, for I do not know anything more difficult than to stop short in a delightful talk, only just for the sake of going to sleep.'

'Yes, it requires some self-control,' said Lady Merton.

'Self-control!' repeated Anne. 'Mamma, I am sure that "Patient cautious self-control is wisdom's root," must be your motto, for you are sure to tell me of it on every occasion.'

'I hope you are not tired of it, Anne,' said Lady Merton, 'for most probably I shall often tell you of it again.'

'Oh yes, I hope you will,' said Anne; 'there will be more need of it than ever, in this visit to Abbeychurch.'

'Yes,' said Lady Merton, 'you live so quietly here, excepting when Rupert is at home, that you must take care that all the excitement and pleasure there does not make you wild.'

'Indeed I must,' said Anne; 'I cannot fancy enjoying anything much more than the Consecration of a church for which Papa has done so much, and going with Lizzie, and meeting Rupert. Really, Mamma, it is lucky there is that one drawback, to keep it from seeming too pleasant beforehand.'

'You mean the Hazelbys,' said her mother.

'Yes, Mamma,' replied Anne; 'I am rather surprised to hear that they are to be there. I should not think that a vulgar-minded Scotchwoman, such as Lizzie describes Mrs. Hazleby, would take much delight in a Consecration; but I suppose Uncle Woodbourne could not well avoid asking them on such an occasion, I believe she is rather touchy.'

'You must take care what you say to Lizzie about the Hazlebys,' said Lady Merton; 'a very little might make it appear that we wished to set her against her step-mother's relations.'

'Oh! that would never do,' said Anne, 'but I am afraid it will be very difficult to keep from shewing what we think, if Mrs. Hazleby is all that Lizzie says.'

'Your Papa was pleased with what he saw of Major Hazleby last year,' said Lady Merton.

'Oh yes, Lizzie likes him very much,' said Anne; 'it is the lady of whom she has such a horror.'

'I should fancy,' said Lady Merton, 'that Mrs. Woodbourne's horror of her was almost equal to Lizzie's.'

'Kind gentle Aunt Mildred,' said Anne, 'do you think she ever had a horror of anyone?'

'It is certainly rather a strong word,' said Lady Merton, 'but you will allow me to say that she has a great dread of her; I think Mrs. Hazleby scolds and frightens her.'

'What a fury she must be,' said Anne, laughing, 'to be able to scold and frighten such a gentle Desdomona as Mrs. Woodbourne.'

'Do not say too much on that subject,' said Lady Merton, 'or we shall be forced to call your beloved Lizzie a fury.'

'O Mamma!' cried Anne, 'you cannot say that she is impetuous and violent now. She used, I allow, to be rather overbearing to Mrs. Woodbourne; but that was before she was old enough fully to feel and love her gentleness. Then she did take advantage of it, and argue, and dispute, but now--'

'She has her own way without disputing,' said Lady Merton.

'O Mamma, do you think so?' said Anne, as if she thought it a terrible accusation. 'Yes, I really think that she has, but then her way is generally right.'

'Yes,' said Lady Merton, 'she is in some respects more fit to govern herself than most girls of sixteen. Her good sense will keep her from going very far wrong.'

'Very far, Mamma?' repeated Anne.

'Yes, for such an excitable impetuous creature is not likely to escape going wrong, without steady control from herself or from someone else,' said Lady Merton.

'But I can hardly imagine Lizzie's actually doing wrong,' said Anne; 'we were certainly both naughty children, but I think the worst we did, was rather what makes nurses scold, than what would seriously displease you or Papa.'

'Oh! she was always an upright, noble-spirited child,' said Lady Merton.

'And now,' continued Anne, 'when she is much interested in anything, when her brilliant dark eyes are lighted up, and her beautiful smile is on her lips, and her whole face is full of brightness, and she looks slight and airy enough to be a spirit, and when she is talking about some things--I could fancy her some higher kind of creature.'

Lady Merton smiled. 'I think I know what you mean,' said she; 'I used to feel something of the kind with her mother.'

'What a wonderful person Aunt Katherine must have been!' cried Anne. She paused, and presently added, 'Mamma, I do not know whether I ought to say so, but much as I like Mrs. Woodbourne, I do rather wonder that Uncle Woodbourne married again.'

'So did your Papa and I,' said Lady Merton; 'but you must excuse him, when you think of his three little girls, Elizabeth especially, requiring such anxious care of body and mind.'

'But you do not think Mrs. Woodbourne could manage Lizzie?' said Anne.

'No,' said Lady Merton, 'she could not manage her in the least, but her mild influence has, I think, been of great service to her. Lizzie has certainly grown more gentle of late, and I think it is from consideration for her and the little children.'

'And I suppose,' said Anne, 'that Mrs. Woodbourne has done as much for Kate as anyone could.'

'Not quite,' said Lady Merton; 'I think your Aunt Katherine would have made her a little less trifling and silly.'

'But no one could ever have made her like Lizzie,' said Aune.

'No, but I think she might have been rather more than a mere good-natured gossip,' said Lady Merton.

'It is curious to see how much difference expression makes in those two sisters,' said Anne; 'their features are so much alike, that strangers never know them apart; the only difference between them, that I could mention, is that Lizzie is the most delicate looking; yet how exceedingly unlike they are to each other!'

'Yes,' said Lady Merton; 'though Lizzie's whole countenance and air is almost exactly her mother's, yet there is nothing about Kate but her voice, which they have in common, that reminds me of her.'

'Helen is very unlike the others in everything,' said Anne.

'Helen will be the handsomest as far as regularity of features goes,' said Lady Merton.

'Do you think so?' said Anne.

'Certainly,' said Lady Merton; 'her features are less prominent, and her colour has not that fixed hectic look that both the others have, especially Lizzie.'

'But she wants brightness and animation,' said Anne, 'and she so often looks dismal and fretful, that I cannot fancy admiring her.'

'There has never been much sympathy between you and Helen,' said Lady Merton, smiling.

'No,' said Anne, 'I never felt as if I knew or liked her. I believe Rupert and I were very unkind to her in our younger days; but, oh! she was the most tiresome whining child I ever knew.'

'I believe that, though she was too young to know it,' said Lady Merton, 'poor little Helen suffered more from your aunt's death than either of her sisters.'

'How so, Mamma?' said Anne, looking rather alarmed.

'She was a very delicate baby, requiring a great deal of care,' said Lady Merton; 'indeed, we have always thought that your aunt laid the foundation of her illness, by sitting up with her while she was cutting her large teeth, and during your aunt's illness, it was painful to see how the poor child missed her. And after her mother died, though Helen had grown strong and healthy, old Margaret still made her the pet; and uncertain nursery treatment, without her mother's firm kindness, was not the best cure for such a temper as hers.'

'Yes,' said Anne, 'I remember she was always called Baby, and allowed to have her own way, till she was six years old, when Horace was born. How very ill-natured I must have been to her, and how cruel it really was of me. But I wonder my uncle did not prevent Margaret from spoiling her.'

'My dear, a man with a parish of fifteen hundred inhabitants, cannot watch his own nursery very minutely,' said Lady Merton; 'he taught Elizabeth admirably, and that was all that could be expected of him. Besides, with all his perfections, managing little girls is not what he is best fitted for.'

Anne laughed. 'No, he is too grave and cold; I am rather afraid of him still, I do not think he has any toleration for nonsense; but of course he must be different with his own children. And how do you think Mrs. Woodbourne trained Helen?'

'I can hardly tell,' said Lady Merton; 'I used to admire her patience and sweetness of temper, when Helen's fretfulness was most wearisome; at the same time that I thought it might have been better for the child to speak sharply to her, and punish her if she did not leave off whining directly. I believe I should have done so, though I do not know that it would have been the best way, or in accordance with what you call my motto.'

'Well,' said Anne, 'if Dykelands has done such wonders for Helen, as they say, I hope I shall make friends with her, if she will let me, which I do not think I deserve after my ill-usage of her. Last time I saw her, it was but for two days, and she was so odd, and grave, and shy, that I could not get on with her, besides that I wanted to make the most of my time with Lizzie.'

'I hope Rupert will not teaze her as he used to do,' said Lady Merton; 'last time she was here, his teazing and her whining were nearly unbearable.'

'Oh! she must have outgrown whining,' said Anne.

'I am afraid you cannot promise me that he has outgrown teazing,' said Lady Merton.

'The one depends upon the other,' said Anne; 'if she does not whine, he will not teaze. But had I not better finish my letter to him, and tell him he must shorten his stay on the Border?'

'Yes, do so,' said Lady Merton; 'and tell him not to lose his keys as usual.'

'I suppose they are gone by this time,' said Anne, as Lady Merton left the room, and she sat down to her desk to write to her brother.

CHAPTER II.

Abbeychurch St. Mary's was a respectable old town, situated at the foot of St. Austin's Hill, a large green mound of chalk, named from an establishment of Augustine Friars, whose monastery (now converted into alms-houses) and noble old church were the pride of the county. Abbeychurch had been a quiet dull place, scarcely more than a large village, until the days of railroads, when the sober inhabitants, and especially the Vicar and his family, were startled by the news that the line of the new Baysmouth railway was marked out so as to pass exactly through the centre of the court round which the alms-houses were built. Happily, however, the difficulty of gaining possession of the property required for this course, proved too great even for the railway company, and they changed the line, cutting their way through the opposite side of St. Austin's Hill, and spoiling three or four water-meadows by the river. Soon after the completion of this work, the town was further improved, by the erection of various rows of smart houses, which arose on the slope of the hill, once the airy and healthy play-place of the rising generation of Abbeychurch, and the best spot for flying kites in all the neighbourhood. London tradesmen were tempted to retire to 'the beautiful and venerable town of Abbeychurch;' the houses were quickly filled, one street after another was built, till the population of the town was more than doubled. A deficiency in church accommodation was soon felt, for the old church had before been but just sufficient for the inhabitants. Various proposals were made--to fill up the arches with galleries, and to choke the centre aisle with narrow pews; but all were equally distasteful to Mr. Woodbourne, who, placing some benches in the aisle for the temporary accommodation of his new parishioners, made every effort to raise funds to build and endow an additional church. He succeeded, as we have heard; and it was the tall white spire of the now Church of St. Austin's, which greeted Anne Merton's delighted eyes, as on the 27th of August, she, with her father and mother, came to the top of a long hill, about five miles from Abbeychurch. What that sight was to her, only those who have shared in the joys of church-building can know. She had many a time built the church in her fancy; she knew from drawing and description nearly every window, every buttress, every cornice; she had heard by letter of every step in the progress of the building; but now, that narrow white point, in the greyish green of the distance, shewed her, for the first time, what really was the work of her father--yes, of her father, for without him that spire would never have been there; with the best intentions, Mr. Woodbourne could not have accomplished more than a solid well-proportioned building, with capabilities of embellishment. It was not till they had nearly reached the town, that her thoughts turned to the pleasure of seeing her cousins, or even of meeting her brother, whom she expected to find at the Vicarage, on his return from Scotland, where he had been spending the last six weeks.

In this anticipation, however, she was disappointed; he was not among the group who stood in the hall, eager to greet the travellers, and no tidings had been heard of him. After talking over the chances of his arriving in the course of the evening, Sir Edward went with Mr. Woodbourne to see the new church, and the ladies were conducted to their apartments; Mrs. Woodbourne making apologies to Anne for lodging her with Elizabeth, and Anne laughingly declaring that she enjoyed Elizabeth's company much more than solitary grandeur. The two cousins were followed by the whole tribe of children, flaxen-haired and blue-eyed little sprites, the younger of whom capered round Anne in high glee, though with a little shyness, sometimes looking upon her as a stranger, sometimes recollecting former frolics, till Elizabeth declared that it was time to dress; and Dorothea, the eldest, a quiet and considerate little maiden of seven years old, carried off Winifred and Edward to their own domains in the nursery.

Elizabeth's room had been set to rights for the accommodation of the visitor, so that it suited most people's ideas of comfort better just then, than in its usual state. A number of books and papers had been cleared from the table, to leave it free for Anne's toilette apparatus, and a heap of school girls' frocks and tippets, which had originally been piled up on two chairs, but, daily increasing in number, had grown top-heavy, fallen down and encumbered the floor, had that morning been

given away, so that there was at least room to sit down. Elizabeth's desk and paint-
ing box were banished to the top of her chest-of-drawers, where her looking-glass
stood in a dark corner, being by no means interesting to her. Near the window
was her book-case, tolerably well supplied with works both English and foreign,
and its lower shelf containing a double row of brown-paper covered volumes, and
many-coloured and much soiled little books, belonging to the lending library. The
walls were hung with Elizabeth's own works, for the most part more useful than
ornamental. There were genealogical and chronological charts of Kings and Kaisars,
comparisons of historical characters, tables of Christian names and their deriva-
tions, botanical lists, maps, and drawings--all in such confusion, that once, when
Helen attempted to find the Pope contemporary with Edward the First, she asked
Elizabeth why she had written the Pope down as Leo Nonus Cardinal, on which she
was informed, with a sufficient quantity of laughter, that the word in question was
the name of a flower, Leonurus Cardiaca, looking like anything but what it was intended for in Elizabeth's writing, and that Pope Martin the Fourth was to be found
on the other side of the Kings of France and Spain, and the portrait of Charles the
First. The chimney-piece was generally used as a place of refuge for all small things
which were in danger of being thrown away if left loose on the table; but, often
forgotten in their asylum, had accumulated and formed a strange medley, which
its mistress jealously defended from all attacks of housemaids. In the middle stood
a plaster cast of the statue of the Maid of Orleans, a present from her little brother
Horace; above it hung a small Geneva watch, which had belonged to Elizabeth's
own mother; and there were besides a few treasures of Horace's, too tender to be
trusted in the nursery in his absence at school.

The window looked out upon the empty solitary street of the old town, and
though little was to be seen from it which could interest the two girls, yet after the
little ones were gone, they stood there talking for some minutes; Elizabeth inquiring after half the people about Merton Hall, a place which she knew almost as well
as her own home.

'When does Mrs. Hazleby come?' said Anne, beginning to dress.

'Oh! do not ask me,' said Elizabeth, 'I do not know, and hardly care; quite late,
I hope and trust.'

'But, Lizzie,' asked Anne, 'what have these unfortunate Hazlebys done to offend you?'

'Done!' answered Elizabeth, 'oh! a thousand things, all too small to be described, but together they amount to a considerable sum, I can tell you. There has been a natural antipathy, an instinctive dislike, between Mrs. Major Hazleby and me, ever since she paid her first visit here, and, seeing me listening to something she was saying to Mamma, she turned round upon me with that odious proverb, "Little pitchers have long ears."'

'Perhaps she meant it as a compliment,' said Anne; 'you know, Mary of Scotland says, that "Sovereigns ought to have long ears."'

'I suppose her son was of the same opinion,' said Elizabeth, 'when he built his famous lug. As to Mrs. Hazleby, she is never happy but when she is finding fault with someone. It will make you sick to hear her scolding and patronizing poor Mamma.'

'She has been in India, has she not?' said Anne, in order to avoid answering.

'Yes,' replied Elizabeth, 'she married the poor Major there, and the eldest son was born there. I often think I should like to ask old Mrs. Hazleby how she felt on her first meeting with her fair daughter-in-law. They were safe in Ireland when Papa married, and did not burst upon us in full perfection till Horace's christening, when the aforesaid little pitcher speech was made.'

'And her daughters?' said Anne, 'I never heard you mention them.'

'Lucy is a nice quiet girl, and a great ally of Helen's, unless she has cast her off for her new friends at Dykelands,' said Elizabeth; 'she is rather creep-mouse, but has no *other* fault that I know of. She is like her father's family, something like Mamma. But as for Harriet, the eldest, and her mother's darling, you will soon be sensible of some of her charms. I only hope she will not teaze the children into naughtiness, as she did last year. I do not know what would be done if Horace was at home. One day he had a regular battle with her. It began of course in fun on both sides, but he soon grew angry, and at last tore her frock and trod pretty hard on her foot. I could not be sorry for her, she deserved it so completely; but then poor Horace had to be punished. And another time, she shut Dora up in a dark room, and really it did the poor little girl a great deal of harm; she could not sleep quietly for three nights after. Dora is old enough to take care of herself now; and Edward is quieter than Horace, which is a great comfort; but, oh! I wish the Hazlebys were forty miles off!'

'Now, Lizzie,' said Anne, 'is it not a very strange thing to hear you talk in this manner?--you, the most good-natured person in the world!'

'Thank you,' said Elizabeth; 'that is as much as to say that I am the greatest goose in the world.'

'And you had rather be a goose than ill-natured,' said Anne.

'It does not follow that I should be a goose for want of ill-nature,' said Elizabeth.

'But you say that to be good-natured is to be a goose,' said Anne.

'Yes; but good-nature is too poor a thing to be the reverse of ill-nature,' said Elizabeth, 'it is only a negative quality.'

'I thought good-natured people were those who never used the negative,' said Anne, laughing.

'Do not pun in the middle of a serious argument, Miss Anne,' said Elizabeth, putting on a solemn face.

'Well, I will be quite as grave as the occasion requires,' said Anne. 'I believe I ought to have used the word kindness, as that is as active in good as ill-nature in evil. But pray, Lizzie, do not let us get into any of these abstruse metaphysical discussions, or we shall arrive at conclusions as wise as when we reasoned ourselves into saying, nine years ago, that it was better to be naughty than good, because good people in books were always stupid.'

'Idle as we were,' said Elizabeth, smiling, 'I do not think that we ever intended to act on that maxim. But really, Anne, I do believe that if you had been a prim pattern of perfection, a real good little girl, a true Miss Jenny Meek, who never put her foot in a puddle, never tore her frock, never spoke above her breath, and never laughed louder than a sucking dove, I should never have cared two straws for you.'

'I think little Dora might convince you that goodness and stupidity need not always be united,' said Anne, after a short pause.

'Demure Dolly, as Horace calls her,' said Elizabeth, 'yes, she is a very choice specimen; but, sweet little thing as she is, she would not be half so good a subject for a story as our high-spirited Horace and wild Winifred. Dora is like peaceful times in history--very pleasant to have to do with, but not so entertaining to read about.'

'Poor Dora, I thought she looked disconsolate as well as demure, without Horace,' said Anne.

'She has been very forlorn, poor child,' said Elizabeth; 'there was quite a beautiful chivalrous friendship between the brother and sister, he delighting in her gentleness, and she in his high daring spirit. Edward and Winifred are scarcely companions to her yet, so that she is forced to turn to us and be one of the elders.'

'You think Horace is happy at Sandleford,' said Anne; 'I should hope he would be; Rupert always looks back to his days there with a great deal of pleasure.'

'I hope Horace's teeth will not meet with the same disaster as Rupert's,' said Elizabeth, 'he has not quite so much beauty to spare; but he really is a very fine looking boy, and just the bold merry fellow to get on well at school, so that he is quite happy now that he has recovered the leaving home. But I am afraid my classical lore will die of his departure, for my newly acquired knowledge of Virgil and the Greek declensions will not be of use to Edward these three years. He is only just conquering "Lapis, lapidis."'

'But you can go on with Latin and Greek, alone, as you did with German, cannot you?' said Anne.

'I do sometimes construe a little Virgil,' said Elizabeth; 'but Horace is his natural contemporary, and he is not happy without him. Besides, when I have nothing to oblige me to learn regularly, I do not know when to do it, so Dido has been waiting an unconscionable time upon her funeral pile; for who could think of Jupiter and Venus in the midst of all our preparations for the Consecration?'

'I am glad Helen came home in time for it,' said Anne.

'I began to think we should never see her more,' said Elizabeth; 'there was no gentleman at Dykelands to escort her, and Papa was too busy to fetch her, till at last, Captain Atherley, Mrs. Staunton's brother, took pity upon her, or rather on us, and brought her home.'

'Captain Atherley is the only one of the family whom I have ever seen,' said Anne; 'I have always wished to know something more of them, they were all such friends of Papa's and Mamma's and Aunt Katherine's.'

'If you wish to hear anything of Mrs. Staunton and her daughters,' said Elizabeth, 'you have only to ask Helen; you will open the flood-gates of a stream, which has overwhelmed us all, ever since she came home.'

'Then I hope Helen likes them as well as they seem to like her,' said Anne; 'Mrs. Staunton spoke very highly of her in her letter to Mamma.'

'Oh yes,' said Elizabeth, 'they seem to have done nothing but sit with their mouths open, admiring her; and she really is very much improved, positively grown a reflective creature, and the most graceful as well as the prettiest of the family. She would be almost a beau ideal of a sister, if she had but a few more home feelings, or, as you say, if she did not like the Stauntons quite so much. I wonder what you will think of her. Now are you ready? Let us come down.'

When the two cousins came into the drawing-room, they found the rest of the ladies already there. Katherine and Helen Woodbourne were busy arranging a quantity of beautiful flowers, which had been brought from Merton Hall, to decorate the Vicarage on this occasion. Mrs. Woodbourne was sitting at her favourite little work-table, engaged, as usual, with her delicate Berlin embroidery. A few of the choicest of the flowers had been instantly chosen out for her, and were placed on her table in a slender coloured glass, which she held up to Elizabeth as she entered the room.

'Oh, how beautiful!' cried Elizabeth, advancing to the table, which was strewn with a profusion of flowers. 'What delightful heliotrope and geranium! Oh, Anne! how could you tear off such a branch of Cape jessamine? that must have been your handiwork, you ruthless one.'

'Anne has been more kind to us than to her greenhouse,' said Mrs. Woodbourne; 'I am afraid she has displeased Mr. Jenkins; but I hope the plants are not seriously damaged.'

'Oh no, indeed,' said Anne, 'you should see the plants before you pity them, Aunt Mildred; we never let Mr. Jenkins scold us for helping ourselves or our friends out of our own garden, for making a great glorious nosegay is a pleasure which I do not know how to forego.'

'Do you call this a nosegay?' said Elizabeth, 'I call it a forest of flowers. Really, a Consecration opens people's hearts;--I do not mean that yours is not open enough on ordinary occasions, Aunt Anne; but when the children took their walk in the alms-house court this morning, they were loaded with flowers from all quarters, beginning with old Mr. Dillon offering Winifred his best variegated dahlia, by name Dod's Mary.'

'Mr. Dillon!' exclaimed Katherine; 'I thought he never gave away his flowers on any account.'

'I know,' said Elizabeth; 'but I have also heard him say that he could not refuse little Miss Winifred if she asked him for the very house over his head.'

'Did she ask him for the dahlia?' said Mrs. Woodbourne.

'No,' said Elizabeth, 'it was a free offer on his part. Dora the discreet tried to make her refuse it, but the dahlia had been gathered long before Winifred could make up her mind to say no; and when the little things came in this morning they looked like walking garlands. Did you see the noble flower-pot in the hall?'

'You must go and look at the fruit which Lady Merton has been so kind as to bring us, Lizzie,' said Mrs. Woodbourne; 'you never saw such fine grapes and pines.'

'I hear you have undertaken that part of the arrangement, young ladies,' said Lady Merton.

'Yes,' said Elizabeth; 'but I am afraid we do not know much about the matter.'

'I am sure I cannot tell what I should do if you did not undertake it, my dears,' said Mrs. Woodbourne.

'Do not begin thanking us till we have done the deed, Mamma,' said Elizabeth; 'it may turn out a great deal worse than if we had left it to the unassisted taste of the maids.'

The four girls continued to arrange the flowers: Elizabeth, inquiring after many of the plants at Merton Hall; Anne, telling how the myrtle was prospering, how well the geraniums had flowered, describing a new fuchsia, and triumphing in the prize which the salpiglossis had gained from the Horticultural Society; Helen, comparing the flora of Merton Hall with that of Dykelands; Mrs. Woodbourne, rejoicing in cuttings to be saved from the branches gathered by Anne's unsparing hand; and Lady Merton, promising to send her seeds and young plants by Rupert, when he should return to Oxford.

When the forest of flowers had been dispersed in the epergne, and in various bowls and glasses, to ornament the drawing-room, the three sisters began to collect the green leaves and pieces of stalks remaining on the table, and as they bent down to sweep them off into a basket, their heads chanced to be almost close together.

'Why, Lizzie,' said Lady Merton, 'where are your curls? Have you made yourself look so very different from Kate, to prevent all future mistakes between you? and, Helen, have you really become a Pasha of two tails?'

'Is it not very silly of Helen to wear them, Aunt Anne?' said Elizabeth.

'Indeed, dear Aunt Anne,' said Helen, 'my hair never will curl well, and Mrs. Staunton always said it made me look like an old woman in the way I wore it before, so what could I do but try it in the way in which Fanny and Jane wore theirs?'

'Oh! we must all bow before Dykelands,' said Elizabeth.

'And I have been wondering what made you look so altered, Lizzie,' said Lady Merton, 'and now I see it is your hair being straight. I like your curls better.'

'Ah, so do I,' said Mrs. Woodbourne; 'but Lizzie docs not like the trouble of curling it.'

'No,' said Elizabeth, 'I think it a very useless plague. It used really to take me two hours a day, and now I am ready directly without trouble or fuss. People I care about will not think the worse of me for not looking quite so well.'

'Perhaps not,' said Lady Merton, 'but they would think the better of you for a little attention to their taste.'

'They might for attention to their wishes, Aunt Anne,' said Elizabeth, 'but hardly to their taste. Taste is such a petty nonsensical thing.'

'I shall leave you and Anne to argue about the fine distinction between taste and wishes,' said Lady Merton; 'it is more in your line than mine.'

'You mean to say that I have been talking nonsense, Aunt Anne,' said Elizabeth.

'I say nothing of the kind, Lizzie,' said her aunt; 'I only say that you are in the habit of splitting hairs.'

Elizabeth saw that her aunt was not pleased. She went to the chimney-piece, and employed herself in making a delicate piece of ixia get a better view of itself in the looking-glass. Presently she turned round, saying, 'Yes, Aunt Anne, I was very wrong; I was making a foolish pretence at refinement, to defend myself.'

'I did not mean to begin scolding you the very moment I came near you, Lizzie,' said Lady Merton.

'Indeed I wish you would, Aunt Anne,' said Elizabeth; 'pray scold me from morning till night, there is no one who wants it more.'

'My dear child, how can you say so?' cried Mrs. Woodbourne.

'Many thanks for the agreeable employment you propose to me, Lizzie,' said Lady Merton.

'If Rupert docs not come to-night, I mean to undertake a little of that agreeable employment myself, when he arrives,' said Elizabeth, 'and to make Anne help me.'

'I believe Rupert is so fond of being scolded, that it only makes him worse,' said Lady Merton.

'Here are Papa and Uncle Edward coming back at last,' said Katherine, who was, as usual, sitting in the window.

Mrs. Woodbourne looked greatly relieved; she had been for some time in trouble for the dinner, not being able to console herself in the way in which Elizabeth sometimes attempted to re-assure her in such cases--'Never mind, Mamma, the dinner is used to waiting.'

CHAPTER III.

As soon as dinner was over, the girls proposed to walk to the new church, that Anne might see it at her leisure before the Consecration. The younger children were very urgent to be allowed to accompany them, but Mrs. Woodbourne would only consent to Dora's doing so, on her eldest sister's promise to return before her bed-time.

'And, Mamma,' said Elizabeth, as soon as this question was decided, and the other two children had taken out their basket of bricks at the other end of the room, 'have you settled whether Edward is to go to the Consecration to-morrow?'

'I really think he is almost too young, my dear,' said Mrs. Woodbourne; 'you know it is a very long service.'

'Oh! Mamma,' said Dora, 'he is five years old now, and he says he will be very good, and he will be very much disappointed if he has to stay at home, now he has had his new frock and trousers; and Winifred and I are going.'

'Really, Dora,' said Elizabeth, 'I think he had better not go, unless he has some reason for wishing to do so, better than what you have mentioned.'

'I believe he understands it all as well as we do,' said Dora; 'we have all been talking about it in the nursery, this evening, at supper:--and you know, Mamma, he has quite left off being naughty in church.'

'Still, my dear,' said Mrs. Woodbourne, 'I scarcely think that we can take him; I cannot have him sitting with me, among the people whom we have invited, and he will certainly grow tired and restless.'

'I do not think his being tired just at last will signify,' said Elizabeth; 'he will attend at first, I am sure, and it is a thing he must never forget all his life. I will take care of him and Winifred, and Dora can behave well without being watched.'

'Very well, my dear,' said Mrs. Woodbourne in her plaintive voice, 'I shall be glad for him to go, if you can undertake to keep him in order, but you must take care you do not tire yourself. You will have almost too much to do afterwards, and you must not let yourself be harassed by his restlessness.'

'Oh no, Mamma, thank you,' said Elizabeth, 'he will not fidget, and I am not afraid of anything in the summer, and on such a great day as to-morrow. I could walk to Johnny Groat's house, and take care of fifty children, if need were.'

Edward was called, examined as to his reasons for wishing to go to the Consecration, made to promise to behave well, and sent back in high glee to play with Winifred. Elizabeth and Dorothea then followed the others up-stairs to prepare for the walk.

'It is very strange,' remarked Mrs. Woodbourne, as they left the room, 'that Elizabeth can manage the children so much better than anyone else can; they always like best to be with her, though she always makes them mind her, and Kate is much more what people would call good-natured.'

'Do you not think Lizzie good-natured?' said Lady Merton, rather surprised.

'Oh yes, indeed I do,' said Mrs. Woodbourne, 'she is a most kind-hearted creature. I really believe there is nothing she would not do for the children or me, I do not know what would become of me without her: but you know her way of speaking, she does not mean any harm; but still when people are not used to her, it vexes them; indeed I did not mean to say anything against her, she is a most excellent creature, quite her Papa's right hand.'

'Horace grew almost too much for her to manage before he went to school, did not he?' said Lady Merton.

'Poor little boy!' said Mrs. Woodbourne, 'we miss him sadly, with his merry face and droll ways. You know, he was always a very high-spirited child, but Lizzie could always make him mind her in the end, and he was very obedient to his papa and me. Edward is a quiet meek boy, he has not his brother's high spirits, and I hope we shall keep him at home longer.'

'Horace is certainly very young for a school-boy,' said Lady Merton; 'Rupert was ten years old when he went to Sandleford, but Sir Edward afterwards regretted that he had not gone there earlier, and the little boys are very well taken care of there.'

'Yes, Mr. Woodbourne said everything looked very comfortable,' said Mrs.

Woodbourne, sighing; 'and I suppose he must rough it some time or other, poor little fellow, so that it may be as well to begin early.'

'And he has taken a good place,' said Lady Merton; 'Lizzie wrote in high glee to tell Anne of it.'

'Yes,' said Mrs. Woodbourne, 'she had brought him on wonderfully; I am sure I wonder how she could, with only a little occasional assistance from her papa; but then, Horace is certainly a very clever child, and few have Lizzie's spirits and patience, to be able to bear with a little boy's idleness and inattention so good-humouredly. And I do believe she enjoyed playing with him and the others as much as the children themselves; I used to say it was no use to send Lizzie to keep the children in order, she only promoted the fun and noise.'

'She is a merry creature,' said Lady Morton, 'her spirits never seem to flag, and I think she is looking stronger than when I saw her last.'

'Indeed, I am very glad to hear you say so,' said Mrs. Woodbourne; 'she has seemed very well and strong all the summer, but she still has that constant cough, and we must always be anxious about her, I wish she would take a little more care of herself, but she will not understand how necessary precautions are; she goes out in all sorts of weather, and never allows that anything will give her cold; indeed, I let Dora go out with them this evening, because I knew that Lizzie would stay out of doors too long, unless she had her to make her come in for her sake.'

'How bright and well Helen looks!' said Lady Merton; 'she seems to have been very happy at Dykelands.'

'Very happy indeed,' said Mrs. Woodbourne; 'I am sure we are exceedingly obliged to Mrs. Staunton for asking her. She has come back quite a different creature, and can speak of nothing but the kindness of her friends at Dykelands.'

Here the conversation dropped for a minute or two, for Lady Morton found it difficult to reply. Mrs. Staunton had lived in the village where Merton Hall was situated, and where both Lady Merton and her sister-in-law had spent their childhood. She had been much attached to Mrs. Woodbourne, and was Helen's godmother; but having settled in a distant county, had scarcely kept up any intercourse with the Woodbourne family since her friend's death, though constantly corresponding with Lady Merton, and occasionally writing and sending presents to her little god-daughter. Chancing however to come to London on business, she had written to Mr. Woodbourne to beg him to bring Helen to meet her there, and allow her to take her back with her into Lincolnshire to spend some time with her and her daughters. Mr. Woodbourne, knowing that his wife had esteemed her very highly, complied after a little deliberation. Helen's visit had lasted longer than at first proposed, and she only returned home, after an absence of five months, just in time to wish her little brother farewell, on his departure for school, a few weeks before the Consecration of St. Austin's. Lady Merton would have been glad to read Mrs. Woodbourne all the admiration of Helen, which Mrs. Staunton had poured forth to her in a letter written a short time before; but the terms in which it was expressed were more exaggerated than Lady Merton liked to shew to one who was not acquainted with Mrs. Staunton, and besides, her praise of Helen was full of comparison with her mother.

Visiting Abbeychurch was always painful to Lady Merton, and her manner, usually rather cold, was still more constrained when she was there; for, although both she and Sir Edward had been very careful not to shew any want of cordiality towards Mr. and Mrs. Woodbourne, they could not but feel that the Vicarage never could be to them what it once had been. It was certainly quite impossible not to have an affection for its present gentle kind-hearted mistress; and Lady Merton felt exceedingly grateful to her, for having, some years ago, nursed Rupert through a dangerous attack of scarlet-fever, with which he had been seized at Abbeychurch, when on his way from school, when she herself had been prevented by illness from coming to him; and Mrs. Woodbourne, making light of her anxiety for her own children, had done all that the most affectionate mother could have done for him, and had shewn more energy than almost anyone had believed her to possess, comforting Sir Edward with hopes and cheerful looks, soothing the boy's waywardness, and bearing with his fretfulness in his recovery, as none but a mother, or a friend as gentle as Mrs. Woodbourne, could have done. Still, much as she loved Mrs. Woodbourne for her own sake, Lady Merton could not help missing Katherine, her first play-fellow, the bright friend of her youth, her sister-in-law; Mrs. Woodbourne, a shy timid person, many years younger, felt that such must be the case, and always feared that she was thinking that the girls would have been in better order under their own mother; so that the two ladies were never quite at their ease when alone together.

In the mean time, Elizabeth, quite unconscious that Dora was intended to act as a clog round her neck, to keep her from straying too far, was mounting the hill, the merriest of the merry party.

'It is certainly an advantage to the world in general to have the church on a hill,' said Anne, 'both for the poetry and beauty of the sight; but I should think that the world in particular would be glad if the hill were not quite so steep.'

'Oh!' said Elizabeth, 'on the side towards the new town it is fair and soft enough to suit the laziest, it is only on our side that it resembles the mountain of fame or of happiness; and St. Austin's, as the new town is now to be called, is all that has any concern with it.'

'I wish it was not so steep on our side,' said Katherine; 'I do not think I ever was so hot in all my life, as I was yesterday, when we carried up all the cushions ourselves, and Papa sent me all the way back to the Vicarage, only just to fetch a needle and thread for Mamma to sew on a little bit of fringe.'

'Really, Kate,' said Elizabeth, 'you might have thought yourself very happy to have anything to do for the Church.'

'All! it was all very well for you to say so,' said Katherine; 'you were sitting in the cool at home, only hearing Edward read, not toiling in the sun as I was.'

'That is not fair, Kate,' said Helen; 'you know it is sometimes very hard work to hear Edward read; and besides, Mamma had desired Lizzie to sit still in the house, because she had been at the church ever since five, helping Papa to settle the velvet on the pulpit after the people had put it on wrong.'

'You would not imagine, Anne,' said Elizabeth, 'how fearfully deficient the world is, in common sense. Would you believe it, the workmen actually put the pulpit-cloth on with the embroidery upside-down, and I believe we were five hours setting it right again.'

'Without any breakfast?' said Anne.

'Oh! we had no time to think of breakfast till Mr. Somerville came in at ten o'clock to see what was going on, and told us how late it was,' said Elizabeth.

By this time, they had reached the brow of the hill, from whence they had a fine view of Abbeychurch, old and new. Anne observed upon the difference between the two divisions of the town.

'Yes,' said Elizabeth, 'our town consists of the remains of old respectable England, and the beginning of the new great work-shop of all nations, met together in tolerably close companionship. I could almost grudge that beautiful Gothic church to those regular red-brick uniform rows of deformity.'

'I do not think even the new church can boast of more beauty than St. Mary's,' said Anne.

'No, and it wants the handiwork of that best artist, old Time,' said Elizabeth; 'it will be long before Queen Victoria's head on the corbel at the new church is of as good a colour as Queen Eleanor's at the old one, and we never shall see anything so pretty at St. Austin's as the yellow lichen cap, and plume of spleen-wort feathers, which Edward the First wears.'

'How beautiful the old church tower is!' said Anne, turning round to look at it; 'and the gable ends of your house, and the tall trees of the garden, with the cloistered alms-houses, have still quite a monastic air.'

'If you only look at the tower with its intersecting arches and their zig-zag mouldings,' said Elizabeth, 'and shut your eyes to our kitchen chimney, on which rests all the fame of the Vicar before last.'

'What can you mean?' said Anne.

'That when anyone wishes to distinguish the Reverend Hugh Puddington from all other Vicars of Abbeychurch, his appellation is "The man that built the kitchen chimney."'

'That being, I suppose, the only record he has left behind him,' said Anne.

'The only one now existing,' said Elizabeth, 'since Papa has made his great horrid pew in the chancel into open seats.--Do not you remember it, Kate? and how naughty you used to be, when Margaret left off sitting there with us, and there was no one to see what we were about--oh! and there is a great fat Patience on a monument on the wall over our heads, and a very long inscription, recording things quite as unsuitable to a clergyman.'

'I do not understand you, Lizzie,' said Helen; 'unsuitable as what? Patience, or building chimneys, or making pews?'

'Patience is a virtue when she is not on a monument,' said Elizabeth.

'And neither pews nor chimneys can be unsuitable to a clergyman,' said little Dora; 'there are four pews in the new church, and Papa built a chimney for the school.'

Everyone laughed, much to Dora's surprise, and somewhat to Helen's, and Elizabeth was forced to explain, for Dora's edification, that what she intended by the speech in question, was only that it was unsuitable to a clergyman to leave no record behind him, but what had been intended to gratify his own love of luxury.

'I am sorry I said anything about him,' said she to Anne; 'it was scarcely right to laugh at him, especially before Dora; I am afraid she will never see the monument without thinking of the chimney.'

At this moment they arrived at the church, and all their attention was bestowed upon it. It was built in the Early English style, and neither pains nor expense had been spared. Anne, who had not been there since the wall had been four feet above the ground, was most eager to see it; and Elizabeth, who had watched it from day to day, was equally eager to see whether Anne would think of everything in it as she did herself.

As the door opened, a flood of golden light poured in upon the pure white stone Font, while the last beams of the evening sun were streaming through the western window, shining on the edges of the carved oak benches, and glancing upon the golden embroidery of the crimson velvet on the Altar, above which, the shadows on the groined roof of the semi-octagonal chancel were rapidly darkening, and the deep tints of the five narrow lancet windows within five arches, supported and connected by slender clustered shafts with capitals of richly carved foliage, were full of solemn richness when contrasted with the glittering gorgeous hues of the west window.

'Oh! Anne,' whispered Elizabeth, as they stood together in the porch, giving a parting look before she closed the door, 'it is "all glorious within," even now; and think what it will be to-morrow!'

Nothing more was said till they had left the churchyard, when Anne exclaimed, looking wistfully towards the railroad, 'Then there is but one chance of Rupert's coming to-night.'

'When the eight o'clock train comes in,' said Katherine; 'it is that which is to bring the Hazlebys.'

'I really think,' said Helen, 'that the gas manufactory and the union poor-house grow more frightful every day. I thought they looked worse than ever when I came home, and saw the contrast with Lincolnshire. I hope the old and new towns will long be as different as they are now.'

'I am afraid they hardly will,' said Anne; 'the old town will soon begin to rival the new one. You must already find new notions creeping into it.'

'Creeping!' cried Elizabeth, 'they gallop along the railroad as fast as steam can carry them. However, we are happily a quiet dull race, and do not take them in; we only open our eyes and stare at all the wonders round. I do not know what we may come to in time, we may be as genteel as Kate's friend, Willie Turner, says the people are in Aurelia Place--that perked-up row of houses, whose windows and doors give them such a comical expression of countenance, more like butterflies than aurelias.'

'Who is Kate's friend?' asked Anne, in a wondering tone.

'Willie Turner!' said Elizabeth; 'oh! the apothecary's daughter, Wilhelmina. You must have heard of Mr. Turner. Rupert has made a standing joke of him, ever since the scarlet-fever.'

'Oh yes!' said Anne, 'I know Mr. Turner's name very well; but I never knew that Miss Turner was a friend of Kate's.'

'She was not,' said Elizabeth, 'till Helen went to Dykelands, and poor Kitty was quite lonely for want of someone to gossip with, and so she struck up a most romantic friendship with Willie Turner; and really, it has done us one most important service.--May I mention it, Kate, without betraying your confidence?'

'Nonsense, Lizzie,' said Katherine.

'Oh! you do not object,' said Elizabeth; 'then be it known to you, Anne, that once upon a time, Kitty confided to me, what I forthwith confided to Papa, that Mrs. Turner was working in cross-stitch a picture of St. Augustine preaching to the Saxons, which she intended to present as a cushion for one of the chairs of St. Austin's Church.'

'Oh! dreadful!' cried Anne.

'Papa walked up and down the room for full ten minutes after he heard of it,' said Elizabeth; 'but Mamma came to our rescue. She, the mild-spoken, (Mildred, you know,) set off with the Saxon Winifred, the peace-maker, to reject the Saint of the Saxons, more civilly than the British bishops did. She must have managed most beautifully, so as to satisfy everybody. I believe that she lamented that the Austin Friars who named our hill were not called after the converter of our forefathers, looking perfectly innocent of Kitty's secret all the time; and Winifred eat Mrs. Turner's plum-cake, and stared at her curiosities, so as to put her into good humour. Thus far is certain, from that day to this no more has been heard of St. Augustine or King Ethelbert.'

'Oh! her work is made up into a screen now,' said Katharine, 'and is very pretty.'

'And last time Mrs. Turner called at the Vicarage, she was very learned about the Bishop of Hippo,' said Elizabeth; 'she is really very clever in concealing her ignorance, when she does not think herself learned.'

'I thought they were not likely to promote the decoration of the new church,' said Anne.

'Oh! she does not trouble herself about consistency,' said Elizabeth; 'anything which attracts notice pleases her. She thinks our dear papa has done more for the living than nine out of ten would have thought of; and if there was any talk of presenting him with some small testimonial of respect, her mite would be instantly forthcoming; and Sir Edward Merton, he is the most munificent gentleman she ever heard of; if all of his fortune were like him now!--"Only, my dear Miss Lizzie, does not your papa think of having a lightning conductor attached to the spire? such an elevation, it quite frightens me to think of it! and the iron of the railroad, too--"'

'Oh! is she scientific, too?' aaid Anne.

'Yes; you see how the march of intellect has reached us,' said Elizabeth; 'poor Kate is so much afraid of the electric fluid, that she cannot venture to wear a steel buckle. You have no idea of the efforts we are making to keep up with the rest of the world. We have a wicked Radical newspaper all to ourselves; I wonder it has the face to call itself the Abbeychurch Reporter.'

'Your inns are on the move,' said Anne; 'I see that little beer-shop near the Station calls itself "The Locomotive Hotel."'

'I wish it were really locomotive,' said Elizabeth, 'so that it would travel out of Abbeychurch; it is ruining half the young men here.'

'Well, perhaps the new town will mend,' said Anne; 'it will have a Christian name to-morrow, and perhaps the influence of the old town will improve it.'

'I think Papa has little hope of that kind,' said Elizabeth; 'if the new town does grow a little better, the old will still grow worse. It is grievous to see how much less conformable Papa finds the people of the old town, than even I can remember them. But come, we must be locomotive, or Dora will not be at home in time.'

CHAPTER IV.

The clock was striking eight as the young ladies entered the house; but Dora was allowed to sit up a little longer to see her aunt, Mrs. Hazleby. It was not long before a loud knock at the door announced that lady's arrival.

Mrs. Hazleby was a tall bony Scotchwoman, with fierce-looking grey eyes. She gave Mrs. Woodbourne a very overpowering embrace, and then was careful to mark the difference between her niece, little Dora, whom she kissed, and the three elder girls, with whom she only shook hands. She was followed by her daughters--Harriet, a tall showy girl of sixteen, and Lucy, a pale, quiet, delicate-looking creature, a year younger. Rupert Merton was still missing; but his movements were always so uncertain, that his family were in no uneasiness on his account.

As Mrs. Woodbourne was advancing to kiss Harriet, a loud sharp 'yap' was heard from something in the arms of the latter; Mrs. Woodbourne started, turned pale, and looked so much alarmed, that Anne could not laugh. Harriet, however, was not so restrained, but laughed loudly as she placed upon a chair a little Blenheim spaniel, with a blue ribbon round his neck, and called to her sister Lucy to 'look after Fido.' It presently appeared that the little dog had been given to them at the last place where they had been staying on the road to Abbeychurch; and Mrs. Hazleby and her eldest daughter continued for some time to expatiate upon the beauty and good qualities of Fido, as well as those of all his kith and kin. He was not, however, very cordially welcomed by anyone at the Vicarage; for Mr. Woodbourne greatly disliked little dogs in the house, his wife dreaded them much among her children, and there were symptoms of a deadly feud between him and Elizabeth's only pet, the great black cat, Meg Merrilies. But still his birth, parentage, and education, were safe subjects of conversation; and all were sorry when Mrs. Hazleby had exhausted them, and began to remark how thin Elizabeth looked--to tell a story of a boy who had died of a fever, some said of neglect, at the school where Horace was--to hint at the possibility of Rupert's having been lost on the Scottish mountains, blown up on the railroad, or sunk in a steam-vessel--to declare that girls were always spoiled by being long absent from home, and to dilate on the advantages of cheap churches.

She had nearly all the conversation to herself, the continual sound of her voice being only varied by Harriet's notes and comments, given in a pert shrill, high key, and by a few syllables in answer from Lady Merton and Mrs. Woodbourne. The two gentlemen, happily for themselves, had a great quantity of plans and accounts of the church to look over together, which were likely to occupy them through the whole of Sir Edward's visit. Elizabeth was busy numbering the Consecration tickets for the next day, and Anne in helping her, so that they sat quietly together in the inner drawing-room during the greater part of the evening.

When they went up-stairs to bed, Elizabeth exclaimed, 'Oh! that horrid new bonnet of mine! I had quite forgotten it, and I must trim it now, for I shall not have time to-morrow morning. I will run to Kate and Helen's room, and fetch my share of the ribbon.'

As she returned and sat down to work, she continued, 'It is too much plague to quill up the ribbon as the others have theirs. It will do quite well enough plain. Now, Anne, do not you think that as long as dress is neat, which of course it must be, prettiness does not signify?'

'Perhaps I might think so, if I had to trim my own bonnets,' said Anne, laughing.

'Ah! you do not think so--Anne, you who have everything about you, from your shoe-strings upwards, in the most complete order and elegant taste. But then, you know, you would do quite as well if the things were ugly.'

'If I wore yellow gowns and scarlet bonnets, for instance?' asked Anne.

'No, no, that would not be modest,' said Elizabeth; 'you would be no longer a lady, so that you could not look lady-like, which I maintain a lady always is, whether each morsel of her apparel is beautiful in itself or not.'

'Indeed, Lizzie,' said Anne, 'I cannot say that I think as you do, at least as far as regards ourselves, I think that it may be possible to wear ugly things and still be lady-like, and I am sure I honour people greatly who really deny themselves for the sake of doing right, if anyone can seriously care for such a thing as dress; but I consider it as a duty in such as ourselves, to consult the taste of the people we live with.'

'As your mother said about my hair,' said Elizabeth thoughtfully; 'I will do as she advised, Anne, but not while she is here, for fear Mamma should fancy that I do so because Aunt Anne wished it, though I would not to please her. I believe you are right; but look here, will my bonnet do?'

'I think it looks very well,' said Anne; 'but will it not seem remarkable for you to be unlike your sisters?'

'Ah! it will give Mrs. Hazleby an opportunity of calling me blue, and tormenting Mamma,' said Elizabeth; 'besides, Mamma wished us all to be alike down to the little ones, so I will make the best of it, and trim it like any London milliner. But, Anne, you must consider it is a great improvement in me to allow that respectable people must be neat. I used to allow it in theory, but not in practice.'

'I do not think I ever saw you untidy, Lizzie,' said Anne, 'except after a day's nutting in the hanging wood.'

'Oh yes, I could generally preserve a little outward tidiness,' said Elizabeth; 'besides, a visit at Merton Hall is very different from every day in shabby old Abbeychurch. No, you must know that when I was twelve years old, I was supposed to be capable of taking care of my own wardrobe; and for some time all went on very smoothly, only that I never did a stitch towards mending anything.'

'Did a beneficent fairy do it for you, then?'

'Not a sprite, nor even a brownie, but one of the old wrinkled kind of fairies. Old Margaret, that kindest of nurses, could not bear to see her dear Miss Lizzie untidy, or to hear her dear Miss Lizzie scolded, so she mended and mended without saying anything, encouraging me in habits of arrant slovenliness, and if I had but known it, of deceit. Dear old Margery, it was a heart-breaking thing when she went away, to all from Winifred upwards, and to none more than to me, who could remember those two melancholy years when she often seemed my only friend, when I was often naughty and Papa angry with me, and I feeling motherless and wretched, used to sit on her lap and cry. Dear old Margery, it is a shame to abuse her in spite of the mischief her over-kindness did us all. Well, when our new maid came, on the supposition that Miss Woodbourne took care of her own clothes, she never touched them; and as Margaret's work was not endowed with the fairy power of lasting for ever, I soon grew as ragged as any ragged-robin in the hedge. Mamma used to complain of my slovenliness, but I am afraid I was naughty enough to take advantage of her gentleness, and out-argue her; so things grew worse and worse, till at last, one fatal day, Papa was aware of a great hole in my stockings. Then forth it all came; he asked question after question; and dear kind Mamma, even more unwilling to expose me than I was myself, was forced to answer, and you may suppose how angry he was. Oh! Anne, I can hardly bear to think of the stern kindness of his voice when he saw I was really quite wretched. And only think how kind it was in him, he spoke seriously to me, he shewed me that building the church, helping our poor people, even Mamma's comforts, and the boys' education, depend upon home economy; and how even I could make a difference by not wasting my clothes, and making another servant necessary.'

'Then could you really gain neat habits immediately?' asked Anne; 'there could be no doubt of your resolving to do so, but few people could or would persevere.'

'Oh! I am not properly tidy now,' said Elizabeth, opening a most chaotic table-drawer, 'see, there is a proof of it. However, I do not think I have been shamefully slovenly in my own person since that explosion, and I have scarcely been spoken to about it. Who could disregard such an appeal? But, Anne, are you not enchanted with sweet Mrs. Hazleby?'

'I wish you would not ask me, Lizzie,' said Anne, feeling very prudent, 'you know that I know nothing of her.'

'No, and you never will know enough of her to say such savage things as I do,' said Elizabeth, 'but at any rate you saw her when she came in.'

'Certainly.'

'I mean the kissing; I am sure I am glad enough to escape it, and always think Mamma and the children seem to be hugged by a bear; but you know making such distinctions is not the way to make us like her, even if we were so disposed. Oh! and about me in particular, I am convinced that she thinks that Mamma hates me as much as she does, for she seems to think it will delight her to hear that I am thinner than ever, and that such bright colour is a very bad sign, and then she finishes off with a hypocritical sigh, and half whisper of "It can be no wonder, poor thing!" trying to put everyone, especially Papa and Uncle Edward, in mind of my own poor mother. I declare I have no patience with her or Harriet, or that ugly little wretch of a dog!'

In the mean time, Katherine and Helen were visiting their guests, Harriet and Lucy Hazleby, whom, contrary to Elizabeth's arrangement, Mrs. Woodbourne had lodged in the room where her own two little girls usually slept. Harriet was sitting at the table, at her ease, curling her long cork-screw ringlets, with Fido at her feet; Lucy was unpacking her wardrobe, Katherine lighting her, and admiring each article as it was taken out, in spite of her former disapprobation of Harriet's style of dress. Helen stood lingering by the door, with her hand on the lock, still listening or talking, though not much interested, and having already three times wished her guests good night. Their conversation, though not worth recording for any sense or reflection shewn by any of the talkers, may perhaps display their characters, and add two or three facts to our story, which may be amusing to some few of our readers.

'Oh! Lucy,' cried Harriet, with a start, 'take care of my spotted muslin, it is caught on the lock of the box. You always are so careless.'

Katherine assisted Lucy to rescue the dress from the threatened danger, and Harriet continued, 'Well, and what do you wear to-morrow, Kate?'

'White muslin, with pink ribbons,' said Katherine.

'I have a green and orange striped mousseline de laine, Mamma gave only fifteen-pence a yard for it; I will shew it to you when Lucy comes to it, and you will see if it is not a bargain. And what bonnets?'

'Straw, with ribbon like our sashes,' said Katherine. 'Oh! we had so much trouble to get--'

'My bonnet is green satin,' said Harriet, 'but if I had been you, Kate, I would have had Leghorn. Wouldn't you, Lucy?'

'Five Leghorn bonnets would have cost too much,' said Katherine, 'and Mamma wished us all to be alike.'

'Ah! she would not let you be smarter than her own girls, eh, Kitty?' said Harriet, laughing.

'I had been obliged to buy a very nice new straw bonnet at Dykelands,' said Helen, 'and it, would have been a pity not to use that.'

'Well, I have no notion of a whole row of sisters being forced to dress alike,' said Harriet; 'Aunt Mildred might--'

Here Lucy stopped her sister's speech, by bringing the gown forward to display it. When Harriet had sufficiently explained its excellence she began, 'So your cousin, young Merton, is coming, is he?'

'Yes,' said Katherine, 'we expected him last night, or in the course of this day, but he has not come yet.'

'Well, what sort of a young fellow is he?' said Harriet.

'Very clever indeed,' said Katherine.

'Oh! then he will not be in my line at all,' said Harriet; 'those clever boys are never worth speaking to, are they, Lucy?'

'Do you like stupid ones better?' said Helen.

'Capital, isn't it, Lucy?' cried Harriet; 'I did not mean stupid; I only meant, clever boys, as they call them, have no fun, they only read, read for ever, like my brother Allan.'

'I am sure Rupert is full of fun,' said Katherine.

'Oh, but he is quite a boy, is not he?' said Harriet.

'Nineteen, and at Oxford,' said Katherine.

'Oh! I call that quite a boy--don't you, Lucy?' said Harriet; 'is he handsome?'

'Yes, very,' said Katherine.

'Not like his sister, then, I suppose,' said Harriet.

'Oh! do not you, think Anne pretty?' said Katherine.

'I do not know--no, too small and pale to suit me,' said Harriet.

'Rupert is not like Anne,' said Katherine, 'he has a very bright pink and white complexion, and light hair.'

'Is he tall?'

'No, not so tall as your brother George, but slighter. He has had two of his front teeth knocked out by a stone at school,' said Katherine.

'What a fuss they did make about those teeth!' muttered Helen.

'Was that the school where Horace is?' said Harriet.

'Yes,' said Katherine, 'Sandleford.'

'How you must miss Horace!' said Lucy.

'Poor little fellow, yes, that we do,' said Katherine, 'but he was so riotous, he would pull all my things to pieces. Nobody could manage him but Lizzie, and she never minds what she has on.'

'What a tear he did make in my frock!' said Harriet, laughing; 'didn't he, Lucy?'

'How tired you look, Lucy,' said Helen, 'I am sure you ought to be in bed.'

'Oh no, I am not very sleepy,' said Lucy, smiling.

'I am dead tired, I am sure,' said Harriet, yawning; 'it was so hot in the railway carriage.'

'Cannot the rest of those things be put away to-morrow morning, Harriet?' said Helen.

'Oh!' said Harriet, yawning, 'there will not be time; Lucy may as well do them all now she has begun. How sleepy I am! we walked about London all the morning.'

'Come, Helen,' said Katherine, 'it is quite time for us to be gone; we must be up early to-morrow.'

CHAPTER V.

The morning of the twenty-eighth of August was as fine as heart could wish, and the three sisters rose almost as soon as it was light, to fulfil their promise of attending to all the small nondescript matters of arrangement, needful when a large party is expected by a family not much in the habit of receiving company. Katherine, who had quite given up all thoughts of equalling her elder sister in talent, and who prided herself on being the useful member of the family, made herself very busy in the store-room; Helen, arranged the fruit with much taste; and Elizabeth was up-stairs and down, here, there, and everywhere, till it was difficult to find anything which she had not rectified by labour of head or hand.

'Well,' said she, as she brought Helen a fresh supply of vine leaves from the garden, 'I wonder whether Rupert will come in time. I shall be very sorry if he does not, for he has done a great deal for the church.'

'Has he indeed?' said Helen, with an air that expressed, 'I should not have thought it.'

'O Helen, how can you take so little interest in the church?' said Elizabeth; 'do not you remember how much trouble Rupert took to find a pattern for the kneeling-stools, and what a beautiful drawing he sent of those at Magdalen Collegia Chapel? I am sure he would be very much vexed to miss the Consecration.'

'I suppose he might come if he pleased,' said Helen; 'but perhaps he did not choose to get up early enough.'

'That is the first time I ever heard Rupert accused of indolence,' said Elizabeth.

'I do not mean that he does not generally get up in good time,' said Helen; 'he is not lazy; but I do not think he chooses to put himself out of the way; and besides, he rather likes to make people anxious about him.'

'I know you have never liked Rupert,' said Elizabeth drily.

'Papa thinks as I do,' said Helen; 'I have heard him say that he is a spoiled child, and thinks too much of himself.'

'Oh! that was only because Aunt Anne worked that beautiful waistcoat for him,' said Elizabeth; 'that was not Rupert's fault.'

'And Papa said that he was quite fond enough already of smart waistcoats,' said Helen; 'and he laughed at his wearing a ring.'

'That is only a blood-stone with his crest,' said Elizabeth, 'and I am sure no one can accuse Rupert of vulgar smartness.'

'Not of **vulgar** smartness,' said Helen, 'but you must allow that everything about him has a--kind of--what shall I say?--recherche air, that seems as if he thought a great deal of himself; I am sure you must have heard Papa say something of the kind.'

'Really, Helen,' said Elizabeth, 'I cannot think why you should be determined to say all that you can against that poor Rupert.'

Helen made no answer.

'I do believe,' said Elizabeth, 'that you have had a grudge against him ever since he made you an April fool. Oh! how capital it was,' cried she, sitting down to laugh at the remembrance. 'To make you believe that the beautiful work-box Uncle Edward sent you, was a case of surgical instruments for Mr. Turner, to shew his gratitude for his attendance upon Rupert when he had the fever, and for setting his mouth to rights when his teeth were knocked out at school. Oh! there never was such fun as to see how frightened you looked, and how curious Kate and Horace were, and how Mamma begged him not to open the box and shew her the horrid things.'

'I wish Rupert would keep to the truth with his jokes,' said Helen.

'Helen,' said Elizabeth, 'you cannot mean to say that he ever says what is untrue. You are letting yourself be carried much too far by your dislike.'

'If he does not positively assert what is not true, he often makes people believe it,' said Helen.

'Only stupid people, who have no perception of a joke,' said Elizabeth; 'he never deceived me with any joke; it is only that you do not understand.'

'I wonder how such a candid person as you are, can defend the slightest departure from truth for any purpose,' said Helen.

'I would not defend anyone whom I did not believe to be upright and open,' said Elizabeth; 'but it is only your slowness, and old spite against Rupert because he used to joke you, that puts these fancies into your head. Now I must go to the children; I hope, Helen, you will really enter into the spirit of the day, little as you seem to care about the church.'

Helen gave a deep sigh as her sister left the room; she was vexed at having been laughed at, at the disregard of her arguments, at the reproach, and perhaps a little at Elizabeth's having taken no notice of the beautiful pyramid of cherries which had cost her half an hour's labour.

There was some truth in what Helen said of her cousin, though few would have given his faults so much prominence. Rupert Merton was an only son, and very handsome, and this was the history of nearly all his foibles. No one could say that his career at school, and so far at college, had not been everything that could be wished, and most people had nearly as high an opinion of him as he had of himself; but Helen, who had almost always been made a laughing-stock when he was with her, had not quite so agreeable a recollection of his lively, graceful, pleasant manners as her sisters had, and was glad to find that his tormenting ways were not entirely caused by her own querulous temper, as Elizabeth sometimes told her they were.

When Mrs. Woodbourne came down, Helen's handiwork received its full share of admiration, and Mrs. Woodbourne was much pleased by the girls' forethought and activity, which had saved her from a great deal of fatigue.

The breakfast was quickly finished, and immediately afterwards the four eldest Miss Woodbournes, together with Anne, went to the school to see if the children were ready to go to church. It was pleasant to see the smiling courtesying row of girls, each with her Prayer-book in her hand, replying to Elizabeth's nods, greetings, and questions, with bright affectionate looks, or a few words, which shewed that they were conscious of the solemnity of the service in which they were about to bear a part.

Elizabeth left her sisters and Anne to assist the school-mistress in marshalling them on their way to church, and returned home to fetch Edward and Winifred, whom she had engaged to take with her. She found that nearly all the party were gone, and report said that the Bishop had arrived at the house of Mr. Somerville, who was to be curate of St. Austin's. Winifred and Edward were watching for her at the door, in great dread of being forgotten, for they said, 'Papa had come for Mamma, and fetched her away in a great hurry, and then Harriet and Lucy set off after them, and Uncle Edward had taken Aunt Anne long before to look at the church.' Elizabeth was rejoicing in the prospect of a quiet walk with the children, and was only delaying in a vain attempt to reduce the long fingers of Winifred's glove to something more like the length of the short fingers of its owner, when a sharp voice at the top of the stairs cried out, 'Wait for me!' and Mrs. Hazleby appeared, looking very splendid in a short black silk cloak trimmed with scarlet.

'Where have you been all this time?' said she to Elizabeth, while she caught hold of Winifred's hand, or, more properly speaking, of her wrist; 'we shall all be too late.'

'I have been at the school,' said Elizabeth.

'What! do you keep school to-day?' asked Mrs. Hazleby.

'No,' said Elizabeth, 'but the children are going to the Consecration.'

'Poor little things!' exclaimed Mrs. Hazleby; 'how will they sit out such a service?'

'None under seven years old are to be there,' said Elizabeth, 'and of the older ones only those who are tolerably good; and I should think they could join in the service sufficiently to prevent them from finding it tedious.'

'Well, I hope so,' said Mrs. Hazleby, in a voice which meant, 'What nonsense!' 'How steep the hill is!' added she presently; 'what a fatigue for old people!'

'It is not nearly so steep on the other side,' replied Elizabeth, 'and the people on this side have the old church.'

'Why did they choose such an exposed situation?' continued Mrs. Hazleby; 'so hot in summer, and so cold in winter.'

'There was no other open piece of ground to be had near enough to the new town,' answered Elizabeth, keeping to herself an additional reason, which was, that tradition said that there had once been a little chapel dedicated in the name of St. Augustine, on the site of the new church. Mrs. Hazleby was silent for a few moments, when, as they came in sight of what was passing at the top of the hill, she saw a gentleman hasten across the church-yard, and asked who he was.

'Mr. Somerville, the new curate,' was the answer.

'What! another curate? I thought Mr. Walker might have been enough!' exclaimed Mrs. Hazleby.

'Papa did not think so,' said Elizabeth drily.

'Well, I suppose that is another hundred a year out of Mr. Woodbourne's pocket,' said Mrs. Hazleby; 'enough to ruin his family.'

'I am sure,' said Elizabeth, beginning to grow angry, 'Papa had rather do his duty as a clergyman, than lay up thousands for us.'

'Fine talking for young things,' said Mrs. Hazleby; 'besides, it is nothing to you, you three elder ones will be well enough off with your mother's fortune.'

Elizabeth was more annoyed and provoked by this speech than by anything Mrs. Hazleby had ever said to her before; her cheeks burnt with indignation, and something which felt very like shame, but her bonnet concealed them, and she attempted no reply. Mrs. Hazleby began talking to Winifred about her new sash, and criticizing Elizabeth's dress; and though Elizabeth could have wished Winifred's mind to have been occupied with other things at such a time, yet she was glad of the opportunity this diversion gave her to compose herself before entering the church.

Almost everyone who has ever joined in our beautiful Consecration Service, can imagine the feelings of some of the party from the Vicarage--can figure to themselves Mrs. Woodbourne's quiet tears; Dora's happy yet awe-struck face; Anne sympathizing with everyone, rather than feeling on her own account; can think of the choking overwhelming joy with which Elizabeth looked into little Edward's wondering eyes, as the name of their father was read, the first among those who petitioned the Bishop to set that building apart from all ordinary and common uses; can feel, or perhaps have known, the exultation with which she joined in the Psalms, and the swelling of heart as she followed the prayer for a blessing on the families of those who had been the means of the building of that House. But we must go no farther; for, such thoughts and scenes are too high to be more than touched upon in a story of this kind; therefore we will only add, that Winifred and Edward behaved quite as well as Elizabeth had engaged that they should do, only beginning to yawn just before the end of the service.

After they had returned from the church, the luncheon at the Vicarage gave ample employment to Elizabeth's hands, and nearly enough to her thoughts, in carving cold chicken, and doing the honours of Merton Hall peaches, at the side-table; and she was very glad, when at three o'clock the company adjourned to the quadrangle, to see the school-children's feast.

The quadrangle was enclosed on the north side by the old church, on the south and west by the alms-houses, and on the east by the low wall of the Vicarage garden; there was a wide gravel path all round the court, and here tables were spread, around which were to be seen the merry faces of all the children of the two schools--the boys, a uniform rank arrayed in King Edward's blue coats and yellow stockings, with but a small proportion of modern-looking youths in brown or blue, and deep white collars--the girls, a long party-coloured line, only resembling each other in the white tippets, which had lately encumbered Elizabeth's room.

Much activity was called for, from all who chose to take part in supplying the children; the young ladies' baskets of buns were rapidly emptied, and Mr. Somerville's great pitcher of tea frequently drained, although he pretended to be very exclusive, and offer his services to none but the children of St. Austin's, to whom Winifred introduced him. The rest of the company walked round the cloisters, which were covered with dark red roses and honeysuckles, talking to the old people, admiring their flowers, especially Mr. Dillon's dahlias, and watching the troop of children, who looked like a living flower-bed.

Mrs. Hazleby chanced to be standing near Mrs. Bouverie, a lady who lived at some distance from Abbeychurch, and who was going to stay and dine at the Vicarage. She was tolerably well acquainted with Mr. Woodbourne, but she had not seen the girls since they were quite young children, and now, remarking Elizabeth, she asked Mrs. Hazleby if she was one of Mr. Woodbourne's daughters.

'Oh yes,' said Mrs. Hazleby, 'the eldest of them.'

'She has a remarkably fine countenance,' said Mrs. Bouverie.

'Do you admire her?' said Mrs. Hazleby; 'well, I never could see anything so remarkably handsome in Lizzie Woodbourne. Too thin, too sharp, too high-coloured; Kate is twenty times prettier, to say nothing of the little ones.'

'I should not call Miss Woodbourne pretty,' said Mrs. Bouverie, 'but I think her brow and eye exceedingly beautiful and full of expression.'

'Oh yes,' cried Mrs. Hazleby, 'she is thought vastly clever, I assure you, though for my part I never could see anything in her but pertness.'

'She has not the air of being pert,' said Mrs. Bouverie.

'Oh! she can give herself airs enough,' said Mrs. Hazleby; 'my poor sister-in-law has had trouble enough with her; just like her mother, they say.'

'So I was thinking,' said Mrs. Bouverie, looking at Elizabeth, who was stooping down to a little shy girl, and trying to hear her whispered request.

Mrs. Bouverie spoke in a tone so different from that which Mrs. Hazleby expected, that even she found that she had gone too far, and recollected that it was possible that Mrs. Bouverie might have known the first Mrs. Woodbourne. She changed her note. 'Just like her poor mother, and quite as delicate, poor girl.'

'Is she indeed?' said Mrs. Bouverie, in a tone of great interest.

'Yes, that she is, scarcely ever without a cough. Full of spirits, you see--rather too, much of it; but I should not be surprised any day--'

At this moment Winifred came running up, to cry, 'Look, Aunt Hazleby, at the basket of balls; I have been to the house to fetch them, and now the boys are going away to the cricket-ground, and the girls are to have a famous game at play.'

Mrs. Hazleby only said, 'Hm,' but the other lady paid more attention to the little girl, who was very little troubled with shyness, and soon was very happy--throwing the balls to the girls, and--at the same time--chattering to Mrs. Bouverie, and saying a great deal about 'Lizzie,' telling how Lizzie said that one little girl was good and another was naughty, that Lizzie said she should soon begin to teach her French; Lizzie taught her all her lessons, Mamma only heard her music; Lizzie had shewn her where to look in her Consecration-book, so that she should not be puzzled at Church to-day; Lizzie said she had behaved very well, and that she should tell Papa so; she had a red ribbon with a medal with Winchester Cathedral upon it, which Lizzie let her wear to shew Papa and Mamma when she was good at her lessons; she hoped she should wear it to-day, though she had not done any lessons, for Lizzie said it was a joyful day, like a Sunday. All this made Mrs. Bouverie desirous of being acquainted with 'Lizzie,' but she could find no opportunity of speaking to her, as Elizabeth never willingly came near strangers, and was fully occupied with the school-children, so that she and Anne were the last to come in-doors to dress.

They were surprised on coming in to find Helen sitting on the last step of the stairs, with Dora on her lap, the latter crying bitterly, and Helen using all those means of consolation, which, with the best intention, have generally the effect of making matters worse. As soon as Elizabeth appeared, Dora sprang towards her, exclaiming, 'Lizzie, dear Lizzie, do you know, Aunt Hazleby says that my mamma is not your mamma, nor Kate's, nor Helen's, and I do not like it. What does she mean? Lizzie, I do not understand.'

Elizabeth looked up rather fiercely; but, kissing her little sister, said, gently, 'Yes, Dora, it is really true, my own mother lies in the churchyard. I will shew you where.'

'And are you, not my sisters?' asked Dora, holding firmly by the hands of Elizabeth, and Helen.

'Oh yes, yes, Dora!' cried Helen, 'we are your sisters, only not quite, the same as Winifred.'

'And have you no mamma, really no mamma?' continued Dora looking frightened, although soothed by Elizabeth's manner, and by feeling that the truth was really told her.

'Not really, Dora; but your mamma is quite the same to us as if she really was our mother,' said. Elizabeth, leading the little girl away, and leaving Anne and Helen looking unutterable things at each other.

Helen then went into the large, drawing-room, to fetch some, of her out-of-door apparel which she had left there, and Anne followed her. No one was in the room but Mrs. Hazleby, who looked more disconcerted than Helen had ever seen her before. She seemed to think, it necessary to make some apology, and began, 'I am sure I had no notion that, the child did not know it all perfectly at her age.'

'Mamma has always wished to keep the little ones from knowing of any difference as long as possible,' said Helen, rather indignantly; but recollecting herself, she added, 'I think Dora is rather tired, and perhaps she was the more easily overcome for that reason.'

'Ah! very likely, poor child,' said Mrs. Hazleby; 'it was folly to take her to such a ceremony.'

'She seemed to enjoy it, and enter into it as much as any of us,' said Helen.

'Ah! well, some people's children are vastly clever,' said Mrs. Hazleby. 'Do you know where Fido is, Miss Helen? if one may ask you such a question.'

Helen replied very courteously, by an offer to go and look for him. He was quickly found, and as soon as she had brought him to his mistress, she followed Anne to Elizabeth's room, where in a short time they were joined by the latter, looking worn and tired, and with the brilliant flush of excitement on her cheeks.

'Is Dora comforted?' was the first question asked on her entrance.

'Oh yes,' said Elizabeth, 'that was soon settled; she was only scared, so I took her to Mamma, who kissed us both, told Dora she loved us all the same, and so on; which made her quite happy again.'

'Dear little affectionate creature!' exclaimed Helen warmly.

'How very angry with her Mrs. Hazleby seemed!' said Anne.

'Yes,' said Helen, 'because Dora came to me in her distress, and would not let Mrs. Hazleby kiss her.'

'How came Mrs. Hazleby to begin upon it?' said Elizabeth; 'was it from her instinctive perception of disagreeable subjects?'

'I can hardly tell,' said Helen, 'I was not there at first; I rather think--' but here she stopped short, and looked confused.

'Well, what do you think?'

'Why, I believe it arose from her seeing Uncle Edward playing with Edward on the green,' began Helen, with a good deal of hesitation, 'saying that he was his god-father, and--and she--she hoped he would be would be as--he would do as much for him, as if he was actually his uncle.'

'Horrid woman!' said Elizabeth, blushing deeply.

'My dear Lizzie,' said Anne, laughing, 'do you hope he will not?'

'Nonsense, Anne,' said Elizabeth, laughing too; 'but I hope you quite give up the Hazlebys after this specimen.'

'Now, Lizzie,' said Helen, 'that is quite in your unjust sweeping style of censuring. You do not mean to say that Lucy, or the Major, or the boys, are disagreeable.'

'Root and branch, they are all infected,' said Elizabeth; 'who could help it, living with Mrs. Hazleby?'

'Pray do not be so unfair, Lizzie,' continued Helen; 'I am sure that Lucy is a most amiable, sensible, gentle creature; the more to be admired for having such a mother and sister.'

'By way of foil, I suppose,' said Elizabeth; 'still, saving your presence, Helen, I think that if Lucy had all the sense you ascribe to her, she might keep things a little more straight.'

'Really, Lizzie,' said Helen, 'it is not like you to blame poor Lucy for her misfortunes; but I know very well that you only do it to contradict me.'

'Well,' said Elizabeth impatiently, 'I do allow that she is a redeeming point, but I do not give her such hyperbolical praise as you do; I may say she is the best of them, without calling her a paragon of perfection.'

'I never called her any such thing!' exclaimed Helen; 'but you will always wrest my words, and pretend to misunderstand me.'

'I am sorry I have vexed you, Helen,' said Elizabeth, more kindly; and Helen left the room.

'Indeed, Lizzie,' said Anne, 'I cannot think why you argued against this poor girl, after what you said yesterday.'

'Because I cannot bear Helen's sententious decided manner,' said Elizabeth; 'and she exaggerates so much, that I must sometimes take her down.'

'But,' said Anne, 'do you not exaggerate the exaggeration, and so put her more in the right than yourself?'

'You mean by turning her string of superlatives into a paragon of perfection,' said Elizabeth; 'I certainly believe I was unjust, but I could not help it.'

Anne did not see that her cousin might not have helped it, but she thought she had said enough on the subject, and let it pass.

'Now, Anne,' said Elizabeth, presently after, 'what strange people we are, to stand here abusing Helen and the Hazlebys, instead of talking over such wonderful happiness as it is to think that your father and mine have been allowed to complete such a work as this church.'

'Indeed it is wonderful happiness,' said Anne, her eyes filling with tears, 'but I do not know whether you feel as I do, that it is too great, too overwhelming, to talk of now it is fresh. We shall enjoy looking back to it more when we are further from it.'

'Yes,' said Elizabeth; 'this morning I was only fit to laugh or cry, at I did not know what, and now I am vexed with myself for having been too much occupied and annoyed with little things to be happy enough. This Consecration day will be a glorious time to look back to, when it is alone on the horizon, and we have lost sight of all that blemishes it now. I will tell you what it will be like. I once saw the Church, on a misty day, from a great distance. It was about the middle of the day, and the veil of mist was hanging all round the hill, but there stood the Church, clear and bright, and alone in the sunshine, all the scaffold poles and unfinished rough- ness lost sight of in the distance. I never saw a more beautiful sight.'

'And do you expect that distance of time will conceal all blemishes as well as distance of place?' said Anne.

'Yes, unless I take a telescope to look at them with,' answered Elizabeth; 'per- haps, Anne, in thirty years time, if we both live so long, we may meet and talk over this day, and smile, and wonder that we could have been vexed by anything at such a time.'

'You like looking forward,' said Anne; 'I suppose I am too happy, for I am afraid to look forward; any change of any sort must bring sorrow with it.'

'I suppose you are right,' said Elizabeth; 'that is, I believe the safest frame of mind to be that which resigns itself to anything that may be appointed for it, rather than that which makes schemes and projects for itself.'

'Oh! but, Lizzie,' said Anne, 'I did not mean that. Mine is rather an indolent frame, which does not scheme, because my present condition is, I do believe, hap- pier than any I could imagine upon earth. I do not think that is resignation--there are some things under which I do not think I could be resigned, at least not with my present feelings.'

'Yes, you would, Anne,' said Elizabeth; 'you are just the calm tempered person who would rise up to meet the trial in peace.--But I do not know what I am talking about; and so I shall go on with what I meant to say before--that bright visions are my great delight. I like to fancy what Horace and Edward may be, I like to imagine my own mind grown older, I like to consider what I shall think of the things that occupy us now. But then I am not likely to be disappointed, even if my castles in the air should fall down. You know I am not likely to be a long-lived person.'

'Oh! do not say so, my dear Lizzie,' cried Anne; 'I cannot bear it.'

'Indeed, Anne,' said Elizabeth, 'I did not mean to say anything which could shock you. I only touched upon what you must have known half your life, and what Mrs. Hazleby has taken good care that I should not forget. I am perfectly well now, and have nothing the matter with me; but then I know that a little illness has a great effect upon me, and my colds are much sooner caught than cured.'

Before Anne could answer, there was a knock at the door, and Lady Merton's maid appeared, ready to dress her young lady for the evening; and thus the conversation ended.

The girls were to drink tea in the inner drawing-room, as soon as the company were gone into the dining-room; and Anne and Elizabeth waited to come down-stairs till dinner had begun.

As soon as they entered the room, Harriet began to admire the lace trimming of Anne's dress, asking many questions about it, to all of which Anne replied with great good nature. As soon as the lace had been sufficiently discussed, Harriet turned round to Elizabeth, exclaiming, 'Why, Lizzie, why in the world have you taken to that fashion of doing your hair? it makes you look thinner than ever. Such dark hair too! it wants a little colour to relieve it; why do you not wear a red band in it, like mine?'

'I thought this way of wearing it saved time,' said Elizabeth; 'but I believe I shall curl it again.'

'Indeed I hope you will; you have no notion how thin it makes you look,' said Harriet.

'Of course I must look thin if I am thin,' said Elizabeth, a good deal annoyed by Harriet's pertinacity.

'Thin you are, indeed,' continued Harriet, taking hold of her wrist. Elizabeth drew back hastily, and Harriet relinquished it; conscious perhaps, that however thin the arm might look, her own broad ruddy hand would hardly bear a compari-son with Elizabeth's long slender white fingers, and returned to the subject of the hair, shaking her profusion of ringlets.

'And straight hair is all the fashion now, but I think it gives a terrible dowdy look. Only that does not signify when you are not out.--By-the-bye, Miss Merton, are you out?'

'I shall not be seventeen these three months,' said Anne.

'Well, I am not seventeen yet, nor near it,' pursued Harriet; 'but I always dine out, and at home too. Don't I, Lucy?'

Elizabeth did not think it necessary to make any apology for Harriet's not hav-ing been asked to dine with the company, since Mrs. Woodbourne had already settled that matter with Mrs. Hazleby; but Katharine, who, though younger, had more idea of manner, said, after a little hesitation, 'Mamma talked of it, but Papa said that if one dined all must, and there would be too many.'

'Oh, law! Kate,' said Harriet, 'never mind; I do not mind it a bit, I would just as soon drink tea here, as dine.--You are not out, are you, Lizzie?'

'If you consider that dining constitutes being out, I generally am,' said Elizabeth, rather coldly and haughtily.

'Ay, ay,' cried Harriet, laughing, 'you would be out indeed, to go without your dinner.--Capital, is not it, Kate? but I wanted to know whether you are regularly come out?'

'I do not know,' replied Elizabeth.

'Oh, then, you are not,' said Harriet; 'everyone knows who is out: I should not have been out now, if it had not been for Frank Hollis, (he is senior lieutenant at last, you know)--well, when our officers gave the grand ball at Hull, Frank Hollis came to Mamma, and said they could do nothing without the Major's daughter, and I must open the ball. Such nonsense he talked--didn't he, Lucy? Well, Mamma gave way, and said she'd persuade the Major. Papa was rather grumpy at first, you know, Lucy, but we coaxed him over at last. Oh, it was such fun! I danced first with Frank Hollis--just out of gratitude, you know, and then with Captain Murphy, and then--O Lucy, do you remember *who*?--and I had a silk dress which Mamma brought from India, trimmed just like yours, Miss Merton, only with four rows of lace, because I am taller, you know, and a berthe of--'

Elizabeth could endure this no longer, and broke in, 'And pray, Harriet, did you learn the book of fashions by heart?'

'Not quite,' said Harriet, with provoking obtuseness, or good humour; 'I did very nearly, though, when I was making my dress. Now, Lizzie, do not you wish you were out?'

'No, not in the least,' said Elizabeth, by this time quite out of patience; 'I think society a nuisance, and I am glad to be free of it as long as I can.'

'Lizzie,' said Helen gravely, 'you are talking rhodomontade.'

'By no means, Helen,' said Elizabeth; 'it is my serious opinion, that, unless you can find real friends, minds that suit you, you should keep to yourself, and let bores and geese keep to themselves.'

'Becoming yourself one of the interesting tribe of bears, or perhaps of crabs,' whispered Anne.

'Well, what an odd girl you are!' cried Harriet; 'well, if ever--!'

'But, Lizzie, what would become of the world if there was no society?' said Katherine.

'And, Lizzie,' began Helen, very seriously, 'do not you know that it is a duty to take part in society, that--'

'Oh yes, Helen!' answered Elizabeth; 'I know all that books and wise people say; but what I say is this: if a sumptuary law could decree that wits should be measured by one standard, like the ruffs and rapiers in Queen Elizabeth's time, so that those found wanting might be banished, there might be some use in meeting people; but in the present state of things there is none.'

'But how would you choose your standard?' said Anne; 'everyone would take their own degree of sense as a measure.'

'Let them,' said Elizabeth; 'there would be a set of measures like the bolters in a mill, one for the pastry-flour, one for the bread-flour, one for the blues, one for the bran.'

'I am glad you put the blues after the bread,' said Anne; 'there is hope of you yet, Lizzie.'

Elizabeth was too far advanced in her career of nonsense to be easily checked, even by Anne; and she continued, 'Sir Walter Scott says in one of his letters, that he wishes there could be a whole village of poets and antiquaries isolated from the rest of the world. That must be like what I mean.'

'I do not think he meant what he said there,' said Helen.

'And pray remember,' said Anne, 'that your favourite brown bread is made of all those kinds mixed--bran, and pastry-flour, and all.'

'Yes,' said Helen, 'all the world would turn idiots if there were not a few sensible people to raise the others.'

'Well,' said Elizabeth, 'you know the Veillees du Chateau says, there is a village where all the people do turn idiots at fourteen.'

'You are just the right age, Helen,' said Anne, 'you had better take care, since Lizzie says you live in such a foolish world.'

Helen had not tact enough to perceive that it was better to turn off the discussion by a joke, and continued, 'And you forget how useful it is to the sensible people to be obliged to bear and forbear.'

'I should be content, if the foolish people would be raised by the wise, instead of debasing them,' said Elizabeth.

'If people are really wise, they will not let themselves be debased,' said Anne.

Helen glanced towards Lucy, Elizabeth caught her eye, and smiled in a way which almost compensated for all her unkindness in their dispute an hour before.

Harriet and Katherine, who had not been much interested by this argument, now started another subject of conversation, which they had almost entirely to themselves, and which occupied them until tea was over, somewhat to Anne's amusement and Elizabeth's disgust, as they listened to it.

As soon as the tea-things were removed, Elizabeth and Anne went to fetch the children. Elizabeth let loose her indignation as soon as she was out of the drawing-room.

'Did you ever hear anything so vulgar?' said she.

'Indeed it was very ridiculous,' said Anne, beginning to laugh at the remembrance.

'How can you be diverted with things that enrage me?' said Elizabeth.

'It is better than taking them to heart, as you do, my poor Lizzie,' said Anne; 'they are but folly after all.'

'Disgusting provoking folly,' said Elizabeth; 'and then to see Kate looking as if she thought it must be so delectable. Really, Kate is quite spoiled between Harriet and the Abbeychurch riff-raff, and I can do nothing to prevent it.'

'But,' said Anne diffidently, seeing that her cousin was in a graver mood this evening, 'do not you think that perhaps if you could be a little more companionable to Kate, and not say things so evidently for the sake of contradiction, you might gain a little useful influence?'

'Well,' said Elizabeth, smiling, 'I believe I do deserve a good scolding; I fancy I was outrageously rude; but when people talk such stuff, I do not much care what I say, as long as I am on the other side of the question.'

'Still the reverse of wrong is not always right,' said Anne.

They now found themselves at the nursery door, and summoned the children from that scene of playthings, and bread and butter. Down-stairs, one of those games at romps arose, for which little children are often made an excuse by great ones, and which was only concluded by the entrance of the ladies from the drawing-room, which caused Harriet hastily to retreat into the inner drawing-room, to smoothe her ruffled lace; while Katherine was re-tying Winifred's loosened sash, and laying a few refractory curls in their right places.

Mrs. Woodbourne called Elizabeth, and introduced her as 'my eldest daughter,' to Mrs. Bouverie, and to Mrs. Dale, a lady who had lately come to live in the neighbourhood, and who discovered a most striking resemblance between Mrs. Woodbourne and Elizabeth, certainly at the expense of a considerable stretch of imagination, as Mrs. Woodbourne was a very little and very elegant looking person, very fair and pale, and Elizabeth was tall, dark-eyed, dark-haired, her figure much too slender for her height, and her movements too rapid to be graceful, altogether as different a style of person as could well be imagined.

Not much prepossessed in favour of the party in general by this specimen, Elizabeth, after shaking hands with Miss Maynard and her niece, people whom she seldom saw, and did not much like, retreated to one of the windows, and there began to meditate, as was her usual custom on such occasions. Once, when accompanying Mrs. Woodbourne on a morning visiting expedition, she had translated the Erl King, which she knew by heart, into English, far more literal than Sir Walter Scott's, and with no fault, except that not above half the couplets professed to rhyme, and most of those that did were deficient in metre. Another time she had composed three quarters of a story of a Saxon hero, oppressed by a Norman baron, and going to the Crusades; and at another time she had sent back the whole party to the times of Queen Elizabeth, and fancied what they might be saying about the Spanish Armada. But now, whether because there was too much talking in the room, or because the Consecration had lately left no room for the fancies on which she was accustomed to feed, she could find nothing more sublime to reflect upon than the appearance of her cousin Anne, who was entertaining the young Miss Maynard, a shy girl, yet pleased with notice, by a conversation, which, if not very interesting, saved her from belonging to any of the four agreeable tribes mentioned at tea-time.

Now, Anne, though she did not posses the tall figure or striking countenance of her cousins, the Woodbournes, or the brilliant complexion of her brother, was one of those people who always look well. She was small and slightly made, and very graceful; and everything she wore was appropriate and becoming, so that, without bestowing much thought on the matter, she never looked otherwise than perfectly well dressed. She was rather pale; her eyes were grey, with long dark lashes; and her hair brown; her features were well formed and animated; and though by no means remarkable, everyone called her nice-looking; some said she was pretty, and a few thought and felt that her countenance was lovely. So much had lately been said about dress--about Elizabeth's curls, and Helen's tails, and Anne's lace-- that, wonderful to say, it was the readiest subject Elizabeth could find to meditate upon. As she looked at her cousin's white muslin frock, with its border of handsome Moravian work, and its delicate blue satin ribbons, at her well arranged hair, and pretty mosaic brooch, she entered upon a calculation respecting the portion of a woman's mind which ought to be occupied with her dress--a mental process, the result of which might perhaps have proved of great benefit to herself, and ultimately to Dora and Winifred, had it not been suddenly cut short in the midst by a piercing scream from the latter young lady, who had been playing on the floor with Edward and Fido.

Mrs. Woodbourne instantly caught up the little girl in her arms, and sat down on the sofa with her on her lap, while Winifred buried her hand in her pocket-handkerchief, screaming and sobbing violently. Fido slunk away under the sofa; and Elizabeth hastily made her way through the circle of ladies who surrounded Mrs. Woodbourne.

'That is what comes of teazing him,' said Mrs. Hazleby reproachfully to Edward; who answered in a loud voice, 'I am sure I did not make him do it.'

Elizabeth knelt down by Mrs. Woodbourne, and began to unroll the handkerchief in which Winifred had wound up her hand; but she was prevented by a fresh scream from the patient.

'Oh! my dear, never mind, do not cry; come, be a brave woman,' said poor Mrs. Woodbourne, her voice quivering with alarm.

'Poor little dear!' exclaimed Mrs. Dale, 'she bears it like a little angel; but it is quite a severe bite.'

'Mamma,' said Elizabeth, rising, 'I think she had better come up-stairs with me. Do not you come, Mamma; I will send for you, if--if it is more than a scratch.'

She took Winifred in her arms and carried her off, followed by Mrs. Dale, Miss Maynard, Harriet, Katherine, and Dora, the last-mentioned looking quite pale with fright.

'If you please,' said Elizabeth, turning round at the foot of the stairs, 'I can manage her better alone.'

She gained her point, though at the expense of politeness. Mrs. Dale and Miss Maynard retreated, and Harriet and Katherine followed in their train. Dora looked inquiringly at her eldest sister.

'Yes, Dora, you may come,' said she, running up-stairs to her own room, where she shut the door, and set Winifred on her feet again. 'Well, Winifred, let us see,' said she cheerfully, 'are you much hurt?'

'It bleeds,' said Winifred, withholding her hand.

'Not very much,' said Elizabeth, removing the handkerchief, and washing off the blood, which had been more the cause of the scream than the pain. She soon satisfied herself and her sisters that the bite was scarcely more than a scratch; and a piece of sticking-plaster, fetched by Dora, whose ready eye and clear thoughtful head had already made her the best finder in the family, had covered the wound before Mrs. Woodbourne came up to satisfy herself as to the extent of the injury. Winifred had by this time been diverted from the contemplation of her misfortunes by the fitting on of the sticking-plaster, and by admiration of Anne's bright rose-wood dressing-box, and was full of the delight of discovering that A. K. M., engraven in silver upon the lid, stood for Anne Katherine Merton, when her mamma came in. It appeared that the little girl and her brother had been playing rather too roughly with Fido, and that he had revenged himself after the usual fashion of little dogs, especially of those not come to years of discretion. Winifred was quite ready to assure her mamma that he had scarcely hurt her, and that she was very sorry she had cried so much. Mrs. Woodbourne and Elizabeth, however, agreed that it would be better for her to appear no more that evening, and Dora undertook to keep her company in the nursery--glad, as Elizabeth could see, to escape from the presence of Aunt Hazleby, who had sunk much in Dora's good graces since her conversation with her in the afternoon.

'If people would but let children alone,' said Elizabeth, as the two little girls departed hand in hand; 'it puts me out of all patience to see her first made silly by being pitied, and then told she is an angel. Too bad and too silly, I declare.'

'You should consider a little, my dear, and not speak so hastily,' said gentle Mrs. Woodbourne; 'they mean it kindly.'

'Mistaken kindness,' said Elizabeth, as she opened the drawing-room door.

In a moment they were overwhelmed with inquiries for 'the sweet little sufferer,' as Mrs. Dale called her.

'I only hope there is no fear of the dog's being mad,' observed that lady.

'Oh! there is no danger of that,' said Elizabeth, knowing how such a terror would dwell on Mrs. Woodbourne's spirits. 'See, he can drink.'

Mrs. Hazleby had taken possession of the cream-jug, which had accompanied the coffee, and was consoling the offender by pouring some of its contents into a saucer for him.

'But I thought it was water that mad dogs refuse,' said Mrs. Dale.

'Mad dog!' cried Mrs. Hazleby, 'he is as mad as I am, I fancy; it was quite enough to make him bite when Edward there was pulling his ears.'

'I did not pull his ears, Aunt Hazleby; I did not make him bite Winifred,' vociferated Edward; 'I told you so before, Aunt Hazleby, and you will say so.'

'Fine little fellow,' whispered Mrs. Dale, quite loud enough for Edward to hear her; 'I quite admire his spirit.'

'Do not be rude, Edward my dear,' said his mother.

'But Aunt Hazleby will say that I made Fido bite Winifred, Mamma,' said Edward; 'and I did not, he did it of himself.'

'Never mind now, my love, pray be quiet, my dear boy,' said Mrs. Woodbourne imploringly; and Edward, who was really a very tractable boy, walked off to his sister Katherine.

Mrs. Dale then seized upon Mrs. Woodbourne, to tell her some horrible stories of hydrophobia; and Elizabeth, in hopes of lessening the impression such stories were likely to make on Mrs. Woodbourne's mind, listened also, sometimes not very courteously correcting evident exaggerations, and at others contradicting certain statements. At last, just as the subject, fertile as it was, was exhausted, Anne's going to the piano, and carrying off a train of listeners, brought Mrs. Bouverie next to Elizabeth, and she took the opportunity of entering into conversation with her.

'Do you play, Miss Woodbourne?'

'No, I do not,' replied Elizabeth, who particularly disliked this mode of beginning a conversation.

'Do not you like music?' continued Mrs. Bouverie.

'I seldom have heard any I liked,' said Elizabeth shortly.

'Indeed you have been unfortunate,' said Mrs. Bouverie; 'but perhaps you are not fond of the piano?'

'No,' said Elizabeth, with rather less of the manner of a suspected criminal examined in sight of the rack; 'I am sick of all the Abbeychurch pianos; I know them all perfectly, and hear nothing else.'

Mrs. Bouverie laughed, and was glad to obtain something like an answer. 'Your cousin plays very well,' said she.

'Yes,' said Elizabeth, 'I like her music better than most people's, and she does not make a great fuss about it, she plays when she thinks people like it, and not when they ask only out of politeness, without caring about it.'

'Do you think many people ask in that manner?' said Mrs. Bouverie.

'Oh yes, everyone,' said Elizabeth; 'what can they do when they see a disconsolate damsel sitting in a corner with nothing to say, and only longing to be at the piano by way of doing something? It would be too cruel not to ask her.'

'Did you ever do so?' said Mrs. Bouverie, smiling.

'No,' said Elizabeth, 'luckily it is no affair of mine yet; but if ever it was, there would be a hard struggle between my politeness and sincerity.'

'Sincerity would be most likely to gain the day,' thought Mrs. Bouverie. 'Perhaps,' said she, 'you are not a fair judge of other people's sincerity, since you do not like music yourself.'

'I think,' said Elizabeth, 'that even if I did play, I could see in people's faces whether they meant what they said; that is, if vanity and love of applause did not blind me.'

Mrs. Bouverie was silent for a moment, and then said, 'Well, I must say, I am disappointed to find that you do not play.'

Elizabeth remembered how well her mother had, played, and it was plain to her that Mrs. Bouverie was noticing her for her mother's sake. She looked down and coloured as she replied, 'Both my sisters are musical, and Helen is said to be likely to sing very well. I believe the history of my want of music to be,' added she, with a bright smile, 'that I was too naughty to learn; and now, I am afraid--I am not sorry for it, as it would have taken up a great deal of time, and two singing sisters are surely enough for one family.'

'I was in hopes of hearing,' said Mrs. Bouverie, 'that you had trained your school-children to sing the sixty-fifth Psalm as nicely as they did to-day. I am sure their teacher must have come from the Vicarage.'

'No,' said Elizabeth, 'it was the school-master who taught them. Perhaps, if Helen had not been from home so long, she might have helped the girls, but when she came home three weeks ago, it was hardly worth while for her to begin. That is the only reason I ever wished to understand music.'

Mrs. Bouverie now began talking to her about the church and its architecture, and of the children, in exactly the way that Elizabeth liked, and in half an hour she saw more of Elizabeth's true self than Miss Maynard had ever seen, though she had known her all her life. Miss Maynard had seen only her roughness. Mrs. Bouverie had found her way below it. Elizabeth was as sincere and open as the day, although from seldom meeting with anyone who could comprehend or sympathize with her ideas, her manners had acquired a degree of roughness and reserve, difficult to penetrate, and anything but attractive, suiting ill with her sweet smile and beaming eyes. She was talking quite happily and confidentially to Mrs. Bouverie, when she caught Mrs. Woodbourne's eye, and seeing her look anxious, she remembered Winifred's disaster, and took the first opportunity of hastening up-stairs to see whether the little girl's hand was still in as favourable a state as when she left her.

A few moments after she had quitted the room, Sir Edward Merton approached Mrs. Bouverie, and took the place beside her, which Elizabeth had lately occupied.

'I hope Elizabeth has been gracious to you, as I see you have been so kind as to talk to her,' said he, smiling.

'Oh, I hope we are becoming good friends,' said Mrs. Bouverie; 'I have seldom seen so young a girl shew as much mind as your niece.'

'I am very glad to hear you say so,' said Sir Edward, 'for she is apt to be rather more reserved with strangers than could be wished.'

'Perhaps she did not consider me as an entire stranger; I remember seeing her once when a most engaging little child of four or five years old,' said Mrs. Bouverie;

'and now I hope our acquaintance will continue. Shall we see her at Marlowe Court to-morrow, as I believe we meet you there? Of course we shall see Miss Merton?'

'No, I believe not,' said Sir Edward; 'we are rather too large a number without the girls, who really form quite a troop by themselves.'

'I like to see your daughter and Miss Woodbourne together,' said Mrs. Bouverie; 'I am sure they must be great allies.'

'Yes,' said Sir Edward, 'there is a tolerably strong cousinly friendship between them: Anne has a wholesome feeling of inferiority, which makes her rather proud of her cousin's preference.'

'Do you not think Miss Woodbourne very like her mother?' said Mrs. Bouverie. 'I knew her immediately by the resemblance.'

'Very--very like her, a little darker certainly,' said Sir Edward, 'but she reminds me of her constantly--there--that smile is my sister's exactly.'

Elizabeth had just then re-entered the room, and was assuring her mamma that Winifred had been as playful as ever all the remainder of the evening, and was now fast asleep in bed.

'I am only afraid she is too fragile and delicate a creature,' said Mrs. Bouverie; 'is her health strong?'

'Strong? no, not very,' said Sir Edward, 'she requires care, but there is nothing much amiss with her; I know most people about here are in the habit of lamenting over her as in a most dangerous state; but I believe the fact is, that Mrs. Woodbourne is a nervous anxious person, and frightens herself more than there is any occasion for.'

'Then I hope she generally looks less delicate than she does to-night,' said Mrs. Bouverie.

'Oh! she may well look over-worked to-night,' said Sir Edward; 'she has a spirit in her which would not let her rest on such a day as this.--Come here, Miss Lizzie,' said he, beckoning to her, 'I want you to account for those two red spots upon your cheeks. Do you think they ought to be there?'

'Yes, if they come in a good cause, Uncle,' said Elizabeth.

'Do you mean, then, to wear them any longer than necessary?' said Sir Edward; 'pray have you sat still for five minutes together to-day?'

'Yes, while I was at tea,' said Elizabeth.

'And why are not you in bed and asleep at this moment?' asked her uncle.

'That is the very question Mamma has been asking,' said Elizabeth; 'and I have been promising to depart, as soon as I can make my escape; so good night, Uncle Edward--good night,' said she, giving her hand to her uncle and to Mrs. Bouverie with almost equal cordiality.

'Good night, Lizzie, get you gone,' said Sir Edward; 'and if you can carry off my girl with you, I shall be all the better pleased.'

Elizabeth succeeded in touching Anne's arm; and the two cousins flitted away together, and soon forgot the various delights and annoyances of the day in sleep.

CHAPTER VI.

The next morning was gloomy and rainy, as Elizabeth informed Anne at about seven o'clock; 'and I am not sorry for it,' said she, 'for I want to have you all to myself at home, so we will turn the incubi over to Kate and Helen, and be comfortable together.'

'Will they submit to such treatment?' said Anne.

'Oh yes, my dear,' said Elizabeth; 'they want us as little as we want them; they only want a little civility, and I will not be so sparing of that useful commodity as I was yesterday evening. And now, Anne, I am going to beg your pardon for being so excessively rude to Harriet, as I was last night. She did not mind it, but you did, and much more than if it had been to yourself.'

'I believe I did,' said Anne; 'other people do not know what you mean when you set up your bristles, and I do. Besides, I was sorry for Lucy, who looks as if she had sensitiveness enough for the whole family.'

'Poor Lucy!' said Elizabeth;

"A weary lot is thine, fair maid,
A weary lot is thine."

Yes, Lucy has very deep feeling; you may see it in the painful flushing of her cheek, and the downcast look of her eye, when her mother and sister expose themselves. I really believe that that poor girl has more to endure than most people.'

'O Lizzie,' said Anne, 'how differently you spoke of her yesterday!'

'Yes,' said Elizabeth, 'but then I was furious with Mrs. Hazleby; and besides, I believe the truth was, that I was very tired and very cross, not exactly the way in which I intended to conclude the Consecration day; and now I am in my senses, I am very sorry I behaved as I did. But, Anne, though I hereby retract all I said in dispraise of Lucy, and confess that I was rude to Harriet, do not imagine that I disavow all I said about society last night, for I assure you that I expressed my deliberate opinion.'

'Your deliberate opinion, my dear?' said Anne, laughing.

'Yes, my deliberate opinion, my dear,' repeated Elizabeth. 'Pray why should not I have a deliberate opinion, as well as Hannah More, or Locke on the Human Understanding, or anyone else?'

'Because,' rejoined Anne, 'I think that if the rest of the world were of your deliberate opinion, there would soon be a lock on the human understanding.'

'I am sure I think there is at present,' returned Elizabeth; 'did you see Aunt Anne last night wasted upon Mrs. Dale, obliged to listen to the dullest stuff that ever was invented, and poor Mamma frightened out of her wits? I should not wonder if she had dreamt of mad dogs all night.'

'I do not defend Mrs. Dale's powers of intellect,' said Anne, 'but I should have thought that you at least had little reason to complain. You were very well off next to Mrs. Bouverie.'

'Oh! Mrs. Bouverie is a rara avis, an exception to the general rule,' said Elizabeth; 'but you know, she or my uncle, or aunt, or Papa, are generally forced to put a lock on their understanding. Why, Anne, what are you laughing at?'

'Lizzie, I beg your pardon,' said Anne, trying to check herself, 'but I could not help it. Your speech put me in mind of the prints from Albano's four elements. Do not you remember Juno's visit to AEolus, where he is opening the door of a little corner cupboard where he keeps the puff-cheeked winds locked up? Do you mean to say that Mamma keeps her mighty powers of mind locked up in the same way, for fear they should burst out and overwhelm everybody?'

Elizabeth heartily joined in her cousin's merriment. 'I will tell you what I do mean, Anne, what the great law of society is. Now, do not put on that absurd face of mock gravity, or I shall only laugh, instead of arguing properly.'

'Well, let us hear,' said Anne.

'It is almost more important than the law that you must eat with a knife and fork,' said Elizabeth. 'There is one level of conversation, fit for the meanest capacity; and whoever ventures to transgress it, is instantly called blue, or a horrid bore,

&c., &c.'

'Nonsense, Lizzie,' said Anne, laughing; 'I am sure I have heard plenty of clever people talk, about sensible things too, and never did I hear them called bores, or blue, or any of your awful et ceteras either.'

'Because people did not dare to do so,' said Elizabeth, 'but they thought it all the same.'

'What do you mean by people?' said Anne.

'The dull, respectable, common-place gentry, who make up the mass of mankind,' said Elizabeth.

'Do they?' said Anne.

'Do not they?' said Elizabeth.

'I do not know what the mass of mankind may be at Abbeychurch,' said Anne, 'but I am sure the people whom we see oftenest at home, are such as I think it a privilege to know.' And she began to enumerate these friends.

'Oh! Anne,' interrupted Elizabeth, 'do not, for pity's sake, make me discontented; here am I in Abbeychurch, and must make the best of it. I must be as polite and hypocritical as I can make myself. I must waste my time and endure dullness.'

'As to waste of time,' said Anne, 'perhaps it is most usefully employed in what is so irksome as you find being in company. Mamma has always wished me to remember, that acquiring knowledge may after all be but a selfish gratification, and many things ought to be attended to first.'

'That doctrine would not do for everybody,' said Elizabeth.

'No,' said Anne, 'but it does for us; and you will see it plainer, if you remember on what authority it is said that all knowledge is profitable for nothing without charity.'

'Charity, yes,' said Elizabeth; 'but Christian love is a very different thing from drawing-room civility.'

'Not very different from bearing and forbearing, as Helen said,' answered Anne.

'Politeness is not great enough,' said Elizabeth, 'to belong to charity.'

'You are not the person to say so,' said Anne.

'Because I dislike it so much,' said Elizabeth, 'but that is because I despise it. It is such folly to sit a whole evening with your hands before you doing nothing.'

'But do you not think,' said Anne, 'that enduring restraint, and listening to what is not amusing, for the sake of pleasing others, is doing something?'

'Passively, not actively,' said Elizabeth; 'but it is not to please others, it is only that they may think you well bred, or rather that they may not think about you at all.'

'It is to please our father and mother,' said Anne.

'Yes, and that is the reason it must be done,' said Elizabeth; 'it is the way of the world, and cannot be helped.'

'Rather say it is the trial which has been ordained for us,' said Anne.

'Well,' said Elizabeth, smiling, 'I know all the time that you have the best of the argument. It would not be so if it was not good for us.'

'And as it is,' said Anne, 'I believe that there is more enjoyment in the present order of things, than there would be in any arrangement we could devise.'

'Oh! doubtless,' said Elizabeth, 'just as the corn ripens better with all the disasters that seem to befall it, than it would if we had the command of the clouds.'

'Of course,' said Anne, 'you really are a much more reasonable creature than you pretend to be, Lizzie.'

'Am I?' said Elizabeth. 'Well, I will just tell you my great horror, and I suppose you will laugh at me. I can endure gossip for old people who cannot employ themselves, and must talk, and have nothing to talk of but their neighbours; but only think of those wretched *faineants* who go chattering on, wasting their own time and other people's, doing no good on the face of the earth, and a great deal of harm.'

'But these unfortunates are probably quite as unable to talk on any very wise subjects, as your beloved old people, to whom you give a license to gossip,' said Anne; 'and you do not wish to condemn them to perpetual silence. They are most likely to be estimable people, who ought to be amused.'

'Estimable--yes, perhaps,' said Elizabeth, 'but then I cannot esteem a silly gossip.'

'Why, Lizzie,' cried Anne, 'you are still at the old story that it is better to be wicked than stupid; at least, you reason upon that foundation, though you do not really think so.'

'I believe,' said Elizabeth, 'that there must be some great crook in my mind; for though I know and believe as firmly as I do any other important thing, that mere intellect is utterly worthless, I cannot feel it; it bewitches me as beauty does some people, and I suppose always will, till I grow old and stupid, or get my mind into better order.'

'Really,' said Anne, 'I think the strongest proof of your beginning to grow old and stupid, is your doing such a very common-place thing, as to abuse honest gossip.'

There was service at St. Mary's Church on Wednesday and Friday mornings; but on this day the rain was so violent, that of all the party at the Vicarage, the Mertons, and Elizabeth, Katherine, and Helen, alone ventured to go to church.

When they returned, Anne followed her mother to her room, to talk over the events of the previous day. After much had been said of the Consecration, and also of their wonder and regret at Rupert's absence, Anne said, 'How strange it seems to lose sight of you and Papa as I have done ever since I have been here! Mamma, I have scarcely been with you at all, and never see Papa but when he is talking to Uncle Woodbourne, and everyone else is in the room.'

'But I hope you are enjoying yourself, my dear?' said Lady Merton.

'Oh yes, Mamma,' cried Anne; 'Lizzie is more delightful than ever, when we are alone.'

'Are you taking a sudden romantic turn?' said Lady Merton, smiling; 'do you mean in future to keep one friend all to yourself?'

'Oh no, Mamma,' said Anne, laughing; 'I only meant that Lizzie is more like herself when we are alone together. Sometimes when the others are there, she gets vexed, and says things which I do not like to hear, only for the sake of differing from them.'

'I have seen something of the kind about her before,' said Lady Merton, 'but not enough to be unpleasant.'

'No, Mamma, because you do not talk as Miss Hazleby did yesterday,' said Anne, smiling. 'She certainly did make a very ridiculous oration about officers and flirtations; but Lizzie, instead of putting a stop to it quietly and gently, only went into the other extreme, and talked about disliking all society.'

'I am very sorry to hear this,' said Lady Merton; 'I am afraid she will make herself absurd and disagreeable by this spirit of contradiction, even if nothing worse comes of it.'

'It was not all out of a spirit of contradiction,' said Anne, 'though she said this morning, that she was very tired and very cross yesterday evening. But, Mamma, she also said that she thinks the time she spends in company wasted, and she really believes that no one dares to talk sense, or that if he does, everyone dislikes him.'

'That is only a little unconscious affectation of being wiser than other people, assisted by living in a place where there are the usual complement of dull people, and where her father's situation prevents him from associating only with those whom he would prefer,' said Lady Merton; 'her good sense will get the better of it. I am much more anxious about this spirit of contradiction.'

'Yes, it certainly led her to be very unjust, as she acknowledged this morning,' said Anne, 'and rather unkind to Helen. But then it was no wonder that she was mad with the Hazlebys.'

Anne then told the history of poor Dora's trouble, and was quite satisfied with her mother's displeasure at Mrs. Hazleby, and her admiration of little Dora.

'And what do you think of Helen?' asked she presently.

'I can hardly tell,' said Anne, 'she is still very demure, with very little of Lizzie's sparkling merriment; indeed, she does not seem in the least able to enter into a joke. But then she said some very sensible things. Lizzie said she wondered what we should think of her. She thinks her very much improved, but complains that she has lost her home feelings, and cares only for Dykelands; I scarcely know what she means.'

'I think that I can guess,' said Lady Merton, 'from knowing a little more of Mrs. Staunton's character. She is a very amiable person, and has in reality, I believe, plenty of good sense; but she has allowed herself to fall into an exaggerated style of feeling and expression, which, I dare say, bewitched a girl like Helen, and now makes her find home cold and desolate.'

'Like the letter which Mrs. Staunton wrote to you about Rupert, and which Papa called ecstatic,' said Anne.

'That is an instance of Mrs. Staunton's way of expressing herself,' said Lady Merton; 'now I will give you one of her acuteness of feeling, as she calls it. Your Aunt Katherine was her greatest friend when she was a girl, though I believe the kind epithets she lavished upon me would have been enough to stock two or three moderate friendships. We all used to walk together, and spend at least one evening in the week together. One evening, your aunt, who had a good deal of the same high careless spirit which you observe in Lizzie, chanced to make some observation upon the rudeness of sailors in general, forgetting that Helen Atherley's brother was a sailor.'

'Or if she had remembered it,' said Anne, 'judging by Lizzie, she would have said the same thing; she would have taken it for granted that the present company was always excepted.'

'Captain Atherley was not of the present company,' said Lady Merton, 'he was in the Mediterranean; and it happened that he had not had time to call at Merton Hall in due form, the last time he had been at home, so that poor Helen thought that this speech was aimed at him. She said nothing at the time; but next morning arrived a note to me, to entreat me to find out what her darling Henry could possibly have done to offend dearest Katherine Merton, for she should be wretched till she understood it, and Katherine had forgiven her and him. She assured me that she had lain awake all night, thinking it over, and had at last come to the conclusion that it must be this unfortunate omission, and she promised to write to dear Henry immediately, to make him send all possible apologies.'

'Poor Captain Atherley!' exclaimed Anne; 'and what could my aunt say?'

'Unfortunately,' said Lady Merton, 'both she and I had entirely forgotten the speech, and could not guess what could have given rise to Helen's imaginations. After a consultation, I was deputed to Helen with many assurances that Katherine was very sorry, she could not exactly tell why, but for whatever had grieved Helen; and after a good deal of kissing and lamenting on both sides, which, I believe, Katherine considered as a punishment for her inconsiderate speech, things were set right again.'

'Inconsiderate, Mamma?' said Anne; 'that seems as if you blamed my aunt, when it seems to me that Mrs. Staunton deserved all the blame for her excessive folly, and what I should think want of confidence in her friend's affection.'

'It was certainly very silly,' said Lady Merton; 'but you know, Anne, that when people have once accustomed themselves to get into a habit of making mountains of mole-hills, they cannot see anything as it really is. I thought Katherine quite in the right, as you do now, but I believe she considered that, knowing as she did the over-sensitiveness of her friend, she should have been more cautious in what she said.'

'That was the right way for her to take it,' said Anne; 'but I still think Mrs. Staunton must be an excessively silly person. Of course one would wish to keep from hurting people's feelings, but it really is hardly possible to help it, if they will ride out to meet offence in such a way.'

'Yet, Anne,' said her mother, 'you may comfort yourself with knowing that as long as you do what is commanded, set a watch before your lips, you are not likely to wound the feelings of others, however sensitive.'

'I know, Mamma,' said Anne, 'that would correct every fault of that kind; but then I hardly know how to do so thoroughly. And I think sensitiveness is a good thing--at least, it makes people know better what will hurt others.'

'Be sensitive for others, without being ready to take offence for yourself, then, Anne,' said Lady Merton. 'And now that you have fitted the moral to my story, I must go down and help Mrs. Woodbourne to entertain Mrs. Hazleby.'

'I pity you,' said Anne. 'If everyone, or indeed if half the world were like her, I should be more violent in my opinions than Lizzie is.'

'And what are you going to do?' asked Lady Merton.

'I am going to sit in the school-room,' said Anne; 'I had a special invitation from Dora this morning.'

On going down-stairs, Anne found that Katherine and Harriet had gone to spend the morning with the Mrs. Turner mentioned during the walk to St. Austin's, as her daughter, Miss Wilhelmina, had engaged to teach Harriet to make wax flowers. Lucy was up-stairs, writing to Major Hazleby; and Helen was sitting in the school-room, where Elizabeth was teaching the children. Little Winifred had just finished her lessons, and was skipping off in high glee with her medal round her neck, to tell her mamma that she had gained four good marks. Dora was perched on a high stool, at Elizabeth's desk, with a broadly ruled paper before her, on the top of which the words, 'My dear Horace, St. Austin's Church was consecrated yesterday,' were to be seen in fair round hand. No more was visible, for the little girl laughingly laid down her rosy cheek, and all her light wavy curls, flat upon the letter, as Anne advanced and made a stealthy attempt to profit by the intelligence she was sending to her brother. Edward was standing by Elizabeth, reading Mrs. Trimmer's Fabulous Histories, for, though five years old, he made very slow progress in

English literature, being more backward in learning to read than any of the others had been, excepting Helen. He did not like the trouble of spelling, and was in the habit of guessing at every word he did not know; and on his very composedly calling old Joe the gardener, 'the old gander,' Anne burst into an irrepressible giggle, and Helen, sedate as she was, could not help following her example. They had just composed themselves, when Edward made another blunder, which set them off again, and Elizabeth, who when alone with the children, could bear anything with becoming gravity, also gave way.

Edward, finding that he was diverting them, began to make absurd mistakes on purpose, so that Elizabeth was forced to call him to order. Anne thought it best to leave the room, and Helen followed her, saying, 'We had better leave Lizzie to manage him by herself; she always does better without me.'

'You have never shewn me your drawings, Helen,' said Anne; 'I should like very much to see them, if you will let me.'

'If you please,' said Helen. 'Will you come up to my room? I keep all my own things there, out of the way of the critics.'

'What critics?' inquired Anne.

'Lizzie, to be sure, and Papa,' said Helen; 'I think them the severest people I know.'

'Do you indeed!' said Anne.

'Do not you?' said Helen; 'does not Lizzie say the sharpest things possible? I am sure she does to me, and she never likes anything I do. If there is any little fault in it, she and Papa always look at that, rather than anything else.'

'Well,' said Anne, 'it is a comfort that if they like anything you do, you are sure it is really very good. Their praise is worth more than that of other people.'

Helen sighed, but made no reply, as by this time they had arrived at the door of the room which she shared with Katherine. It was a complete contrast to Elizabeth's; it was larger and lighter, and looked out upon the bright garden, the alms-houses, and the church tower. The upper part of the window was occupied by Katherine's large cage of canary birds, and below was a stand of flower-pots, a cactus which never dreamt of blossoming, an ice-plant, and a columnia belonging to Katherine, a nourishing daphne of Helen's, and a verbena, and a few geranium cuttings which she had brought from Dykelands, looking very miserable under cracked tumblers and stemless wine-glasses. On a small round table were, very prettily arranged, various little knicknacks and curiosities, which Elizabeth always laughed at, such as a glass ship, which was surrounded with miniature watering-pots, humming-tops, knives and forks, a Tonbridge-ware box, a gold-studded horn bonbonniere, a Breakwater-marble ruler, several varieties of pincushions, a pen-wiper with a doll in the middle of it, a little dish of money-cowries, and another of Indian shot, the seed of the mahogany tree, some sea-eggs, a false book made of the wreck of the Royal George, and some pieces of spar and petrifactions which Helen had acquired on an expedition to Matlock with the Stauntons. The book-shelf, however, was to Anne the most attractive object in the room; and whilst Helen was untying the strings of her portfolio, she went up to it.

'What a beautiful little Bishop Wilson!' exclaimed she, taking out one of the books.

'Yes,' said Helen with a sigh, 'that was dear Mrs. Staunton's last present to me before I left Dykelands. She said that perhaps she should not see me again before I was confirmed, and it was the fittest Godmother's gift she could find.'

'And is this pretty Lady of the Lake yours too?' said Anne; 'what a pretty binding, with the Douglas arms on it!'

'Yes,' said Helen, 'that was Fanny's present; and Jane gave me the pretty forget-me-not brooch I wore yesterday. You see I have plenty of keep-sakes from the dear people.'

Anne then turned to the portfolio on the table. Helen shewed her, in the first place, a rather stiff and formal looking forget-me-not, painted by Fanny Staunton, and a carelessly sketched but neatly shaded head drawn by Jane, both which specimens of art Anne tried hard to admire for Helen's sake, but could not find it in her heart to do so. Helen's own drawings, which were landscapes, gave more promise of improvement, and displayed a good deal of taste and freedom of hand, though some were by no means correct in the outline. Helen pointed out several faults which she candidly acknowledged to be wrong, and some others which she said 'Lizzie called blunders.'

'There,' said she, 'is the house at dear Dykelands; there is my window with the Banksia roses clustering round it, so that I could gather them as I stood in my room. That room is still to be called Helen's. But now, Anne, do you think that line ought to be straight? Lizzie says it should, but I think the perspective alters it; I am sure I saw it so.'

'Indeed, Helen,' said Anne, 'I think the shadow must have deceived you.' And with a little trouble she proved that Elizabeth was right.

'Ah!' said Helen, 'if Lizzie would but have shewn me patiently, instead of saying, 'Why, Helen, cannot you draw a straight line?' I should have understood her.' Then she continued, while taking out India-rubber and pencil to rectify the mistake, 'I used to draw a great deal at dear Dykelands; we had a sketching master, and used to go out with him twice a week, but it was very delightful when we three went alone, when one of us used to read while the others drew. I am sure these sketches will for ever remind me of those happy days.'

'Why, Helen,' said Anne, smiling, 'you speak as if you never meant to be happy again.'

'Do I?' said poor Helen; 'I am afraid I do seem rather silly about dear Dykelands. The other day I was singing

"My heart's in the Highlands, my heart is not here,
My heart's in the Highlands, gone chasing the deer,"

when in came Lizzie, and said, "No, Helen,

Your heart is at Dykelands, your heart's in the bogs,
Your heart is at Dykelands, gone chasing the frogs,"

for she is always laughing at it for being so damp, dear place. And it was before Horace went to school, and he would do nothing but sing it at me all day, and make Winifred do so too.'

Anne could not help laughing.

'Then you too think me absurd,' said Helen; 'but if you only knew how happy I was at Dykelands, and how desolate I sometimes feel here, you would not wonder at me.'

'Then you do not like Abbeychurch?' said Anne incredulously; she could not say 'you are not happy at home.'

'Who could prefer a little dismal town to a pleasant house in the country?' said Helen; 'you like Merton Hall better than this place, do not you, Anne?'

'Of course,' replied Anne; 'but then Merton Hall is my home.'

'And Abbeychurch is mine,' sighed poor Helen. 'I believe it is very wrong to be discontented with home, but I cannot help it.'

'My dear Helen, what do you mean?' exclaimed Anne, quite aghast.

'Indeed, Anne,' said Helen, 'I do not wonder that you are shocked, but you do not know how I feel here. At Dykelands I felt that people liked me and were pleased with me, but at home nobody wants me, nobody cares for me, I am in the way wherever I go.'

'My dear Helen,' cried Anne, 'that must be fancy!'

'I wish it was,' said poor Helen, shaking her head.

'But only think,' proceeded Anne, 'what you are accusing them of. Not loving you, and wishing you away.'

'No, I do not say it is as bad as that,' said Helen; 'but I am sure I am of no use here, and might as well be away.'

'I suppose,' said Anne, 'that you have been so long away as to have lost all your old home occupations, and you have not yet had time to make new ones.'

'Perhaps it is so,' said Helen; 'but I do not think I had any occupations before I went to Dykelands, at least none worth having, and now I cannot make myself new ones. Lizzie does everything, and will not let me help her, for fear I should do mischief.'

'Now, Helen,' said Anne, who had by this time collected her ideas, which had been completely startled by her cousin's avowal of dislike of home, 'I will tell you what I think Mamma would say to you. I think you used to be indolent and waste your senses, but now Dykelands has given you a spur, and you are very much improved.'

'Do you really think so?' interrupted Helen, who had lately felt quite starved for want of praise.

'Yes,' said Anne, 'and so does everyone, and so Lizzie told me.'

'Lizzie?' said Helen; 'I thought she considered me as great a baby as ever.'

'No, no, my dear,' said Anne; 'I will tell you what she said of you. She said you were almost all she could wish in a sister, and that you were quite a reflective creature; and that is high praise from her.'

'Well, if she thinks so,' said Helen, 'she does not shew it; she is always making game of my opinions and feelings.'

'So she does of almost everyone's,' said Anne; 'but that is no proof that she does not love them.'

'And she will never listen to anything that I say, or take interest in anything I care for,' continued Helen.

'Indeed, Helen, you only think so because you do not understand her ways,' said Anne; 'all last month she could think of nothing but the Consecration, and Horace's going to school. Now all that is over and you are quiet again, after we are gone you will get on capitally together.'

'I am sure she contradicts every word I say,' said Helen.

'That is not out of unkindness, I assure you,' said Anne, who unfortunately could not deny that such was the fact. 'She only likes an argument, which sharpens your wits, and does no harm, if both sides are but good-humoured and cheerful. She will find you out in time, and you will understand her better.'

'Oh! Lizzie is delightful when she does not contradict,' said Helen; 'she is cleverer than anyone I ever saw, even than Fanny Staunton, and Papa says her patience and diligence with Horace were beyond all praise; but I can never be clever enough for her to make me her friend.'

'But you do not think people choose their friends only for their cleverness?' said Anne.

'Why, no,' said Helen, 'I do not think they ought, but Lizzie does. You would not be her friend if you were not clever.'

'Well,' said Anne, 'but try and convince her that you can be her friend without being clever, if you will not allow that you are.'

'Oh!' said Helen, brightening up, 'if Lizzie would but make a friend of me, how happy we should be! if she would but talk to me of her own concerns, and listen to mine! But she never chooses to hear me speak of Dykelands.'

'Then,' said Anne, 'you must remember that she has never been there, and does not know the people.'

'Yes,' said Helen; 'but I think that if she had been there, and I at home, I should have listened for her sake, besides that Mrs. Staunton was our own mamma's dearest friend.'

Anne had always thought that her own mother had been Aunt Katherine's dearest friend; but she had forbearance enough to leave the honour to Mrs. Staunton in Helen's imagination, and answered, 'And for that very reason, and for your sake too, Helen, she will delight to hear about Mrs. Staunton when you are quiet together, if you do not give her too much at a time, or talk of Dykelands when she is thinking of something else. Oh yes, Helen, you and Lizzie will be excellent friends, unless you are much more silly than I think either of you.'

Anne smiled so cheerfully, that Helen could not help smiling too; but she would probably have found another sorrow to lament over, if at this moment Dora had not come up to summon them to their early dinner.

Helen felt exceedingly grateful to Anne for having listened so kindly and patiently to her list of grievances. It was the first sympathy, as she considered, that she had met with since she had left Dykelands, and it atoned in her mind for various little thoughtless ways of Anne's, which had wounded her in former years, and which she had not perhaps striven sufficiently to banish from her memory; and this was a great advantage from this conversation, even if she derived no further benefit from it.

On her side, Anne had some thoughts of telling Elizabeth what Helen's feelings really were, in hopes that she might shew a little regard for them; but, sisterless herself, she thought the bond of sisterhood too sacred to be rashly interfered with by a stranger's hand; besides, she considered Helen's complaints as really confidential, if not expressly so, and resolved to mention them to no one but Lady Merton, and to limit her attempts at being useful to bringing the two sisters before each other in their most amiable light, and at any rate to avoid saying anything that could possibly occasion a discussion between them, though she could hardly imagine that it was possible to dislike one of the merry arguments that she delighted in. However, remembering her mother's story of Mrs. Staunton, she decided that though it was a great misfortune for people to have such strange fancies, yet their friends ought to respect them.

CHAPTER VII.

As soon as dinner was over, Elizabeth went up to her own room, and was followed in a few moments by Anne, who found her putting on her bonnet and cloak. 'Can you be going out in such weather as this?' exclaimed she.

'Yes,' said Elizabeth; 'I must

"Let content with my fortunes fit,
Though the rain it raineth every day."'

'But what are the fortunes which oblige you to go out?' said Anne.

'The fortunes of an old woman to whom Kate or I read every Friday,' said Elizabeth, 'and the fortunes of various young school-children, who must be prepared for Papa or Mr. Walker to catechize in Church on Sunday.'

'Why do not you send Kate or Helen, instead of murdering yourself in the wet?' said Anne.

'Miss Kitty is three inches deep in the mysteries of a spencer, (I do not mean Edmund,)' said Elizabeth, 'and it will not be out of her head these three days, at least not till she has made Mamma's old black satin gown into one after Harriet's pattern; I heard her asking for it as I came up-stairs.'

'And would not Helen go?' said Anne; 'she does not catch cold as easily as you do.'

'Helen has contrived, somehow or other,' said Elizabeth, 'to know no more about the school-children than if they were so many Esquimaux; besides, anyone with any experience of Helen's ways, had rather walk ninety miles in the rain, than be at the pains of routing her out of the corner of the sofa to do anything useful.'

'Indeed,' said Anne, 'I think Helen does wish to make herself useful.'

'I dare say she sits still and wishes it in the abstract, for I think it must be a very disagreeable thing to reflect that she might as well be that plaster statue for any good that she does,' said Elizabeth; 'but she grumbles at every individual thing you propose for her to do, just as she says she wishes to be a companion to Dora and Winifred, yet whenever they wish her to play with them or tell them a story, which is all the companionship children of their age understand, she is always too much at her ease to be disturbed. And now, as she is the only person in the house with whom poor Lucy is tolerably at her ease, it would be cruel to take her away.'

'That is more of a reason,' said Anne; 'what a pity it is that Lucy is so shy!'

'Excessive shyness and reserve is what prevents her mother from being able to spoil her,' said Elizabeth; 'so do not regret it.'

'Still I do not like to see you going out in this way,' said Anne.

'I may truly say that rain never hurts me,' said Elizabeth; 'and if I once let one trifle stop me in these parish matters, I shall be stopped for ever, and never do anything. Perhaps I shall not come back this hour and a half, for old Mrs. Clayton must be dying to hear all about our Consecration, luncheon, dinner, &c., and as she is the widow of the last Vicar, we are in duty bound to be civil to her, and I must go and call upon her. Oh! you poor thing, I forgot how deserted you will be, and really the drawing-room is almost uninhabitable with that Bengal tiger in it. Here is that delightful Norman Conquest for you to read; pray look at the part about Hereward the Saxon.'

Elizabeth would not trust herself to stay with Anne any longer, and ran downstairs, and might soon be heard putting up her umbrella and shutting the front door after her.

Anne found the afternoon pass rather heavily, in spite of the companionship of William the Conqueror and Hereward the Saxon, of assisting the children in a wet day game of romps, and of shewing Dora and Winifred the contents of the box they had admired the day before. Helen and Lucy were sitting at work very comfortably in the corner of the sofa in the inner drawing-room; Harriet and Katherine very busy contriving the spencer in the front drawing-room, keeping up a whispering accompaniment to the conversation of the elder ladies--if conversation it could be called, when Mrs. Hazleby had it all to herself, while giving Lady Merton and Mrs.

Woodbourne an account of the discomforts she had experienced in country quarters in Ireland.

Sir Edward and Mr. Woodbourne were engaged in looking over the accounts of the church in the study, and Fido was trying to settle his disputes with Meg Merrilies, who, with arching back, tail erect, and eyes like flaming green glass, waged a continual war with him over her basket in the hall.

Anne was very glad to hear her cousin's footstep in the hall as she returned. Coming straight to the drawing-room, Elizabeth exclaimed, 'Mamma, did you tell Mrs. Clarke that she might have a frock for Susan?'

'Yes, my dear,' said Mrs. Woodbourne; 'she asked me yesterday when you were not near, and I told her you would give her one. I thought the child looked very ragged.'

'I suppose she must have it,' said Elizabeth, looking much vexed; 'I told her she should not, a month ago, unless she sent the children to school regularly, and they have scarcely been there five days in the last fortnight.'

'I wish I had known it, my dear,' said Mrs. Woodbourne; 'you know I am always very sorry to interfere with any of your plans.'

'O Mamma, there is no great harm done,' said Elizabeth. She then went to fetch the frock, and gave it to the woman with a more gentle and sensible rebuke than could have been expected from the vehemence of her manner towards Mrs. Woodbourne a minute before. When this was done, and she had taken off her bonnet, she came to beckon Anne up-stairs.

'So you have finished your labours,' said Anne, taking up her work, while Elizabeth sat down to rule a copy-book for Winifred.

'Yes,' said Elizabeth, '"we are free to sport and play;" I have read to the old woman, and crammed the children, and given old Mrs. Clayton a catalogue raisonnee of all the company and all their dresses, and a bill of fare of our luncheon and dinner, and where everything came from.'

'And yet you profess to hold gossip in abomination,' said Anne.

'Oh! but this is old gossip, regular legitimate amusement for the poor old lady,' said Elizabeth. 'She really is a lady, but very badly off, and most of the Abbeychurch gentility are too fine to visit her, so that a little quiet chat with her is by no means of the common-place kind. Besides, she knows and loves us all like her own children. It was one of the first pleasures I can remember, to gather roses for her, and carry them to her from her own old garden here.'

'Well, in consideration of all that you say,' said Anne, 'I suppose I must forgive her for keeping you away all this afternoon.'

'And what did you do all that time?' said Elizabeth. 'Have you read Hereward, and do not you delight in him?'

'Yes,' said Anne, 'and I want to know whether he is not the father of Cedric of Rotherwood.'

'He must have been his grandfather,' said Elizabeth; 'Cedric lived a hundred years after.'

'But Cedric remembered Torquilstone before the Normans came,' said Anne.

'No, no, he could not, though he had been told what it had been before Front-de-Boeuf altered it,' said Elizabeth.

'And old Ulrica was there when Front-de-Boeuf's father took it,' said Anne.

'I cannot tell how long a hag may live,' said Elizabeth, 'but she could not have been less than a hundred and thirty years old in the time of Richard Coeur-de-Lion.'

'Coeur-de-Lion came to the throne in 1189,' said Anne. 'No, I suppose Torquil Wolfganger could not have been dispossessed immediately after the Conquest. But then you know Ulrica calls Cedric the son of the great Hereward.'

'Her wits were a little out of order,' said Elizabeth; 'either she meant his grand-son, or Sir Walter Scott made as great an anachronism as when he made that same Ulrica compare Rebecca's skin to paper. If she had said parchment, it would not have been such a compliment.'

'How much interest Ivanhoe makes us take in the Saxons and Normans!' said Anne.

'And what nonsense it is to say that works of fiction give a distaste for history,' said Elizabeth.

'You are an instance to the contrary,' said Anne; 'no one loves stories so well, and no one loves history better.'

'I believe such stories as Ivanhoe were what taught me to like history,' said Elizabeth.

'In order to find out the anachronisms in them?' said Anne; 'I think it is very ungrateful of you.'

'No indeed,' said Elizabeth; 'why, they used to be the only history I knew, and almost the only geography. Do not you remember Aunt Anne's laughing at me for arguing that Bohemia was on the Baltic, because Perdita was left on its coast? And now, I believe that Coeur de Lion feasted with Robin Hood and his merry men, although history tells me that he disliked and despised the English, and the only sentence of their language history records of his uttering was, "He speaks like a fool Briton." I believe that Queen Margaret of Anjou haunted the scenes of grandeur that once were hers, and that she lived to see the fall of Charles of Burgundy, and die when her last hope failed her, though I know that it was not so.'

'Then I do not quite see how such stories have taught you to like history,' said Anne.

'They teach us to realize and understand the people whom we find in history,' said Elizabeth.

'Oh yes,' said Anne; 'who would care for Louis the eleventh if it was not for Quentin Durward? and Shakespeare makes us feel as if we had been at the battle of Shrewsbury.'

'Yes,' said Elizabeth; 'and they have done even more for history. They have taught us to imagine other heroes whom they have not mentioned. Cannot you see the Black Prince, his slight graceful figure, his fair delicate face full of gentleness and kindness--fierce warrior as he is--his black steel helmet, and tippet of chain-mail, his clustering white plume, his surcoat with England's leopards and France's lilies? Cannot you make a story of his long constant attachment to his beautiful cousin, the Fair Maid of Kent? Cannot you imagine his courteous conference with Bertrand du Guesclin, the brave ugly Breton?--Edward lying almost helpless on his couch, broken down with suffering and disappointment, and the noble affectionate Captal de Buch, who died of grief for him, thinking whether he will ever be able to wear his black armour again, and carry terror and dismay to the stoutest hearts of France.'

'Give Froissart some of the credit of your picture,' said Anne.

'Froissart is in some places like Sir Walter himself,' said Elizabeth; 'but now I will tell you of a person who lived in no days of romance, and has not had the advantage of a poetical historian to light him up in our imagination. I mean the great

Prince of Conde. Now, though he is very unlike Shakespeare's Coriolanus, yet there is resemblance enough between them to make the comparison very amusing. There was much of Coriolanus' indomitable pride and horror of mob popularity when he offended Beaufort and his kingdom in the halles, when, though as 'Louis de Bourbon' he refused to do anything to shake the power of the throne, he would not submit to be patronized by the mean fawning Mazarin. Not that the hard-hearted Conde would have listened to his wife and mother, even if he had loved them as Coriolanus did, or that his arrogance did not degenerate into wonderful meanness at last, such as Coriolanus would have scorned; but the parallel was very amusing, and gave me a great interest in Conde. And did you ever observe what a great likeness there is in the characters of the two apostates, Julian and Frederick the Great?'

'Then you like history for the sake of comparing the characters mentioned in it?' said Anne.

'I think so,' said Elizabeth; 'and that is the reason I hate abridgements, the mere bare bones of history. I cannot bear dry facts, such as that Charles the Fifth beat Francis the First, at Pavia, in a war for the duchy of Milan, and nothing more told about them. I am always ready to say, as the Grand Seignior did about some such great battle among the Christians, that I do not care whether the dog bites the hog, or the hog bites the dog.'

'What a kind interest in your fellow-creatures you display!' said Anne. 'I think one reason why I like history is because I am searching out all the characters who come up to my notion of perfect chivalry, or rather of Christian perfection. I am making a book of true knights. I copy their portraits when I can find them, and write the names of those whose likenesses I cannot get. I paint their armorial bearings over them when I can find out what they are, and I have a great red cross in the first page.'

'And I will tell you of something else to put at the beginning,' said Elizabeth, 'a branch of laurel entwined with the beautiful white bind-weed. One of our laurels was covered with wreaths of it last year, and I thought it was a beautiful emblem of a pure-hearted hero. The glaring sun, which withers the fair white spotless flower, is like worldly prosperity spoiling the pure simple mind; and you know how often it is despised and torn away from the laurel to which it is so bright an ornament.'

'Yes,' said Anne, 'it clings more safely and fearlessly round the simplest and most despised of plants. And would you call the little pink bindweed childish innocence?'

'No, I do not think I should,' said Elizabeth, 'it is not sufficiently stainless. But then innocence, from not seeing or knowing what is wrong, is not like the guilelessness which can use the world as not abusing it.'

'Yet Adam and Eve fell when they gained the knowledge of good and evil,' said Anne.

'Yes, because they gained their knowledge by doing evil,' said Elizabeth, 'but you must allow that what is tried and not found wanting is superior to what has failed only because it has had no trial. St. John's Day is placed nearer Christmas than that of the Holy Innocents.'

'And St. John knew what evil was,' said Anne; 'yes you are right there.'

'You speak as if you still had some fault to find with me, Anne,' said Elizabeth.

'No, indeed I have not,' said Anne, 'I quite agree with you; it was only your speaking of knowledge of evil us a kind of advantage, that startled me.'

'Because you think knowledge and discernment my idol,' said Elizabeth; 'but we have wandered far away from my white convolvulus, and I have not done with it yet. When autumn came, and the leaves turned bright yellow, it was a golden crown.'

'But there your comparison ends,' said Anne; 'the laurel ought to vanish away, and leave the golden wreath behind.'

'No,' said Elizabeth; 'call the golden wreath the crown of glory on the brow of the old saint-like hero, and remember that when he dies, the immortality the world prizes is that of the coarse evergreen laurel, and no one dreams of his white wreath.'

'I wish you would make a poem of your comparison, for the beginning of my book of chivalry,' said Anne.

'It will not do,' said Elizabeth, 'I am no poet; besides, if I wished to try, just consider what a name the flower has--con-vol-vu-lus, a prosaic, dragging, botanical term, a mile long. Then bindweed only reminds me of smothered and fettered raspberry bushes, and a great hoe. Lily, as the country people call it, is not distinguishing enough, besides that no one ever heard of a climbing lily. But, Anne, do tell me whom you have in your book of knights. I know of a good many in the real heroic age, but tell me some of the later ones.'

'Lord Exmouth,' said Anne; 'I am sure he was a true knight.'

'And the Vendeen leaders, I suppose,' said Elizabeth.

'Yes, I have written the names of M. de Lescure and of Henri de la Rochejaquelein; I wish I knew where to find their pictures, and I want a Prussian patriot. I think the Baron de la Motte Fouque, who was a Knight of St. John, and who thought so much of true chivalry, would come in very well.'

'I do not know anything about himself,' said Elizabeth, 'though, certainly, no one but a true knight could have written Sintram. I am afraid there was no leader good enough for you among the Spanish patriots in the Peninsular war.'

'I do not know,' said Anne; 'I admire Don Jose Palafox for his defence of Zaragoza, but I know nothing more of him, and there is no chance of my getting his portrait. I am in great want of Cameron of Lochiel, or Lord Nithsdale, or Derwentwater; for Claverhouse is the only Jacobite leader I can find a portrait of, and I am afraid the blood of the Covenanters is a blot on his escutcheon, a stain on his white wreath.'

'I am sorry you have nothing to say to bonnie Dundee,' said Elizabeth, 'for really, between the Whiggery and stupidity of England, and the wickedness of France, good people are scarce from Charles the Martyr to George the Third. How I hate that part of history! Oh! but there were Prince Eugene and the Vicomte de Turenne.'

'Prince Eugene behaved very well to Marlborough in his adversity,' said Anne: 'but I do not like people to take affront and abandon their native country.'

'Oh! but Savoy was more his country than France,' said Elizabeth, 'however, I do not know enough about him to make it worth while to fight for him.'

'And as to Turenne,' said Anne, 'I do not like the little I know of him; he was horribly cruel, was he not?'

'Oh! every soldier was cruel in those days,' said Elizabeth; 'it was the custom of their time, and they could not help it.'

Anne shook her head.

'Then you will be forced to give up my beloved Black Prince,' continued Elizabeth piteously; 'you know he massacred the people at Limoges.'

'I cannot do without him,' said Anne; 'he was ill and very much exasperated at the time, and I choose to believe that the massacre was commanded by John of Gaunt.'

'And I choose to believe that all the cruelties of the French were by the express order of Louis Quatorze,' said Elizabeth; 'you cannot be hard on a man who gave all his money and offered to pawn his plate to bring Charles the Second back to England.'

'I must search and consider,' said Anne; 'I will hunt him out when I go home, and if we have a print of him, and if he is tolerably good-looking, I will see what I can do with him.'

'You have Lodge's portraits,' said Elizabeth, 'so you are well off for Cavaliers; do you mean to take Prince Rupert in compliment to your brother?'

'No, he is not good enough, I am afraid,' said Anne, 'though besides our own Vandyke there is a most tempting print of him, in Lodge, with a buff coat and worked ruffles; but though I used to think him the greatest of heroes, I have given him up, and mean to content myself with Charles himself, the two Lindsays, Ormond and Strafford, Derby and Capel, and Sir Ralph Hopton.'

'And Montrose, and the Marquis of Winchester,' said Elizabeth; 'you must not forget the noblest of all.'

'I only forgot to mention them,' said Anne, 'I could not leave them out. The only difficulty is whom to choose among the Cavaliers.'

'And who comes next?' said Elizabeth.

'Gustavus Adolphus and Sir Philip Sydney.'

'Do not mention them together, they are no pair,' said Elizabeth. 'What a pity it was that Sir Philip was a euphuist.'

'Forgive him for that failing, in consideration of his speech at Zutphen,' said Anne.

'Only that speech is so hackneyed and commonplace,' said Elizabeth, 'I am tired of it.'

'The deed was not common-place,' said Anne.

'No, and dandyism was as entirely the fault of his time as cruelty was of Turenne's,' said Elizabeth; 'Sir Walter Raleigh was worse than Sydney, and Surrey quite as bad, to judge by his picture.'

'It is not quite as bad a fault as cruelty,' said Anne, 'little as you seem to think of the last.'

'Now comes the chivalric age,' said Elizabeth; 'never mind telling me all the names, only say who is the first of your heroes--neither Orlando nor Sir Galahad, I suppose.'

'No, nor Huon de Bordeaux,' said Anne.

'The Cid, then, I suppose,' said Elizabeth, 'unless he is too fierce for your tender heart.'

'Ruy, mi Cid Campeador?' said Anne, 'I must have him in consideration of his noble conduct to the King who banished him, and the speech the ballad gives him:

"For vassals' vengeance on their lord,   Though just, is treason still;
The noblest blood is his, who best   Bears undeserved ill."

And the loyalty he shewed in making the King clear himself of having any share in his brother's death, even though Alphonso was silly enough to be affronted.'

'Like Montrose's feeling towards his lady-love,' said Elizabeth; 'not bearing the least stain on what he loved or honoured.'

'But he is not our earliest knight,' said Anne; 'I begin with our own Alfred, with his blue shield and golden cross.'

'King Alfred!' exclaimed Elizabeth, 'do you consider him a knight?'

'Certainly,' said Anne; 'besides that I care more for the spirit of chivalry than for the etiquette of the accolade and golden spurs; we know that Alfred knighted his grandson Athelstane, so that he must have been a knight himself.'

'By-the-bye,' said Elizabeth, 'I think I have found out the origin of the golden spurs being part of a knight's equipment. Do you remember when the Cid's beloved king Don Sancho was killed, that Rodrigo could not overtake the traitor Bellido Dolfos, because he had no spurs on, whereupon he cursed every knight who should for the future ride without them. Now that was at the time when the laws of chivalry were attaining their perfection, but--'

'Not so fast,' said Anne; 'I have a much earlier pair of golden spurs for you. Do not you remember Edmund, the last King of East Anglia, being betrayed to the Danish wedding-party at Hoxne, by the glitter of his golden spurs, and cursing every new married pair who should ever pass over the bridge where he was found. I think that makes for my side of the question. Here is Edmund, a knight in golden spurs when Alfred was a child. Ah ha, Miss Lizzie!'

Before Elizabeth could answer, Winifred came to tell her that her mamma wanted her, and she was forced to leave the question of King Alfred's and King Edmund's chivalry undecided; for, to her praise be it spoken, she was much too useful a person ever to be able to pursue her own peculiar diversions for many minutes together. She had to listen to some directions, and undertake some messages, so that she could not return to her own room till after Anne had gone down-stairs. She herself was not ready till just as the elders were setting off to the dinner-party at Marlowe Court, and rejoicing in the cessation of the rain and the fineness of the evening.

About half an hour afterwards, the young ladies assembled in the inner drawing-room to drink tea. Helen, however, remained in the outer drawing-room, practising her music, regardless of the sounds of mirth that proceeded from the other room, until Elizabeth opened the door, calling out,

"Sweet bird, that shunnest the noise of folly,
Most musical, most melancholy,"

come in to tea, so please your highness.'

'What can you mean?' said Helen; 'I am sure I am not melancholy.'

'I am sure you shun the noise of folly,' said Elizabeth.

'I am sorry you consider all our merriment as folly,' said Anne, hoping to save Helen.

'Indeed I do not,' said Elizabeth; 'it was no more folly than a kitten's play, and quite as much in the natural course of things.'

'Helen's occupation being out of the natural course of things,' said Anne, 'I should think she was better employed than we were.'

'In making a noise,' said Elizabeth; 'so were we, I do not see much difference.'

'O Lizzie, it was not the same thing!' said Helen, exceedingly mortified at being laughed at for what she considered as a heroic piece of self-denial, and so it was, though perhaps not so great in her as it would have been in one who was less musical, and more addicted to the noise of folly.

'How touchy Helen is this evening!' thought Elizabeth; 'I had better let her alone, both for her sake and my own.'

'How foolish I was to interfere!' thought Anne; 'it was the most awkward thing I ever did; I only roused the spirit of contradiction, and did Helen more harm than good; I never will meddle between sisters again.'

Presently after, Elizabeth asked Harriet Hazleby whether she had ever been at Winchester.

'Yes,' was the answer, 'and a duller place I would not wish to see.'

'It is a handsome old town, is it not?' inquired Anne, turning to Lucy; but Harriet caught up the word, and exclaimed, 'Handsome, indeed! I do not think there is one tolerable new looking street in the whole place, except one or two houses just up by the railroad station.'

Anne still looked towards Lucy, as if awaiting her answer; Lucy replied, 'The Cathedral and College and the old gateways are very beautiful, but there are not so many old looking houses as you would expect.'

'It must be badly off indeed,' said Elizabeth, 'if it has neither old houses nor new; but I wanted to know whether William Rufus' monument is in a tolerable state of preservation.'

'Oh! the monuments are very grand indeed,' said Harriet; 'everyone admired them. There are the heads of some of the old kings most beautifully painted, put away in a dark corner. They are very curious things indeed; I wonder they do not bring them out.'

'Those are the heads of the Stuart kings,' whispered Lucy.

'Why, Harriet,' exclaimed Dora, 'William Rufus was not a Stuart, he was the second of the Normans.'

'Very likely, very likely, Dora, my dear,' answered Harriet; 'I have done with all those things now, thank goodness; I only know that seeing the Cathedral was good fun; I did not like going into the crypts, I said I would not go, when I saw how dark it was; and Frank Hollis said I should, and it was such fun!'

Dora opened her eyes very wide, and Elizabeth said, 'There could certainly never be a better time or place.'

Looking up, she saw poor Lucy's burning cheeks, and was sorry she had not been silent. No one spoke for a few moments, but presently Anne said, 'Alfred the Great is not buried in the Cathedral, is he?'

No one could tell; at last Helen said, 'I remember reading that he was buried in Hyde Abbey, which is now pulled down.'

'There is a street at Winchester, called Hyde Street,' said Lucy.

'Yes, I know,' said Harriet, 'where the Bridewell is, I remember--'

'By-the-bye, Anne,' said Elizabeth, anxious to cut short Harriet's reminiscences, 'I never answered what you said about Alfred and Athelstane. I do not think that Alfred did more than present him with his sword, which was always solemnly done, even to squires, before they were allowed to fight, and might be done by a priest.'

'But when Athelstane is called a knight, and the ceremony of presenting him with his weapons is mentioned,' said Anne, 'I cannot see why we should not consider him to have been really knighted.'

'Because,' said Elizabeth, 'I do not think that the old Saxon word, knight, meant the sworn champion, the devoted warrior of noble birth, which it now expresses. You know Canute's old rhyme says, "Row to the shore, knights," as if they were boatmen, and not gentlemen.'

'I do not think it could have been beneath the dignity of a knight to row Canute,' said Anne, 'considering that eight kings rowed Edgar the Peaceable.'

'Other things prove that Knight meant a servant, in Saxon,' said Elizabeth.

'I know it does sometimes, as in German now,' said Anne; 'but the question is, when it acquired a meaning equivalent in dignity to the French Chevalier.'

'Though it properly means anything but a horseman,' said Elizabeth; 'we ought to have a word answering to the German Ritter.'

'Yes, our language was spoilt by being mixed with French before it had come to its perfection,' said Anne; 'but still you have not proved that King Alfred was not a knight in the highest sense of the word, a preux chevalier.'

'I never heard of Alfred on horseback, nor did I ever know him called Sir Alfred of Wessex.'

'Sir is French, and short for seigneur or senior,' said Anne; 'besides, I suppose, you never heard Coeur-de-Lion called Sir Richard Plantagenet.'

'I will tell you how you may find out all about it,' interrupted Katherine; 'Mrs. Turner's nephew, Mr. Augustus Mills, is going to give a lecture this evening, at seven o'clock, upon chivalry, and all that. Mrs. Turner has been telling us all day how much she wishes us to go.'

'Mr. Augustus Mills!' said Elizabeth; 'is he the little red-haired wretch who used to pester me about dancing all last year?'

'No, no,' said Katherine, 'that was Mr. Adolphus Mills, his brother, who is gone to be clerk to an attorney somewhere. This is Mr. Augustus, a very fine young man, and so clever, Willie says, and he has most beautiful curling black hair.'

'It wants a quarter to seven now,' said Elizabeth, 'and the sky is most beautifully clear, at last. Do you like the thoughts of this lecture, Anne?'

'I should like to go very much indeed,' said Anne; 'but first I must go and seal and send some letters for Mamma, so I must depart while you finish your tea.' So saying, she left the room.

'Pray, Kate,' said Helen, as Anne closed the door, 'where is this lecture to be given?'

'At the Mechanics' Institute, of course,' said Katherine.

'So we cannot go,' said Helen.

'And pray why not, my sapient sister?' said Elizabeth; 'what objection has your high mightiness?'

'My dear Lizzie,' said Helen, 'I wish you had heard all that I have heard, at Dykelands, about Mechanics' Institutes.'

'My dear Helen,' said Elizabeth, 'I wish you would learn that Dykelands is no Delphos to me.'

'Nay, but my dearest sister,' exclaimed Helen, clasping her hands, 'do but listen to me; I am sure that harm will come of your going.'

'Well, ope your lips, Sir Oracle,' said Elizabeth impatiently, 'no dog shall bark, only make haste about it, or we shall be too late.'

'Do you not know, Lizzie,' said Helen, 'that Socialists often hold forth in Mechanics' Institutes?'

'The abuse of a thing does not cancel its use,' said Elizabeth, 'and I do not suppose that Mr. Mills preaches Socialism.'

'Captain Atherley says,' persisted Helen, 'that all sorts of people ought not to mix themselves up together on equal terms.'

'Oh! then he never goes to church,' retorted Elizabeth.

'No, no, that was only my foolish way of expressing myself,' said Helen; 'I meant that he says that it is wrong for Church people to put themselves on a level with Dissenters, or Infidels, or Socialists, for aught they know to the contrary.'

'Since you have been in the north, Helen,' said Elizabeth, 'you have thought every third man you met a Chartist or a Socialist; but as I do not believe there are specimens of either kind in Abbeychurch, I see no harm in taking our chance of the very few Dissenters there are here, and sitting to hear a lecture in company with our own townspeople.'

'Really, I think we had better not go without asking leave first,' said Katherine.

'In the first place,' said Elizabeth, 'there is no one to ask; and next, I know that Mrs. Turner has offered hundreds of times to take us there, and I suppose Papa would have refused once for all, if he had been so very much afraid of our turning Chartists as Helen seems to be. I can see no reason why we should not go.'

'Then you consider my opinion as utterly worthless,' cried Helen, losing all command of temper, which indeed she had preserved longer than could have been expected. 'I might have known it; you never care for one word I say. You will re-pent it at last, I know you will.'

'It is not that I never care for what you say, Helen,' said Elizabeth, 'it is only when you give me Dykelands opinions instead of your own, and talk of what you do not understand. I suppose no one has any objection to a walk, at least. Shall we get ready?'

Everyone consented, and they went to prepare. It should be said, in excuse for Elizabeth, that both she and Helen had been absent from home at the time of the establishment of the Mechanics' Institute at Abbeychurch, so that they had not known of their father's opposition to it. Helen, who, when at Dykelands, had been nearer the manufacturing districts, had heard more of the follies and mischiefs committed by some of the favourers of these institutions. Unfortunately, however, her temper had prevented her from reasoning calmly, and Elizabeth had wilfully blinded herself, and shut her ears to conviction, being determined to follow her own course. Anne, who had always lived at Merton Hall, excepting two months of each year, which she spent in London, knew nothing of country town cabals, and thinking the lecture was of the same nature as those she had heard in London, asked no questions, as she had not heard the debate between Elizabeth and Helen. Katherine, however, hesitated to go without the permission of her father and mother; or, in other words, she was afraid they would reprove her, and she was not unwilling to listen to Helen's representations on the subject, while they were putting on their bonnets.

'It is not only,' said Helen, 'that we are sure that it is not right to go anywhere without leave from Papa or Mamma, but that I know that these Mechanics' Institutes are part of a system of--'

'Oh yes, I know,' said Katherine, 'of Chartism, and Socialism, and all that is horrible. I cannot imagine how Lizzie can think of going.'

'Then you will not go,' said Helen.

'Oh, I do not know,' said Katherine; 'it will seem so odd and so particular if Anne and Lizzie and the Hazlebys go, and we do not. It would be like setting ourselves up against our elders.'

'You do not always think much of that, Kate,' said Helen; 'besides, if our eldest sister thinks proper to do wrong, I do not see that we are forced to do so too.'

'Well, but Lizzie said it was not wrong, and she is the eldest,' argued Katherine.

'Lizzie said it was not wrong, that she might have her own way, and contradict me,' said Helen.

'We shall see what Anne says,' said Katherine; 'but if they go, I must, you know. It was to me that Mrs. Turner gave the invitation, and she and Willie would think it so odd to see the others without me; and Mr. Mills too, he said so very politely that he hoped that he should be honoured with my presence and Harriet's, it would be an additional stimulus to his exertions, he said.'

'My dear Kate,' exclaimed Helen, 'how could you listen to such affected nonsense?'

'Why, Lizzie says everybody talks nonsense,' said Katherine, 'but we must listen and be civil, you know; I am sure I wish people would not be so silly, it is very disagreeable to hear it; but I cannot help it, and after this I really think I ought to go, it would be very odd if I did not.'

'Better do what is odd than what is wrong,' said Helen.

In her secret soul, Katherine had been of the same opinion the whole time, and now that she thought she had made a sufficient merit of giving up the expedition, she was about to promise to follow Helen's advice, when she was interrupted by the entrance of Harriet, with her shawl and bonnet in her hand, coming to gossip with Katherine, and thus escape from Lucy, who had been quietly suggesting that in a doubtful case, such as the present seemed to be, it was always best to keep to the safe side. Harriet had laughed at Lucy for not being able to give any reasons, told her that it was plain that Helen knew nothing about the matter, and declared that she thanked goodness that if Mr. Woodbourne was ever so angry, he was not her master, and her own mamma never minded what she did. Lucy could make no answer in words, but her silent protest against her sister's conduct made Harriet so uneasy that she quitted her as soon as she could.

Helen still hoped that Anne would see the folly of the scheme, and persuade Elizabeth to give it up, and content herself with taking a walk, or that her sister's better sense would prevail; but she was disappointed, when, as they left the house, Anne asked where the lecture was to be given, Elizabeth replied, 'At the Mechanics' Institute;' and no further observation was made, Anne's silence confirming Elizabeth in her idea that Helen had been talking nonsense. Still, as St. Martin's Street, where Mr. Turner lived, was their way out of the town, Helen remained in doubt respecting her sister's intentions until they reached Mr. Turner's house, and Elizabeth walked up the steps, and knocked at the door.

Helen immediately wheeled round, and walked indignantly homewards, too full of her own feelings to make any attempt to persuade Katherine to follow her example, and every step shewing how grieved and affronted she was.

Lucy laid her hand on her sister's arm, and looked up imploringly in her face.

'Pooh!' said Harriet pettishly, jerking the ribbon by which she was leading Fido: 'give me one reason, Lucy, and I will come.'

'What Helen said,' answered Lucy.

'Stuff and nonsense!' said Harriet; 'that was no reason at all.'

'What did Helen say?' asked Anne, who had been rather startled by her departure.

'Only some Dykelands fancies about Socialists,' said Elizabeth; 'that is the reason she has gone off like a tragedy queen. I did not think all Abbeychurch was ready for the French Revolution--that was all.'

'There, Lucy, you see,' said Harriet; 'come along, there's a good girl.'

Here Mrs. Turner's page opened the door, and answered that his mistress was at home.

'Dora, my dear,' said Elizabeth, 'this is too late an affair for you; we shall not be at home till after you are gone to bed. Good-night--run after Helen.'

Dora obeyed, and Lucy also turned away; Katherine lingered. 'Come, Kate,' said Harriet, mounting the steps. --'Lucy, you nonsensical girl, come back; every-one can see you out of the window; it is very rude, now; if Mrs. Turner sees you, what will she think? Mamma would be very angry to see you so silly. Come back, I tell you!'

Lucy only looked back, and shook her head, and then hastened away; but Kath-erine, fearing that her friends would be irrecoverably offended if she turned away from their house, thinking that she had gone too far to recede, and trusting to Eliza-beth to shield her from blame, followed the others up-stairs.

Helen turned back, much surprised, as Lucy and Dora overtook her; and they hastened to give explanations.

'Lizzie said I had better come home,' said Dora.

'And I thought it would be the safest thing to do,' said Lucy.

'I am very glad of it,' said Helen; 'I am sure it is not right to go, but when Lizzie has once set her mind on anything, she will listen to no one.'

'Then do you think Papa and Mamma will be displeased?' said Dora; 'I do not think Lizzie thinks so.'

'I cannot be quite sure,' said Helen; 'but I do not think Lizzie chooses to believe that they will.'

'But let me understand you, Helen,' said Lucy; 'I only know that you think that Uncle Woodbourne would not approve of your going. What are your reasons for thinking so? I did not clearly understand you. Church-people and Dissenters put themselves on a level in almost every public place.'

'They do not meet in every public place on what they agree to call neutral ground,' said Helen, 'or profess to lay aside all such distinctions, and to banish re-ligion in order to avoid raising disputes. You know that no subject can be safely treated of, except with reference to the Christian religion.'

'How do you mean?' said Lucy.

'Why,' said Helen, hesitating a little, 'how many people run wild, and adopt foolish and wicked views of politics, for want of reading history religiously! And the astronomers and geologists, without faith, question the possibility of the first chapter of Genesis; and some people fancy that the world was peopled with a great tribe of wild savages, instead of believing all about Adam and Eve and the Patriarchs. Now if you turn religion out, you see, you are sure to fall into false notions; and that is what these Mechanics' Institute people do.'

'Yes,' said Lucy, 'I have heard what you say about those things before, but I never saw them in connection with each other.'

'Nor should I have seen them in this light, if it had not been for a conversation between Captain Atherly and another gentleman, one day at Dykelands,' said Helen. 'But, Lucy, did you leave this party, then, only because I said it was wrong, or because you thought so yourself?'

'Indeed, I can hardly tell,' answered Lucy; 'I scarcely know what to think right and what wrong, but I thought I might be certain that it was safer to go home.'

'I do not see,' said Helen, drawing herself up, and feeling as if she had done a very wise thing, and known her reasons for doing it, too, 'I do not see that it is so very hard to know what is right from what is wrong. It is the easiest way to think what Papa and Mamma would approve, and then try to recollect what reasons they would give.'

'But then you are not always sure of what they would say,' replied Lucy; 'at least I am not, and it is not always possible to ask them. What did you do all the time you were at Dykelands?'

'Oh! dear Mrs. Staunton was quite a mother to me,' said Helen; 'and besides, it was as easy to think what would please Papa there as it is here. You were from home for some time last year, were you not, Lucy?'

'Yes,' replied Lucy, 'I spent several months at Hastings, with Grandmamma; and I am almost ashamed to say that I felt more comfortable there than anywhere else. I liked being by the sea, and having a garden, and being out of the way of the officers. Papa and Grandmamma talked of my always living there, and I hoped I should; but then I should not have liked to leave Papa and the rest, and not to be at home in my brothers' holidays, so I believe things are best as they are.'

'How you must wish to have a home!' said Helen.

'Do not you think that home is wherever your father and mother and brothers and sisters are, Helen?' said Lucy.

'Oh yes, certainly,' said Helen, quickly; 'but I meant a settled home.'

'I do sometimes wish we were settled,' said Lucy; 'but I have been used to wandering all my life, and do not mind it as much as you would, perhaps. We scarcely stay long enough in one place to get attached to it; and some places are so disagreeable, that it is a pleasure to leave them.'

'Such as those in Ireland, that Mrs. Hazleby was talking of yesterday?' said Helen.

'I did not mind those half so much as I do some others,' said Lucy; 'we could easily get into the country, and I used to walk with Papa every day, or ride when Harriet did not want the horse. It was rather uncomfortable, for we were very much crowded when George and Allan were at home; but then they had leave to shoot and fish, and enjoyed themselves very much.'

'Really, Lucy,' said Helen, 'I cannot think how you can be so very contented.'

'I did not know there was anything to be discontented with,' said Lucy, smiling; 'I am sure I am very happy.'

'But what did you say just now you disliked?' said Helen.

'Did I say I disliked anything?' said Lucy. 'Oh! I know what it was. I do not like going to a large town, where we can only walk in the streets, and go out shopping every day, and the boys have nothing to amuse them. And it is worst of all to go to a place where Papa and Mamma have been before, and know all the people; we go out to tea half the days we are there, or to dinner, or have company at home, and I never get a quiet evening's reading with Papa, and Allan has a very great dislike to company.'

As Lucy finished her speech they came to the Vicarage; and as they opened the door, Meg Merrilies came purring out to meet Dora. They looked round for Fido, in order to keep the peace between the two enemies, but he was nowhere to be seen, and Dora remembered to have seen him with Harriet, just as they left the rest of the party at Mr. Turner's door; so dismissing him from their minds, they went to finish their walk in the garden, where Helen gave Lucy a full description of all the beauties of Dykelands, and the perfections of its inhabitants; and finding her an attentive and obliging listener, talked herself into a state of most uncommon good humour and amiability for the rest of the evening. On her side, Lucy, though she had no particular interest in the Stauntons, and indeed had never heard their name before Helen's visit to them, was really pleased and amused, for she had learnt to seek her pleasures in the happiness of other people.

CHAPTER VIII.

I f Helen had not been too much offended by Elizabeth's disregard of her counsel to think of anything but her own dignity, and had waited to remind Katherine of her argument with her, the latter might perhaps have taken the safest course, for it was not without many qualms of conscience that she ascended the stairs to Mrs. Turner's drawing-room.

There was no one in the room; and as soon as the page had closed the door, Elizabeth exclaimed, 'I declare, Anne, there is the bone of contention itself--St. Augustine in his own person! Oh! look at King Ethelbert's square blue eye; and, Kate, is not this St. Austin's Hill itself in the distance?'

'Nonsense, Lizzie!' said Katherine, crossly; 'you know it is no such thing. It was in the pattern.'

'I assure you it is round, and exactly the colour of St. Austin's,' said Elizabeth; 'there can be no doubt about it.'

Elizabeth's criticisms were here cut short by the entrance of Mrs. Turner and her daughter, ready dressed for the evening's excursion.

'Mrs. Turner,' said Elizabeth, with all the politeness she was capable of towards that lady, 'we are come to claim your kind offer of taking us to the Mechanics' Institute this evening.'

'Oh, my dear Miss Lizzie,' cried Mrs. Turner, 'I am so delighted to have the honour, you cannot think! It is my nephew, Augustus Mills, who lectures to-night. Most talented young man, poor fellow, is Augustus--never without a book in his hand; quite in your line, Miss Lizzie.'

At this moment the gentleman quite in Elizabeth's line came into the room. He had a quantity of bushy black hair, a long gold chain round his neck, a plaid velvet waistcoat, in which scarlet was the predominant colour--and his whole air expressed full consciousness of the distinguished part which he was about to act. Poor Elizabeth! little reliance as she usually placed in Katherine's descriptions, she had expected to see something a little more gentleman-like than what she now beheld; and her dismay was increased, when Mrs. Turner addressed her nephew--'Augustus, Augustus, my dear, you never were so flattered in your life? Here *is* Miss Merton, and Miss Hazleby, and Miss Lizzie Woodbourne, all come on purpose to hear your lecture!'

Mr. Augustus said something about being very happy, and bowed, but whether to the young ladies or to his own reflection in the looking-glass was doubtful. He was then regularly introduced to Anne and Elizabeth; and upon Mr. Turner making his appearance, they arranged themselves for the walk to the Mechanics' Institute. Mr. Turner, a fat silent old gentleman, very ceremoniously offered his arm to Miss Merton, who, though by this time exceedingly amazed and disgusted by all she saw and heard, could scarcely refrain from laughing at the airs and graces of her squire, or at the horror she plainly perceived in Elizabeth's face, when the talking Mrs. Turner exclaimed, 'Now, Augustus, I must have you take Miss Woodbourne--I know you will be such friends!'

Little did Mrs. Turner suspect, as in the overflowing of her pride and delight she bestowed upon Elizabeth the hero of the night, the mingled feeling of shame and repugnance which the poor girl had to encounter as she placed her hand within the offered arm of Mr. Mills, almost groaning at her own folly, and vainly seeking some possible means of escape. Mrs. Turner followed with Harriet; and Katherine and Wilhelmina brought up the rear.

'You are very fond of study, I believe, Miss Woodbourne?' said Mr. Mills, as they left the house.

Elizabeth made some inarticulate answer: she was in the utmost dread of meeting either of the curates, or worse still, her cousin Rupert Merton, if he should chance to arrive that evening.

'Most interesting pursuit!' continued Mr. Mills, wishing to shew his aunt how well he and his companion agreed. 'I am quite devoted to it, always was! You are a classical scholar, I presume?'

Elizabeth was ready to wish she had never learnt to read: she fancied she saw a figure like Rupert's at the other end of the street, and was too much frightened to reply.

While they were traversing one street of the old town, crossing the bridge over the little stream which flowed along the valley, and walking along the principal street of the new town, Mr. Mills continued to talk, and Elizabeth to echo the last word of each sentence; or when that would not serve for a reply, she had recourse to the simple interjection 'Oh!' that last refuge of listeners with nothing to say. After a walk, which she thought was at least as many miles in length as it was yards, they arrived at the Mechanics' Institute, outside which they found sundry loiterers, and a strong scent of tobacco; and inside some crowded benches, a table with some chairs ranged round it, and a strong odour of gas.

After a good deal of pushing and shoving, the ladies were safely deposited on one of the front benches; while Mr. Turner, who was one of the managing committee, seated himself on one of the chairs; and Mr. Augustus Mills stood at the table.

Elizabeth felt as if the crimson flush called up by vexation and embarrassment, together with her hasty walk, would never leave her cheeks; she held her head down till Katherine touched her to make her look up, and trusting that her bonnet would screen her heightened colour from observation, she obeyed the sign. A flaring gas-light hung opposite to her; and as she raised her face she encountered the gaze of Mr. Higgins, the Radical and Dissenting editor of a newspaper which had several times abused Mr. Woodbourne. The moment he caught her eye, he bowed with something of a triumphant air; and she, doubly ashamed of herself and provoked with him, bent her head so low that he might well imagine that she returned the bow. She hoped by looking down to escape all further observation, but unfortunately for her, Mrs. Turner had taken care to find a conspicuous place for her party; and Katherine, who had by this time quite forgotten her doubts and misgivings, was nodding and smiling to everyone, with what she considered the utmost grace and affability. Anne, meanwhile, was trying to account for Elizabeth's ever having thought of going to such a place, wondering what Sir Edward and Lady Merton would think of the expedition, and for a moment considering whether Mr. Woodbourne could approve of it, yet at the same time keenly enjoying all that was ludicrous in the scene, and longing to talk it over with Rupert. She was also much diverted with Mr. Augustus Mills's eloquent lecture, in which she afterwards declared that she heard the words 'barbarous institution' fifteen times repeated, and 'civilized and enlightened age,' at least twenty-three times. She was, however, not a little fatigued before it was nearly concluded, and was heartily glad when after an hour and a half it was terminated by a mighty flourish of rhetoric, upon the universal toleration, civilization, and liberty enjoyed in the nineteenth century.

Deafened by the applause of those who had heard little and understood less, half stifled by the heat of the room, and their heads aching from the smell of gas, the girls now hoped to escape; but they were forced to wait till the crowd nearer the door had dispersed, and then to listen to the numerous compliments and congratulations which poured in upon Mrs. Turner from all quarters before they could reach the open air; and then, strenuously refusing all invitations to take tea in St. Martin's Street, they happily regained the Vicarage. Helen and Lucy met them at the door, with hopes that they had had a pleasant evening.

Elizabeth answered quickly, 'Come, come, say no more about it, it was a foolish affair altogether;' but the inquiry, after the feelings she had seen expressed in Elizabeth's face, struck Anne as so excessively ridiculous, that the moment they were in the drawing-room she sank down upon the sofa, giving way to the laughter which, long repressed, now burst forth louder and more merrily upon every fresh remembrance of the scene; while the other girls, though persisting in declaring that they had seen nothing diverting, were soon infected by her joyous merriment, and the room rang again with laughter.

'Well, Lizzie,' said Anne, recovering her breath, 'I hope, as Helen says, you have had a pleasant evening; I hope you were very much edified.'

'How can you be so absurd, Anne?' answered Elizabeth, trying to look serious, but the corners of her mouth relaxing, in spite of her attempts to control her risible muscles.

'I hope,' continued Anne, with a very grave face, 'that Mr. Augustus was fully sensible of your wisdom, love of erudition, and classical scholarship, though I cannot say they appeared on the surface.'

'You may be sure he thought me very wise,' said Elizabeth; 'I only echoed his own words--and what would a man have more?'

'And how tenderly you touched him with the tip of your glove!' continued Anne. 'I wish you could have seen yourself!'

'Indeed, I wish you had, Lizzie,' said Katherine; 'I think you would have been ashamed of yourself.'

'I am ashamed,' said Elizabeth, gravely and shortly.

Lucy here asked where Fido was.

No one knew; no one could recollect anything about him from the time they had left Mr. Turner's house to go to the Mechanics' Institute. Katherine and Harriet went to the front door, they called, they searched, they even went to Mr. Turner's to inquire for him, but all their researches were fruitless; and Harriet turned angrily upon her sister, saying, 'It is all your fault, Lucy, for running home in such a hurry, and never thinking of him. How was I to be watching him there, did you think?'

'I should have supposed,' said Elizabeth, 'that the person who was leading the dog was more likely--'

'No, no, Elizabeth,' hastily interrupted Lucy, 'it was my fault in some degree. I know I ought to have thought of him.'

'Well, say no more about him,' said Elizabeth; 'I dare say he will come home before morning.'

And Elizabeth left the room to take off her bonnet, and to visit the nursery, where the children were in bed. All were asleep excepting Dora; and as Elizabeth leant over her, kissing her and bidding her good-night, the little girl put her arm round her neck, and said, 'Lizzie, will you tell me one thing? Was it naughty to--to go where you went to-night?'

Elizabeth had felt annoyed and provoked and surprised at herself for her folly, but she had not thought herself in fault; but now Dora's soft, sweet, caressing tone sounded in her ears like a serious reproof, and turned her thought upon her sin. She was too upright and sincere to evade such an inquiry as this, even from a younger sister and a pupil, and answered, 'Indeed, Dora, I can hardly tell yet how wrong it was; but I am afraid it was very wrong, for I am sure it is a thing I hope you will never do. Besides, I know I was very self-willed, and unkind to Helen; I have set you a very bad example, Dora, and I believe I ought to beg your pardon for it. Good-night, my dear!'

Was Elizabeth lowered in her sister's eyes by humbling herself?

Just as the girls were arranging themselves in the drawing-room for the evening, a loud knocking was heard at the front-door, and Harriet and Anne both sprang up--the one exclaiming, 'Someone has brought Fido back!'--the other, 'Can that be Rupert?'

The last supposition was proved to be right; and in another moment Rupert Merton was receiving the affectionate greetings of his sister and cousins. Elizabeth felt some embarrassment in performing a regular introduction of Mr. Merton to the Miss Hazlebys; but Rupert's easy well-bred manners rendered the formidable ceremony much easier than she had expected, and the cousins soon fell into their usual style of conversation.

'Well, Mr. Rupert,' said Elizabeth, 'better late than never; that is all that can be said for you!'

'Am I late?' said Rupert; 'I hope no one has waited for me.'

'I hope not indeed,' said Elizabeth; 'pray, did you expect the Bishop and Clergy, and the whole town of Abbeychurch, St. Mary and St. Austin, to wait your pleasure and convenience? Anne, did you ever hear the like? Do you think Prince Rupert himself was ever so favoured and honoured?

'What do you mean?' said Rupert.

'That you have come a day too late, you idle boy!' said Anne.

'I thought next Tuesday was to have been the day of the Consecration,' said Rupert.

'Did you never get my letter?' said Anne; 'I wrote to tell you that the day was altered, and you were to meet us here on the Wednesday.'

'Can I ask you to believe a gentleman's word in opposition to a lady's?' said Rupert, looking round. 'I did indeed receive a letter from my amiable sister, full of--let me see--histories of dogs and cats, and the harvest, and old Dame Philips, and commissions for pencils, which I will produce if I have not lost the key of my portmanteau, but not one word of the Consecration.'

'But indeed I wrote a good many words about it,' said Anne; 'have you the letter, Rupert?'

'Have I the letter?' cried Rupert. 'Young ladies, did you ever hear of such over-weening presumption? Here is a damsel who expects her scraps of angular writing to be preserved with as much care as the Golden Bulls of the Pope!'

'That is to say, you burnt it without reading it,' said Anne.

'The former part of your supposition is true, sweet sister mine,' replied Rupert: 'not knowing what spells it might contain, seeing that Miss Merton's caligraphy is more like the cabalistic characters of a sorceress than the Italian-hand of a gentle demoiselle, I exorcised it--I committed it to the devouring element!'

'Without turning over the second page of the second piece of note-paper, I suppose?' said Anne.

'How was I ever to suppose that anyone would write a letter for the purpose of giving me an important piece of information,' said Rupert, 'and then put the pith of it in a place where no one would ever dream of looking? No, Lady Elizabeth, if by my absence your feast has lost its brightest ornament, its wittiest and wisest cavalier, it is this sister of mine whom you must accuse!'

It was really not a little provoking to be blamed in this manner for Rupert's own carelessness; but Anne was used to her brother's ways, and could bear them with good humour. Elizabeth, however, attacked him. 'Why, Rupert, one would suppose you had never heard where a woman's mind is to be found! These are most futile excuses.'

'I will only attempt one other,' said the truant--'the utter worthlessness of young ladies' letters, which is such as not to encourage their friends to make any very strict researches into them.'

'Worse and worse!' said Elizabeth; 'you have certainly behaved most cavalierly, that must be confessed! We are only considering what punishment you deserve.'

'I deserve the punishment I have had, Lizzie,' said Rupert; 'I have missed the Consecration, and three days of this fair company!'

'Besides that, you will be held up ever after as a warning to Horace and Edward,' said Elizabeth.

'I saw that first-mentioned pupil of yours on Sunday,' said Rupert.

'Oh! how pleased Mamma will be!' cried Elizabeth; 'then you went to Sandleford?'

'Yes; finding myself too late for the coach on Saturday afternoon, by which I had intended to go to Ely,' said Rupert, 'I made up my mind to spend Sunday at Sandleford, and take a cursory view of the young gentleman, and of my old haunts.'

'Thank you,' said Elizabeth, her eyes beaming with pleasure; 'I am sure that was very kind of you. And how did he look, poor little fellow, and what did he say, and was not he delighted to see you?'

'I shall leave you to judge of that,' said Rupert, 'and say that he looked very happy and flourishing, with face and shirt-collar all over ink on Saturday afternoon; and he said more than I can remember on Sunday evening.'

'And what does Dr. Freeman say of him?' said Elizabeth.

'Dr. Freeman assured me--what do you think, young ladies?--that Master Horatio Woodbourne is by far the most promising youth who has entered his celebrated academy since--of course you know whom I mean, and will spare my blushes!'

'Unluckily,' said Anne, 'the evident fabrication of the latter part of that speech destroys our belief in the beginning of it.'

'No, no,' said Elizabeth, 'it is only the most promising, not the most performing. No one can doubt of Rupert's promises!'

'Rupert, you always do talk such nonsense,' said Katherine.

'Many thanks for the compliment, Lady Kate,' said Rupert, with a bow; 'considering how my intelligence is received, I think I shall spare it in future. I have a letter and parcel from Master Horatio in my portmanteau, and they may speak for themselves, if I have not lost my keys, as I said before.'

'O Rupert!' cried Anne, 'how could you lose them again, after all the pains Mamma took to save them?'

'Indeed, Anne, I did behave better than usual,' said Rupert; 'I kept them safe till yesterday, I assure you. I wish you would come and give me the carriage keys; perhaps some of them may unlock the portmanteau.'

Anne did not think they would; she said they had all been tried twice before; but Rupert would not be satisfied till the experiment had been repeated once more; and long after all the other girls were gone to bed, he kept his sister up, looking out some things which had been brought from Merton Hall for him, while he sat by recounting all his adventures in Scotland. Anne was much delighted to listen, and very glad to have her brother with her again; but perhaps, if he had not been quite so much engrossed by his own affairs, he would have seen that she looked very tired, and have remembered that it was much later than her usual bed-time.

While Katherine and Helen were undressing, the former began:

'Helen, I wish you had gone, it was such fun!'

'Was it?' said Helen. 'I thought Lizzie did not seem much gratified.'

'Lizzie? Oh no,' said Katherine; 'she only hung her head and looked vexed, though there were such a number of people, all so civil and bowing--Mr. Wilkins, and the Greens, and Mr. Higgins.'

'Did Mr. Higgins bow to you and Lizzie?' exclaimed Helen.

'Yes, that he did,' said Katherine triumphantly; 'and a very polite bow he made, I assure you, Helen. I was quite glad to see him; I hope he is coming round.'

'How did Lizzie like it?' asked Helen.

'Oh! she is so odd, you know,' said Katherine; 'she seemed really quite angry; I jogged her once or twice to make her look up, but she shook me off quite crossly; I thought she would have been pleased.'

'I should think few things would vex her much more,' said Helen.

'Well,' said Katherine, 'Willie once told me that some people think Lizzie very proud and disdainful, and I really begin to believe so too.'

'Oh no, Kate,' said Helen; 'I am sure she is not proud, it is only--'

'Mercy, Helen!' here interrupted Kate, 'what are you doing to your hair?'

'Curling it,' replied Helen, in her composed manner.

'Why in the world?' said Katherine; 'I thought you liked your plaits better.'

'Lizzie does not,' said Helen.

'Well,' said Katherine, 'I am sure I should never dream of doing such a thing, only because Lizzie chooses to make a fuss.'

'Perhaps not,' said Helen.

There was a silence. Presently Helen said, 'I suppose Mr. Higgins's next Sunday's paper will mention that the Mechanics' Institute was honoured by the presence of the Miss Woodbournes!'

'Dear me, do you think so?' said Katherine, who could not guess from her sister's manner what opinion she intended to express.

'I think it very probable indeed,' said Helen; 'such a sanction to the education-without-religion system is not to be neglected.'

'System!' said Katherine, looking bewildered; 'how are we to sanction anything?'

'Our station here, as the daughters of the clergyman, gives us some weight,' said Helen; 'besides that, what each person does, however trifling, is of importance to others.'

This was not very clearly expressed, and Katherine did not trouble herself to understand it. She only said, 'Well, I hope we have not got into a scrape; however, you know it was Lizzie's doing, not mine.'

'I thought you went,' said Helen.

'Yes,' said Katherine; 'but that was only because Lizzie said it was not wrong. She is the eldest, and you know she is accountable.'

'I should think that poor consolation,' said Helen.

'Well,' said Katherine sleepily, 'good-night. Those horrid gas-lights have made my head ache. I cannot talk any more.'

CHAPTER IX.

Although she had sat up so much later than usual the night before, Anne was dressed on Saturday morning in time to go to her mother's room for a little while before breakfast.

'Mamma,' said she, after they had spoken of Rupert's arrival, 'where do you think we went yesterday evening?'

'Where, my dear?'

'To hear a lecture at the Mechanics' Institute, Mamma.'

'I should not have thought that your uncle would have approved of his daughters going to such a place,' said Lady Merton.

'Do you think we ought not to have gone, Mamma?' said Anne.

'I do not know the circumstances, my dear,' said Lady Merton; 'the Mechanics' Institute may perhaps be under your uncle's management, and in that case--'

'Oh no,' said Anne. 'I do not think it is--at least, I do not think Uncle Woodbourne would have liked the lecture we heard much better than Lizzie and I did; and after it was too late, I found that Helen had declared it was very wrong of us to go. She would not go; and I found that when I was out of the room, she and Lizzie had had a great debate about it.'

Anne then gave a full account of all that had occurred, and ended with, 'Now, Mamma, do you think we could have helped going on after we once came to Mrs. Turner's, and found what kind of a thing it was likely to be?'

'People certainly cannot stop themselves easily when they have taken the first wrong step,' said Lady Merton.

Anne sighed. 'Then I am afraid we have done very wrong,' said she.

'For yourself, Anne,' said her mother, 'I do not think you are much to blame, since I cannot see how you were to know that your cousins were going without their father's consent.'

'I am glad you think so, Mamma,' said Anne; 'but I cannot be quite happy about it, for I might certainly have supposed that there was some reason against our going, when Helen and the youngest Miss Hazleby turned back and went home.'

'You heard none of Helen's remonstrances?' said Lady Merton.

'No, Mamma; I was foolish enough to be satisfied with Lizzie's saying that she had been talking nonsense,' said Anne; 'besides, I could see that Helen was out of temper, and I thought that might account for her objecting.'

'These are very good reasons, Anne,' said Lady Merton.

'Indeed they are not, Mamma,' said Anne; 'I am afraid the real cause was, that my head was so full of the pleasure I expected in going to the lecture, that I did not choose to think that we ought not to go. I am afraid I am growing thoughtless, as you said I should here.'

'No, no, Anne,' said Lady Merton, smiling, 'I did not say you would, I only said you must guard against doing so; and as far as I have seen, you have shewn more self-command than when you and Lizzie were last together.'

'Ah! but when you are not looking on, Mamma,' said Anne; 'that is the dangerous time, especially now Rupert is come; he and Lizzie will make us laugh dreadfully.'

'I hope they will,' said Lady Merton, 'provided it is without flippancy or unkindness.'

'But, Mamma,' said Anne, presently after, 'what do you think about Lizzie? was she in the wrong?'

'I cannot tell without knowing more about it,' said Lady Merton; 'do you know what she thinks herself?'

'No, Mamma,' said Anne; 'she was asleep before I went to bed last night, and up before I awoke this morning. But I do firmly believe, that if Lizzie had had the slightest idea that she was doing wrong in going there, she would as soon have thought of flying as of doing so.'

It was now breakfast-time; and Rupert came up to summon his mother and sister, and to inform them that his portmanteau had just been broken open for the seventh time since it had been in his possession. He said this with some satisfaction, for he was somewhat vain of his carelessness, for of what cannot people be vain?

During breakfast, it was arranged that the three elder ladies should go in the Mertons' carriage to Baysmouth, a large town, which was about ten miles distant from Abbeychurch, and take Winifred and Edward with them; Dora was to accompany the other young people in a long walk, to a farm-house, which report said had been a baronial castle in the days of King Stephen, and from exploring the antiquities of which some of them expected great things, especially as it was known by the mysterious name of Whistlefar. Mr. Woodbourne and Sir Edward expected to be engaged all day in the final settlement of accounts with the architect of the church.

As soon as the two parties of pleasure had been arranged, Elizabeth left the breakfast-table to tell the children of the treat in store for them, and to write a little note to Horace, to accompany Dora's letter, which had been finished that morning before breakfast.

Just after she had quitted the room, Sir Edward asked what the smart-looking building, at the corner of Aurelia Place, was.

'You mean the Mechanics' Institute,' said Mr. Woodbourne.

'Never was new town without one,' said Rupert.

'Is this one well conducted?' inquired Lady Merton.

'Not much worse than such things usually are,' replied Mr. Woodbourne; 'two or three Socialist lectures were given there, but they were stopped before they had time to do much harm.'

'Were you obliged to interfere?' said Sir Edward.

'Yes,' said Mr. Woodbourne; 'I went to some of the managing committee--Mr. Green and old Mr. Turner--and after some rather strong representations on my part, they found means to put a stop to them. Higgins, their chief promoter, made several violent attacks upon me in his newspaper for my illiberality and bigotry; and poor Mr. Turner was so much distressed, that he came to entreat me to go myself, or at least to allow my girls to go, to some lectures, which he promised should be perfectly harmless. I told him that I disapproved of Mechanics' Institutes in general, and especially of the way in which this one is conducted, and that I had resolved long before that none of my family should ever set foot in it. Here the matter ended; and I have heard no more of it, except that Mrs. Turner is constantly tormenting my wife with offers to take the girls to some peculiarly interesting lecture.'

If Elizabeth had been present, she would certainly have immediately confessed her indiscretion of the evening before; but she was not there, and Katherine, who was on the point of speaking, was checked by an imploring glance from Harriet. The conversation was changed, and nothing more was said on the subject. As soon as they could leave the breakfast-table, all the young ladies instantly flew to the school-room, where Elizabeth was sitting alone, writing.

'Lizzie, Lizzie!' exclaimed three voices at once, 'do you know what you have done?'

'Is it anything very fatal?' said Elizabeth, looking quite composed.

'A fine scrape you have got into!' cried Katherine.

'A pretty kettle of fish you have brought us into!' exclaimed Harriet.

'But what is the matter, good ladies?' said Elizabeth; 'why do you look so like the form that drew Priam's curtains at the dead of night?'

'Come, Lizzie,' said Katherine pettishly, 'do not be so provoking with Priam and all that stuff, but tell us what is to be done about that horrid Institute.'

'Oh! that is it, is it?' said Elizabeth; 'so I suppose Fido was stolen there, and you are afraid to tell!'

'I am afraid he was,' said Katherine; 'but that is not the worst of it--I know nothing about him. But do you know what Papa says? Uncle Edward has been asking about the Institute; and, oh dear! oh dear! Papa said he could not bear Mechanics' Institutes, and had resolved quite firmly that none of his family should ever set foot in one!'

Elizabeth really looked quite appalled at this piece of intelligence; and Katherine continued, 'And Chartists, and Socialists, and horrible people, have been lecturing there! I remember now, that when you were at Merton Hall in the spring, there was a great uproar, and the Abbeychurch Reporter behaved very badly to Papa about it. A fine affair you have made of it, indeed, Lizzie!'

'And pray, Miss Kate,' said Elizabeth sharply, 'who was the person who first proposed this fine expedition? Really, I think, if everyone had their deserts, you would have no small share of blame! What could prevent you from telling me all this yesterday, when it seems you knew it all the time?'

'I forgot it,' said Katherine.

'Exactly like you,' continued her sister; 'and how could you listen to all Helen said, and not be put in mind of it? And how could you bring me back such a flaming description of Mrs. Turner's august puppy of a nephew? If we are in a kettle of fish, as Harriet says, you are at the bottom of it!'

'Well, Lizzie,' said Katherine, 'do not be so cross; you know Mamma says I have such a bad memory, I cannot help forgetting.'

And she began to cry, which softened Elizabeth's anger a little.

'I did not mean to throw *all* the blame upon you, Kate,' said she; 'I know I ought not to have trusted to you; besides that, I led you all into it, being the eldest. I only meant to shew you that you are not quite so immaculate as you seem to imagine. We have all done very wrong, and must take the consequences.'

Helen was leaving the room, when Harriet died out, 'O Helen, pray do not go and tell of us!'

'Helen has no such intention,' said Elizabeth; 'I am going to tell Papa myself as soon as he has done breakfast.'

'Oh! Lizzie, dearest Lizzie,' cried Harriet, 'I beg you will not; you do not know what Mamma would do to me!'

'Pray, Harriet,' said Elizabeth scornfully, 'do you think that I am going to conceal my own faults from my own father?'

'But, Lizzie, stop one moment,' said Harriet; 'you know it was you and Kate who took me; I did not know it was wrong to go; and now Fido is lost, Mamma will be certain to say it was by my going, and she will be dreadfully angry with me; and you would not wish me to be scolded for what was your fault!'

'Should not you wish me to tell, Anne,' said Elizabeth, turning her back upon Harriet.

'I told Mamma this morning,' said Anne.

'Told her!' exclaimed Harriet; 'and what did she say--?'

'She said she wondered that my cousins were allowed to go to such a place,' said Anne; 'and she seemed very sorry we had gone.'

'But was she angry with you?' persisted Harriet.

Anne hesitated; and Elizabeth replied, 'No, of course she could not be angry with Anne, when it was all my doing. She must be displeased enough with me, though.'

'But will she tell Mamma and Aunt Mildred?' said Harriet.

'I do not think she will,' answered Anne.

'No, because she trusts to me to tell,' said Elizabeth; 'so that you see I must, Harriet.'

'Must you?' said Harriet; 'I cannot see why; it will only get us all a scolding.'

'Which we richly deserve,' said Elizabeth.

'I am sure, if you like to be scolded,' said Harriet, 'you are very welcome; only do not make Mamma scold me too.'

'I am sure, if you like to be insincere and cowardly,' said Elizabeth, 'you shall not make me so too.'

'I do not want you to tell a fib,' said Harriet; 'I only want you to say nothing.'

'L'un vaut bien l'autre,' said Elizabeth.

'What?' said Harriet; 'do only wait till we are gone, if you are determined to tell--there's a dear girl.'

'Deceive Papa and Mamma for three whole days!' cried Elizabeth; 'I wonder you are not ashamed of yourself. Besides, Harriet, I do not see what you have to fear. It was Kate and I who did wrong; we knew better, and cast away Helen's good advice; we shut our eyes and went headlong into mischief, but you had no reason to suppose that you might not do as we did.'

'No,' said Harriet, 'I should not care if it was not for Fido.'

'But will my silence find Fido?' said Elizabeth.

'No,' said Harriet; 'but if Mamma knows we went there she will scold us for going, because she will be angry about Fido; and if she once thinks that it was I who lost him--oh, Lizzie, you do not know how angry she will be!'

'But, Harriet,' said Katherine, 'I thought you used to say that you could do anything with your Mamma, and that she never minded where you went.'

'Oh! that is when she is in good humour,' said Harriet; 'she is not often cross with me, but when she is, you may hear her from one end of the house to the other. Cannot you, Lucy? And now she will be dreadfully cross about Fido, and the other thing coming upon it, I do not know what she may say. O Lizzie, you will save me!'

'I will only tell of Kate and myself,' said Elizabeth; 'or I will ask Papa not to mention it to Mrs. Hazleby; though, Harriet, there are some people who prefer any suffering, just or unjust, to deceit.'

'Then you mean to tell directly,' said Katherine, in a piteous tone.

'Of course I do,' said Elizabeth; 'there is the dining-room door shut. Come with me, Kate.'

Katherine rather unwillingly followed her sister into the passage; but when there, fear making her ingenious, a sudden thought struck her. 'Lizzie,' whispered she, 'if you tell Papa that you and I went, Mrs. Hazleby will be sure to hear, and if she asks Harriet about it, perhaps she--you know--may tell a story about it.'

'Fine confidence you shew in your chosen friend!' said Elizabeth.

'Why, one must be civil; and Harriet is a sort of cousin,' said Katherine; 'but I am sure she is not half so much my friend as Willie.'

'Well, never mind defending your taste in friends,' said Elizabeth; 'for as I do think your scruple worth answering, I will tell you that I had thought of the same thing; but I do not choose to do evil that good may come, or that evil may not come. I shall tell Papa what an excellent opinion you have of Harriet, and leave him to do as he pleases.'

Elizabeth's hand was on the lock of the door of her father's study, when Katherine exclaimed, 'There is someone there--I hear voices!'

'Uncle Edward,' said Elizabeth. 'I do not mind his being there; we ought to beg his pardon for leading Anne astray.'

'Oh! but do not you see,' said Katherine, 'here are a hat and a roll of papers on the table! Mr. Roberts must be come.'

'Tiresome man!' cried Elizabeth; 'he will be there all day, and I shall not see Papa I do not know when. It really was a very convenient thing when the architects of the old German cathedrals used to take a desperate leap from the top of the tower as soon as it was finished. Well, I must find Mamma now.'

'Cannot you wait till the evening, when you may see Papa?' said Katherine, hoping to put off the evil day.

'I cannot have this upon my mind all day unconfessed,' said Elizabeth; 'besides, Harriet will pester me with entreaties as long as it is untold. Come, Kitty, do not be such a coward.'

'I am sure I do not want you not to tell,' said Katherine, looking rather miserable; 'only I am not in such a hurry about it as you are. You do not know where Mamma is.'

'No, but I will find her,' said Elizabeth.

The sisters set off on the chase; they looked into the drawing-room, the dining-room, Mrs. Woodbourne's room, without success; they ran up to the nursery, but she was not there; and they were going down again, when Katherine, seeing Elizabeth go towards the kitchen stairs, exclaimed, 'Well, I will go no further; it is so ridiculous, as if it was a matter of life and death! You may call if you want me.'

Katherine retreated into her own room, and Elizabeth ran down to the kitchen, where she found Mrs. Woodbourne ordering dinner.

Elizabeth stood by the fire, biting her lip and pinching her finger, and trembling all over with impatience, while Mrs. Woodbourne and the cook were busily consulting over some grouse which Rupert had brought from Scotland.

'Lizzie, my dear,' said Mrs. Woodbourne presently, 'would you just run to my room and fetch down the green receipt-book?'

Elizabeth obeyed: running was rather a relief to her, and she was down-stairs again in another instant.

'Why, Lizzie,' said Mrs. Woodbourne, with a smile, 'you must be wild to-day; you have brought me the account-book instead of--But, my dear child, what is the matter?' said she, perceiving that Elizabeth's face was scarlet, and her eyes full of tears.

'I will tell you presently,' whispered Elizabeth, breathlessly, 'when you have done.' She darted away again, and returned with the right book; but Mrs. Woodbourne was too much alarmed by her manner to spend another moment in giving directions to the cook, and instantly followed her to her own room. Elizabeth hastily shut the door, and sat down to recover her breath.

'My dear Lizzie, there is nothing amiss with any of the--' exclaimed Mrs. Woodbourne, almost gasping for breath.

'Oh no, Mamma,' said Elizabeth, a smile passing over her face in spite of her distress, 'it is not Winifred who is mad. It is I who have been more mad and foolish and self-willed than you would ever believe. Mamma, I have been with Mrs. Turner to the Mechanics' Institute.'

'My dear Lizzie, you do not mean it!' said Mrs. Woodbourne.

'Yes, Mamma, indeed it is so,' said Elizabeth mournfully; 'I did not know what had happened there certainly, but I would not listen to Helen's good advice, and so

I have made Papa seem to consent to what he abhors; I have led Kate and Anne and Harriet all wrong. Oh! Mamma, is not it terrible?'

'Indeed, I wish I had told you what your Papa said to Mr. Turner,' said Mrs. Woodbourne; 'I am afraid your papa will be very much annoyed; but, my dear, do not distress yourself, you could not know that it was wrong.'

'Yes; but, Mamma,' said Elizabeth, 'I did know that it was wrong to go out without asking your leave. Simple obedience might have kept me straight. But now I will tell you all, and you shall judge what had best be done about the Hazlebys and Fido.'

Rather incoherently, and with many sobs, Elizabeth told the history of the preceding evening. Mrs. Woodbourne listened to her with the utmost kindness, and said all she could to soothe and console her, assuring her that Mr. Woodbourne could not be seriously displeased with her for having transgressed a command of which she was ignorant. Elizabeth was much relieved by having been able to talk over her conduct in this manner; and though she still felt that she had been very much to blame, and by no means sure that Mr. Woodbourne would pass over her fault so lightly, was greatly comforted by her mamma's kindness. She went away to bathe her swollen eyes, before she went down to the school-room to read the Psalms and Lessons with her sisters, as was their regular custom when there was no service at the church, before they began their morning's work; Mrs. Woodbourne undertaking to call the children down in a few minutes, and saying that she would speak to Katherine in the course of the day. She willingly promised to say nothing to Mrs. Hazleby, and only wished she was quite sure that there were no symptoms of madness about Fido.

'What a strange girl Lizzie is!' cried Harriet, just as Elizabeth departed on her search for her father or Mrs. Woodbourne.

'But, Harriet,' said Lucy, drawing her aside to the window, 'what difference is her saying nothing to make? Mamma will ask how Fido was lost.'

'I am sure, Lucy, that was more your fault than mine,' said Harriet; 'I could not be watching him all the time we were at that place.'

'Then why did you take him there?' said Helen.

'Because Lucy chose to run away without ever thinking what I was to do,' said Harriet.

'But when you were leading him, and it must have been you who let go his string,' said Helen; 'I cannot see how you can accuse Lucy of having been the means of losing him, when she was safe at home.'

Harriet was saved from the necessity of finding an answer, by hearing her mother calling her in the passage, and she hastened to obey the summons.

'Do you know where Fido is?' was Mrs. Hazleby's question.

'No,' said Harriet, finding she had only escaped one dilemma to fall into another. She avoided any further questions, however, by hastening past her mother and running up-stairs.

'Lucy, Lucy!' then called Mrs. Hazleby; and as Lucy came out of the school-room, she repeated the inquiry.

'I do not know, Mamma,' answered Lucy in a low voice, but standing quite still.

'Go and ask for him in the kitchen then,' said Mrs. Hazleby.

'I am afraid it would be of no use. Ma'am,' said Lucy, firmly, but not daring to raise her eyes; 'we missed him when we came in from walking, yesterday evening.'

'Yesterday evening!' cried Mrs. Hazleby; 'and did you never speak of it? I never knew anyone so careless as you are, in all my life. It is of no use to leave anything in your charge, you care for--'

Here Lucy leant back and shut the door behind her, so that Anne and Helen could distinguish nothing but the sound of Mrs. Hazleby's loud angry voice raised to its highest pitch.

'Poor Lucy!' sighed Helen.

'Dreadful!' said Anne.

'And how can anyone say that Lucy is not one of the noblest, most self-devoted creatures upon earth?' exclaimed Helen, with tears in her eyes; 'there she is, bearing all that terrible scolding, rather than say it was Harriet's fault, as everyone knows it was. I am sure no one is like Lucy. And this is going on continually about something or other.'

'How can she exist?' said Anne.

'With her acute feelings and painful timidity,' said Helen, 'it is worse for her than it would be for anyone else, yet how gently and simply she bears it all! and old

Mrs. Hazleby says that she is often ill after these scoldings, and she would have taken her away to live with her, as the Major proposed, after Miss Dorothea Hazleby died, but that she thought it would be taking away all the comfort of her father's life. Oh! Anne,' cried Helen, walking up and down the room as Mrs. Hazleby's voice became louder and louder, 'I cannot bear it; what shall I do? Oh! if it was but right, if it would not make it worse for Lucy, I could, I would go out and tell Mrs. Hazleby what everybody thinks of her.'

'I do not wonder that Miss Hazleby was ready to do almost anything to avoid such a scene,' said Anne.

'Mean selfish creature!' said Helen; 'she ran away on purpose that Lucy might stay and bear all this. Anne, I do believe that if martyrs are made, and crowns are gained, by daily sufferings and hourly self-denial, that such a crown will be dear dear Lucy's.'

Anne's answer was--

> 'And all the happy souls that rode
> Transfigured through that fresh abode,
> Had heretofore in humble trust,
> Shone meekly 'mid their native dust,
> The glow-worms of the earth!'

'Thank you, Anne,' said Helen, wiping away her tears; 'I will think of Lucy as the light, the glow-worm of her family. Thank you; the thought of her meek clear light in darkness need not be gloomy, as it has been.'

Anne had never thought of Helen as possessing so much enthusiasm, and was almost more inclined to wonder at her than at Lucy. While they had been talking, Mrs. Hazleby's voice had ceased, steps were now heard in the passage, and a letter was brought in and given to Helen. It was from Fanny Staunton, but she had only just time to glance it over, before the three children came in, followed by their mother and Elizabeth. Anne went to call her mother to join them in reading the Psalms and Lessons; and Winifred was sent to summon Katherine, who had purposely lingered up-stairs till all the rest were assembled.

Elizabeth's eyes were very red, and she was afraid to trust her voice to read the first verse of the Psalm, as it was always her part to do; but little Dora, who sat next to her, and who seemed in part to enter into her feelings, although she said nothing, read the first verse for her; and Elizabeth took Edward, who always looked over her book, upon her knee when the Lessons began, so as to screen her face from her aunt. When they had finished, attention was drawn away from her by Edward, who was eagerly assuring Lady Merton that the Bible and Prayer-book which Uncle Edward, his godfather, had given him, were quite safe, and he was to use them himself when Lizzie thought he could read well enough. This Dora explained as meaning when he had for a week abstained from guessing words instead of spelling them; and Elizabeth proposed to him to try whether he could read to-day without one mistake. Edward objected to reading at that time, as he was to go out at half-past twelve, and there would be no time for lessons. Elizabeth demonstrated that it was now only half-past ten, and that it was impossible that he could spend two hours in putting on his best frock and trowsers, and in settling what to buy with the bright half-crown which Uncle Edward had given him; and Winifred assured him that she meant to do all her lessons to-day. Edward looked round to appeal to his mother, but both she and Lady Merton had left the room, and he was forced to content himself with asking Anne whether she thought there was time.

'Oh yes, Edward; I hope you will let me hear how well you can read; I want to know whether the young robins saw any more monsters,' said Anne good-naturedly.

Winifred, rather inopportunely, was ready with the information, that the nest was visited by two more monsters; but Anne stopped her ears, and declared she would hear nothing but from Edward himself, and the young gentleman was thus persuaded to begin his lesson.

Helen did not wait to see how the question was decided, but went up to her own room to enjoy Fanny Staunton's letter. She paused however a few moments, to consider whether she should go to Lucy, but thinking that it must certainly be painful to her to speak of what had passed, she proceeded to her own room, there to send her whole heart and mind to Dykelands.

Fanny Staunton's letter was overflowing with affection and with regrets for Helen's departure; and this, together with her descriptions of her own and her sister's amusements and occupations, made Helen's heart yearn more strongly than ever after the friends she had left. Anne's cheerful manner, and Lucy's quiet content, had, the day before, made Helen rather ashamed of herself, and she had resolved to leave off pining for Dykelands, and to make herself happy, by being useful and obliging, without thinking about little grievances, such as almost everyone could probably find in their own home, if they searched for them. When she had curled her hair, it was with the hope that the sacrifice of her tails would convince Elizabeth that she had some regard for her taste; unfortunately, however, her hair was rather too soft to curl well, and after having been plaited for the last three months, it was most obstinate in hanging deplorably straight, in a way very uncomfortable to her feelings and irritating to her temper; besides which, Elizabeth had been too much occupied by her own concerns all the morning, to observe the alteration, and indeed, if she had remarked it, she was not likely to feel as much flattered by this instance of deference to her opinion, as Helen thought she ought to be. Last night, Helen had lamented that her own petulance had prevented her from reasoning calmly with Elizabeth, and from setting before her all the arguments upon which she had discoursed so fluently to Lucy, after the imprudent step had been taken; but now, she threw the blame upon Elizabeth's impetuosity and unkindness, and felt somewhat aggrieved, because neither of her sisters had expressed a full sense of her firmness and discretion. She compared Fanny's affectionate expressions, with Elizabeth's sharp and hasty manner; the admiration which her friends had made rather too evident, with the wholesome though severe criticisms she sometimes met with at home; the quietness at Dykelands, with the constant bustle at the Vicarage; and ended, by thinking Mrs. Woodbourne the only person of the family who possessed any gentleness or kindness, and making up her mind that Dykelands was the only pleasant place in England, and that she herself was a most ill-used person, whose merits were not in the least appreciated.

Such were the feelings which gradually took possession of her mind, while she was writing her answer to Fanny's letter; and by the time she had finished, had brought her into that agreeable frame, which is disposed to be offended with the first person who does not act up to its expectations.

Katherine's study, through the whole morning, was to avoid a private interview with Mrs. Woodbourne; and she really shewed considerable ingenuity in evading her. If Mrs. Woodbourne called her, she answered, 'Yes, Mamma, I am coming directly,' but she took care not to come till she knew that her mamma was no longer alone; if Lady Merton wanted anything which she had left up-stairs, Katherine would officiously volunteer to fetch it, when particularly told that she was not wanted; if Mrs. Woodbourne moved to the door, and made signs to Katherine to follow her, she worked with double assiduity, and never looked up unless to speak to Rupert or to Harriet; and thus she contrived to elude the reproof she expected, until the whole party, except the two gentlemen, met at twelve o'clock for an early luncheon, so that there was no longer any danger that Mrs. Woodbourne would find an opportunity of speaking to her, at present.

The three children were to dine late with the rest of the party, and were in high glee at the prospect of the afternoon's amusement; Elizabeth seemed to have recovered her spirits; Harriet was as noisy as ever; and Lucy, if possible, a little quieter than was her wont; Anne, as usual, ready to be amused with anything; and Rupert quite prepared to amuse everyone.

Fido was again mentioned, and Rupert, who had heard about half of the history of his loss, suggested the possibility of his having been despatched by the railroad to London, there to be converted into sausages. Harriet, after many exclamations of 'O Mr. Merton!' declared that if she believed such a thing could ever happen, she would never eat another sausage in her life, and concluded as usual with, 'would you, Lucy?' Mrs. Woodbourne inquired anxiously after Winifred's hand. Mrs. Hazleby was on the point of taking fire at the implied suspicion of her lamented favourite's sanity, when Rupert averted the threatened danger, by a grave examination of Winifred and Meg Merrilies, who had both been wounded, and concluded by recommending that as soon as puss shewed symptoms of hydrophobia, Winifred should be smothered between two feather-beds, to prevent further mischief. Everyone laughed, except Dora, who thought the proposal exceedingly shocking; and Rupert argued very gravely with her on the expediency of the measure, until she was called away to prepare for the walk.

CHAPTER X.

Dora re-considered her arguments while putting on her bonnet, and the instant the walking party were outside the front door, she began again. 'But, Rupert, it would be committing murder to kill Winifred, even if she had the Fidophobia.'

'No, no, Dora,' said Rupert, 'it is your mamma and Lizzie who have the Fidophobia.'

'What can you mean?' said Helen; 'how can you frighten the child so, Rupert?'

'Do not you know, Helen,' said Elizabeth, ''tis his vocation. He is a true Knight Rupert.'

'Expound, most learned cousin,' said Rupert; 'you are too deep.'

'You must know,' said Elizabeth, 'that Knecht Ruprecht is the German terrifier of naughty children, the same as the chimney-sweeper in England, or Coeur de Lion in Palestine, or the Duke of Wellington in France.

'Baby, baby, he's a giant,   Tall and black as Rouen steeple;   And he dines and sups, 'tis said,   Every day, on naughty people.'

'I should have thought,' said Rupert, 'that considering my namesake's babe-bolting propensities, and his great black dog, that he would have been more likely to be held up in terrorem in England.'

'I suppose there was some old grim Sir Rupert in Germany,' said Elizabeth; 'but my dictionary is my only authority.'

'You are taking knecht to mean a knight,' said Anne, 'contrary to your argument last night. Knecht Ruprecht's origin is not nearly so sublime as you would make it out. Keightley's Fairy Mythology says he is only our old friend Robin Good-fellow, Milton's lubber fiend, the Hob Goblin. You know, Rupert, and Robert, and Hob, are all the same name, Rudbryht, bright in speech.'

'And a hobbish fellow means a gentleman as clumsy as the lubber fiend,' said Elizabeth.

'No doubt he wore hob-nails in his shoes,' said Rupert.

'And chimney hobs were so called, because his cream bowl was duly set upon them,' said Anne.

'And he was as familiar as the Robin Redbreast,' said Elizabeth.

'And wore a red waistcoat like him, and like Herb Robert,' said Anne.

'As shabby as this flower,' said Elizabeth, gathering a ragged Robin from the hedge.

'Well done, etymology,' said Rupert; 'now for syntax and prosody.'

'I hope we have been talking syntax all this time,' said Elizabeth; 'we will keep prosody for the evening, and then play at Conglomeration.'

They now came to some bright green water-meadows, which bordered the little stream as soon as it left the town. There was a broad dry path by the river side, and as they walked along it, there was no lack of laughter or merriment in anyone but Helen, and she could find no amusement in anything she saw or heard. At last, however, she was highly delighted at the sight of some plants of purple loose-strife, growing on the bank. 'Oh!' cried she, 'that is the flower that is so beautiful at Dykelands.'

'What! the loose strife?' said Elizabeth, 'it is common enough in all damp places.'

Poor Helen! as if this slight to the flower she admired were not a sufficient shock to her feelings, Rupert, perfectly unconscious on what tender ground he was treading, said, 'If it is a lover of damp, I am sure it can nowhere be better suited than at Dykelands. Did you grow web-footed there, Helen?'

'O Rupert,' said Helen, 'I am sure the garden is always quite dry.'

'Except when it is wet,' said Elizabeth.

'That was certainly the case when I was there two years ago,' observed Rupert; 'I could not stir two steps from the door without meeting with a pool deep enough to swim a man-of-war.'

'Rupert,' said Elizabeth, 'I hereby give notice, that whosoever says one single word against the perfect dryness, cleanliness, and beauty, of dear Dykelands, commits high treason against Miss Helen Woodbourne; and as protecting disconsolate damsels is the bounden duty of a true knight and cavalier, I advise you never to mention the subject, on pain of being considered a discourteous recreant.'

'Lizzie, how can you?' said Helen peevishly.

'How strange it is,' said Anne, 'that so many old family houses should have been built in damp places.'

'Our ancestors were once apparently frogs,' said Rupert; unhappily reminding Helen of her sister's parody.

'Well,' said Elizabeth, 'I can understand why monasteries should have been built in damp places, near rivers or bogs, both for the sake of the fish, and to be useful in draining; but why any other mortal except Dutchmen, tadpoles, and newts, should delight in mud and mire, passes my poor comprehension.'

Rupert pointed to a frog which Dora's foot had startled from its hiding-place, and said, 'Pray, why, according to my theory, should not the human kind have once been frogs? leap-frog being only a return to our natural means of progression.'

'And bull-frogs in a course of becoming stalwart gentlemen,' said Anne.

'Yes, we often hear of a croaking disposition, do not we, Helen?' said Elizabeth; 'you see both that propensity, and a love of marshes, are but indications of a former state of existence.'

'And I am sure that your respectable neighbour, Mr. Turner, is a toad on his hind legs,' said Rupert.

'Minus the precious jewel,' said Elizabeth.

'By-the-bye,' said Rupert, 'is there not some mystery about that gentleman? This morning I hazarded a supposition, in the drawing-room, that the lost darling we have heard so much of, might have been dissected for the benefit of Mr. Turner's pupils, and thereupon arose a most wonderful whispering between Kate and one of your sweet cousins there, Lizzie, about some nephew, an Adolphus or Augustus, or some such name; but the more questions I asked, the more dark and mysterious did the young ladies become.'

'I wonder if it is possible!' cried Elizabeth, with a sudden start.

'What is possible?' asked Anne.

'That Rupert should be right,' said Elizabeth; 'was Mrs. Hazleby in the room when you spoke?'

'Yes, but what of that?' said Rupert.

'That you, talking at random,' said Elizabeth, 'very nearly betrayed Harriet's grand secret.'

'Really, the affair becomes quite exciting,' said Rupert; 'pray do not leave me in suspense, explain yourself.'

'I do not think I can, Rupert,' said Elizabeth, not wishing to expose Harriet, for Mrs. Woodbourne's sake.

'Then I am to understand,' said Rupert, 'that Miss Hazleby has presented Fido to this noble Adolphus, as a pledge of the tenderest friendship, and that you and Kate act as confidants.'

'Nonsense, Rupert,' said Anne, trying to check him by a look.

'And I suppose,' proceeded Rupert, 'that the gentleman is to extract poor Fido's faithful heart, and wear it next his own. I never should have devised so refined and sentimental a souvenir. It is far beyond forget-me-nots and arrows. So professional too.'

Elizabeth and Anne laughed so much that they could neither of them speak for some moments; but when Anne recovered, she took her brother by the arm and whispered, 'Rupert, the less you say about the Turners or Fido, the better. I will explain it all to you when we have an opportunity.'

Elizabeth thanked her by a look; and at this moment Dora, who had been far in advance with Katherine and the Hazlebys, came running back to beg Rupert to gather for her some fine bulrushes which grew on the brink of the river. Rupert was very willing to comply with her request; but Elizabeth recommended Dora to leave them till they should return, and not to take the trouble of carrying them to Whistlefar Castle and back again.

Leaving the river, they began to ascend a steep chalky lane, which had been wet all the winter, and was now full of rough hardened wheel-ruts and holes made by slipping horses. Elizabeth thought that Robert Bruce's calthorps could hardly have made the ground more uneven, and she was just going to say so, when Helen groaned out, 'What a horrid place! I slip and bruise my ancle every minute.' Upon which she immediately took the other side of the question, and answered, 'It is not nearly so bad as the long lane on the down, and you never complain of that.'

'Oh! but this is all up-hill,' said Helen.

'I am not in the least tired, Helen,' said Dora, who with Rupert's assistance was taking flying leaps over the ruts.

'You? no, I should think not,' said Helen, in so piteous a tone, that Rupert very good-naturedly waited till she came up to him, and then offered her his arm.

On seeing this, Harriet was rather vexed that she had not been first noticed by the gentleman, and began to make heavy complaints of the badness of the road, but no one paid much attention to her. Elizabeth however gave her arm to Lucy, who never could bear much fatigue.

After they had gained the top of the hill, they walked on for some distance between high hedges, and as none of the party knew the way further than the river, except from some directions given them by Mr. Walker, the Curate, they begun to think that they must have missed a turn to the left, which he had told them to take. Harriet and Helen both declared that they had passed the turning; Katherine was sure they had not; and Elizabeth said that she had seen a turn to the right some way behind them, but that to the left was yet to come. As they could not agree upon this question, Rupert walked onwards to explore, leaving the young ladies to rest on the trunk of a tree lying by the side of the road. While he was gone, Elizabeth drew Helen aside, saying, 'Helen, you had better take care, I hope Rupert has not observed how much out of humour you are.'

'I am not out of humour,' said Helen, according to the usual fashion of denying such a charge.

'Then why do you look and speak as if you were?' said her sister; 'you had better watch yourself.'

'I think you are enough to vex anyone, Lizzie,' said Helen; 'bringing me ever so far out of the way on such a road as this, and then scolding me for saying I do not like it.'

'I see,' answered Elizabeth, 'you are not in a fit state to be reasoned with.'

'No,' retorted Helen, who had indulged in her ill-humour till she hardly knew what she said, 'you will never condescend to hear what I have to say. Perhaps it might be as well sometimes if you would.'

'Yes, Helen,' said Elizabeth, colouring and turning away, 'it would indeed. I know I have given you a right to upbraid me.'

At this moment Rupert came back, cheering the drooping courage of the wearied and heated damsels with intelligence, that 'there is no lane without a turning,' and he had found the one they were seeking.

Things now went on better; they came to a shady green path by the side of a wood, and Helen was more silent, her temper having perhaps been a little improved by the coolness. Soon, however, they had to cross two long fields, where gleaning was going on merrily; Helen made several complaints of the heat and of the small size of her parasol; and Elizabeth had to catch Dora, and hold her fast, to prevent her from overheating herself by a race after Rupert through the stubble. At the first stile, Harriet thought proper to make a great outcry, and was evidently quite disposed for a romp, but Rupert helped her over so quietly that she had no opportunity for one. They now found themselves in a grass field, the length of which made Helen sigh.

'Why, Helen, how soon you are tired!' said Rupert; 'I am afraid Dykelands did not agree with you.'

'Helen is only a little cross, she will be better presently,' said Dora, in so comical a tone, that Rupert, Katherine, and Harriet all laughed, and Helen said sharply, 'Dora, do not be pert.'

Rupert was really a very good-natured youth, but it would have required more forbearance than he possessed, to abstain from teazing so tempting a subject as poor Helen was at this moment.

'And how do you know that Helen is a little cross, Dora, my dear?' said he.

'Because she looks so,' said Dora.

'And how do people look when they are a little cross, Dora?'

'I do not know,' answered Dora.

'Do they look so, my dear?' said Rupert, mimicking poor Helen's woe-begone face in a very droll way.

Dora laughed, and Helen was still more displeased. 'Dora, it is very naughty,' said she.

'What! to look cross?' said Rupert; 'certainly, is it not, Dora?'

Elizabeth and Anne were far in the rear, reaching for some botanical curiosity, on the other side of a wet ditch, or they would certainly have put a stop to this conversation, which was not very profitable to any of the parties concerned. Dora was rather a matter-of-fact little person, and a very good implement for teazing with, as she did not at all suspect the use made of her, until a sudden thought striking her, she stopped short, saying very decidedly, 'We will not talk of this any more.'

'Why not?' said Rupert, rather sorry to be checked in the full enjoyment of his own wit.

'Because Helen does not like it,' said Dora.

'But, Dora,' said Rupert, wishing to try the little girl rather further, 'do not you think she deserves it, for being out of temper?'

'I do not know,' said Dora gravely, 'but I know it is not right or kind to say what vexes her, and I shall not stay with you any longer, Rupert, if you will do it.'

So saying, Dora, well-named Discreet Dolly, ran away to Lucy, of whom she was very fond.

Rupert was both amused and surprised at Dora's behaviour, and perhaps, at the same time, a little ashamed and piqued by a little girl of seven years old having shewn more right feeling and self-command than he had displayed; and to cover all these sensations, he began to talk nonsense to Katherine and Harriet as fast as he could.

In the mean time Helen walked on alone, a little behind the rest of the party; for by this time Elizabeth and Anne had come up with the others, and had passed her. As they entered a little copse, she began to recollect herself. She had from her infancy been accustomed to give way to fits of peevishness and fretfulness, thinking that as long as her ill-humour did not burst forth in open name, as Elizabeth's used formerly to do, there was no great harm in letting it smoulder away, and make herself and everyone else uncomfortable. Some time ago, something had brought conviction to her mind that such conduct was not much better than bearing malice and hatred in her heart, and she had resolved to cure herself of the habit. Then came her visit to Dykelands, where everything went on smoothly, and there was little temptation to give way to ill-humour, so that she had almost forgotten her reflections on the subject, till the present moment, when she seemed suddenly to wake and find herself in the midst of one of her old sullen moods. She struggled hard against it, and as acknowledging ill temper is one great step towards conquering it, she soon recovered sufficiently to admire the deep pink fruit of the skewer-wood, and the waxen looking red and yellow berries of the wild guelder rose, when suddenly the rear of the darkness dim which over-shadowed her spirits was scattered by the lively din of a long loud whistle from Rupert, who was concealed from her by some trees, a little in advance of her. She hastened forwards, and found him and all the others just emerged from the wood, and standing on an open bare common where neither castle nor cottage was to be seen, nothing but a carpet of purple heath, dwarf furze, and short soft grass upon which a few cows, a colt, and a donkey, were browsing. The party were standing together, laughing, some moderately, others immoderately.

'What is the matter?' asked Helen.

'I do not know,' said Elizabeth, 'unless Rupert is hallooing because he is out of the wood.'

'Wait till you have heard my reasons unfolded,' said Rupert; 'did you never hear how this celebrated fortress came by its name?'

'Never,' said several voices.

'Then listen, listen, ladies all,' said Rupert. 'You must know that once upon a time there was a most beautiful princess, who lived in a splendid castle, where she received all kinds of company. Well, one day, there arrived an old grim palmer, just like the picture of Hopeful, in the Pilgrim's Progress, with a fine striped cockle-shell sticking upright in his hat-band. Well, the cockle-shell tickled the Princess's fancy very much, and she made her pet knight (for she had as many suitors as Penelope) promise that he would steal it from him that very night. So at the witching hour of midnight, the knight approached the palmer's couch, and gently abstracted the cockle hat and staff, placing in their stead, the jester's cap and bells, and bauble. Next morning when it was pitch dark, for it was the shortest day, up jumped the palmer, and prepared to resume his journey. Now it chanced that the day before, the lady had ordered that the fool should be whipped, for mocking her, when she could not get the marrow neatly out of a bone with her fingers, and peeped into it like a hungry magpie; so that the moment the poor palmer appeared in the court-yard, all the squires and pages set upon him, taking him for the fool, and whipped him round and round like any peg-top. Suddenly, down fell the cap and bells, and he saw what had been done; upon which he immediately turned into an enchanter, and commanded the Princess and all her train to fall into a deep sleep, all excepting the knight who had committed the offence, who is for ever riding up and down the castle court, repenting of his discourtesy, with his face towards the tail of a cream-coloured donkey, wearing a cap and bells for a helmet, with a rod for a lance, and a cockle-shell for a shield, and star-fishes for spurs, and the Princess can only be disenchanted by her devoted champion doing battle with him. All, however, has vanished away from vulgar eyes, and can only be brought to light by being thrice whistled for. A slight tradition has remained, and the place has ever since been known by the mysterious name of Whistlefar.'

'And has no one ever found it?' said Dora.

'I cannot say,' answered Rupert.

'A deed of such high emprise can only be reserved for the great Prince Rupert himself,' said Elizabeth.

'How can such nonsensical traditions be kept up?' said Harriet; 'I thought everyone had forgotten such absurd old stories, only fit to frighten children.'

'Oh! you know nobody believes them,' said Katherine.

'But, Rupert,' said Helen, 'this must be a modern story, it cannot be a genuine old legend, it is really not according to the spirit of those times to say that a palmer could be an enchanter, or so revengeful.'

'Oh!' said Rupert, 'you know everything bad is to be learnt among the Saracens.'

'Still,' said Helen, 'if you consider the purpose for which the Palmers visited the Holy Land, you cannot think them likely to learn the dark rites of the Infidels, and scarcely to wish to gratify personal resentment.'

'The frock does not make the friar,' said Rupert, 'and this may have been a bad palmer. Think of the Knights Templars.'

'Besides,' said Helen, 'how could the squires see either palmer or jester when it was pitch dark?'

'I suppose there were lamps in the court,' said Rupert; 'but

> "I cannot tell how the truth may be,
> I tell the tale as 'twas told to me."'

'But who told you, Rupert?' said Helen.

'Why, the story of Red Mantle, Helen, cannot you see?' said Elizabeth; 'it was on the table all the morning.'

'O Lizzie, was there ever anything so cruel?' cried Rupert; 'Edie Ochiltree was nothing to you. Everyone was swallowing it so quietly, and you will not even let me enjoy the credit of originality.'

'I am sure I give you credit due,' said Elizabeth; 'it is really an ingenious compound of Red Mantle, the Sleeping Beauty, Robert of Paris, and Triermain, and the cockle-shell shield and star-fish spurs form an agreeable variation.'

'I never will tell another story in your presence, Lizzie,' said Rupert, evidently vexed, but carrying it off with great good humour; 'you are worse than Quarterly, Edinburgh, and Blackwood put together.'

'I really think you deserved it, Rupert,' said Anne; 'I cannot pity you, you ought not to laugh at the pilgrims.'

'Oh! I dare not open my lips before such devotees of crusading,' said Rupert.

'And pray, Rupert,' said Elizabeth, 'what did you mean by comparing me to Edie Ochiltree? did you mean to say that you were like Monkbarns? I never heard that that gentleman fabricated either legends or curiosities, and made them pass for genuine ancient ones.'

At this moment, happily for Rupert, they came to the top of a small rising ground, and beheld a farmhouse at about a hundred yards before them. Rupert whistled long and loud and shrill, and two or three of the young ladies exclaimed, 'Is this Whistlefar Castle?'

'It is only enchanted,' said Elizabeth; 'clear away the mist of incredulity from your eyes, and behold keep, drawbridge, tower and battlement, and loop-hole grates where captives weep.'

It cannot be denied that the young party were a little disappointed by the aspect of the renowned Whistlefar, but they did ample justice to all that was to be seen; a few yards of very thick stone wall in the court, a coat of arms carved upon a stone built into the wall upside down, and the well-turned arch of the door-way. Some, putting on Don Quixote's eyes for the occasion, saw helmets in milk-pails, dungeons in cellars, battle-axes in bill-hooks, and shields in pewter-plates, called the baby in its cradle the sleeping Princess, agreed that the shield must have been reversed by order of the palmer, and that one of the cows was the mischievous knight's cream-coloured donkey; so that laughter happily supplied the place of learned lore.

On the way home the party were not quite so merry, although Helen was unusually agreeable, and enjoyed a very pleasant conversation with Rupert and Anne, who, she was pleased to find, really thought her worth talking to. Elizabeth was occupied with Dora, who was tired, and wanted to be cheered and amused. She did not however forget her bulrushes, and when they came in sight of them, she ran forwards to claim Rupert's promise of gathering some for her and her little brother and sister. This was a service of difficulty, for some of the bulrushes grew in the water, and others on deceitful ground, where a pool appeared wherever Rupert set his foot. With two or three strides and leaps, however, he reached a little dry island, covered with a tuft of sedges, in the midst of the marsh, and was reaching some of the bulrushes with the hook of Anne's parasol, when he suddenly cried out, 'Hollo, what have we here?'

'What?' said some of the girls.

'A dead dog, I believe,' said Rupert.

'Oh! let me see,' cried Harriet, advancing cautiously over the morass.

'Are you curious in such matters. Miss Hazleby?' said Rupert, laughing, as Harriet came splashing towards him through the wet, holding up her frock with one hand, and stretching out the other to him, to be helped upon the island. He pulled her upon it safely, but it quaked fearfully; and there was hardly room for them both to stand on it, while Harriet, holding fast by Rupert's hand, bent forwards, beheld the object of her curiosity, uttered a loud scream, lost her balance, and would have fallen into the river had she not been withheld by Rupert's strength of arm. They both slipped down on the opposite sides of the island, into the black mud, and Harriet precipitately retreated to the mainland.

'Well, what is the matter?' said Elizabeth.

'Oh! my poor dear little doggie!' cried Harriet.

'Is it Fido?' said Elizabeth; 'then, Harriet, there is no fear of your eating him in a sausage; you may be at rest on that score.'

'But can it really be Fido?' said Katherine, pressing forwards.

'Do you wish to see?' said Rupert, 'for if so, I advise you to make haste, the island is sinking fast.'

'I am splashed all over, so I do not care. Can I have one more look?' said Harriet, in a melancholy voice.

Rupert handed her back to the island, where she took her last farewell of poor

Fido, all his long hair drenched with water, and the very same blue ribbon which she had herself tied round his neck the day before, floating, a funeral banner, on the surface of the stream. She contemplated him until her weight and Rupert's had sunk the island so much, that it was fast becoming a lake, while Elizabeth whispered to Anne to propose presenting her with a forget-me-not, on Fido's part.

'I hope,' said Rupert, as they proceeded with their walk, 'that you are fully sensible of poor Fido's generous self-sacrifice; he immolated himself to remove, by the manner of his death, any suspicions of Winifred's having the Fidophobia.'

'Perhaps,' said Elizabeth, 'he had some knowledge of the frightful suspicions which attached to him, and, like the Irish varmint in St. Patrick's days,

> "went flop,
> Slap bang into the water,
> And thus committed suicide
> To save himself from slaughter."'

They now began to consider how Fido could have met with his death. Harriet was sure that some naughty boy must have thrown him in. Lucy thought that in that case he would have lost his blue ribbon; Dora indignantly repelled the charge of cruelty from the youth of Abbeychurch; Elizabeth said such a puppy was very likely to fall off the bridge; and Rupert decided that he had most probably been attacked by a fit, to which, he said, half-grown puppies were often liable.

Rupert and Anne then began talking about a dog which they had lost some time ago in nearly the same manner; and during this dialogue the party divided, Harriet and Katherine walked on in close consultation, and Lucy and Helen began helping Dora to sort and carry her bulrushes, which detained them behind the others.

'What appears to me the most mysterious part of the story,' said Rupert, 'is how the beloved Fido, petted and watched and nursed and guarded as he seems to have been, should have contrived to stray from your house as far as to the river.'

'Oh! that is no mystery at all,' said Elizabeth; 'we crossed the bridge twice yesterday evening, and I dare say we left him behind us there.'

'What could you have been doing on the bridge yesterday evening?' said Rupert. 'Oh! I know; I saw the people coming away from a tee-total entertainment;

you were certainly there, Anne, I hope you enjoyed it.'

'How very near the truth you do contrive to get, Rupert,' said Elizabeth.

'Then,' cried Rupert, with a start, 'I see it all. I thought you all looked very queer at breakfast. I understand it all. You have been to the Mechanics' Institute.'

'Yes, Rupert,' said Elizabeth.

'No, but you do not mean to say that you really have, Lizzie and Anne,' cried Rupert, turning round to look into their faces.

Each made a sign of assent; and Rupert, as soon as he had recovered from his astonishment, burst into a violent fit of laughter, which lasted longer than either his sister or cousin approved, and it was not till after he had been well scolded by both, that he chose to listen to their full account of all that had passed on the subject.

'The worst of it is, now,' said Elizabeth, 'that as soon as Mrs. Hazleby hears that Fido has been found in the river, she will ask how he came near it.'

'And what then?' said Anne.

'Why, she well knows that the bridge is not a place to which we are likely to resort; she will ask what took us there; I would not trust Harriet to tell the truth, and I have promised not to betray her, so what is to be done if Mrs. Hazleby asks me?' said Elizabeth.

'I hope she will not ask her youngest daughter,' said Anne.

'That she shall not do,' said Elizabeth: 'I will tell her myself that Fido was found in the river, and answer all her questions as best I can.'

'It is rather a pity,' said Anne archly, 'that Miss Hazleby did not actually fall into the river, for the sensation caused by Rupert's rescuing her would quite have absorbed all the interest in Fido's melancholy fate.'

'Thank you, Anne,' said Rupert; 'I am sure I only wonder she was not submerged. I never could have guessed any fair lady could be so heavy. I am sure I feel the claw she gave my arm at this moment.'

'How very ungallant!' said Anne.

'Still,' said Rupert, 'without appearing as the preserver of the fair Harriet from a watery grave, I think I have interest enough with Mrs. Hazleby to be able to break the fatal news to her, and calm her first agonies of grief and wrath.'

'You, Rupert?' said Anne.

'Myself, Anne,' replied Rupert; 'you have no notion what friends Mrs. Hazleby and I have become. We had a tete-a-tete of an hour and a half this morning.'

'What could you find to talk about?' said Anne.

'First,' said Rupert, 'she asked about my grouse shooting; where I went, and with whom, and whether I had seen any of the Campbells of Inchlitherock. Of course we embarked in a genealogy of the whole Campbell race; then came a description of the beauties of Inchlitherock. Next I was favoured with her private history; how she, being one of thirteen, was forced, at eighteen, to leave the lovely spot, and embark with her brother for India.'

'On speculation,' said Elizabeth.

'And finally, how she came to marry the Major.'

'O Rupert, that is too much; you must have invented it!' cried Anne.

'Indeed I did not, Anne,' said Rupert; 'it is a fact that she lived somewhere in the Mofussil with her brother, and there she encountered the Major. You, young ladies, may imagine how she fascinated him, and how finally her brother seems to have bullied the Major into marrying her.'

'Poor man!' said Elizabeth, 'I always wondered how he chanced to fall into her clutches. But did you hear no more?'

'No more of her personal history,' said Rupert; 'she kindly employed the rest of her time in giving me wise counsels.'

'Oh! pray let us have the benefit of them,' said Anne, who had by this time pretty well forgotten her prudence.

'There were many regrets that I was not in the army,' said Rupert, 'and many pieces of advice which would have been very useful if I had, but which I am afraid were thrown away upon me, ending with wise reflections upon the importance of a wise choice of a wife, especially for a young man of family, exposed to danger from designing young ladies, with cautions against beauty because of its perishable nature, and learning, because literary ladies are fit for nothing.'

'Meaning to imply,' said Elizabeth, 'how fortunate was Major Hazleby in meeting with so sweet a creature as the charming Miss Barbara Campbell, possessed of neither of these dangerous qualities.'

'I do not know,' said Anne; 'I think she might have possessed some of the former when she left Inchlitherock.'

'Before twenty years of managing and scolding had fixed her eyes in one perpetual stare,' said Elizabeth. 'But here we are at home.'

They found the hall table covered with parcels, which shewed that Mrs. Woodbourne and her party had returned from their drive, and the girls hastened up-stairs.

Anne found her mamma in her room, as well as Sir Edward, who was finishing a letter.

'Well, Mamma, had you a prosperous journey?' said she.

'Yes, very much so,' said Lady Merton: 'Mrs. Hazleby was in high good-humour, she did nothing but sing Rupert's praises, and did not scold Mrs. Woodbourne as much as usual.'

'And what have you been doing, Miss Anne?' said Sir Edward; 'you are quite on the qui vive.'

'Oh! I have been laughing at the fun which Rupert and Lizzie have been making about Mrs. Hazleby,' said Anne; 'I really could not help it, Mamma, and I do not think I began it.'

'Began what?' said Sir Edward.

'Why, Mamma was afraid I should seem to set Lizzie against her step-mother's relations, if I quizzed them or abused them,' said Anne.

'I do not think what you could say would make much difference in Lizzie's opinion of them,' said Sir Edward, 'but certainly I should think they were not the best subjects of conversation here.'

'But I have not told you of the grand catastrophe,' said Anne; 'we have found poor Fido drowned among the bulrushes.'

'I hope Mrs. Woodbourne will be happy again,' said Lady Merton.

'And, Mamma, he must have fallen in while we were at the Mechanics' Institute,' said Anne; 'there is one bad consequence of our folly already.'

'I cannot see what induced you to go,' said Sir Edward; 'I thought Lizzie had more sense.'

'I believe the actual impulse was given by a dispute between Lizzie and me on the date of chivalry,' said Anne.

'And so Rupert's friends, the Turners, are great authorities in history,' said Sir Edward; 'I never should have suspected it.'

'Now I think of it,' said Anne, 'it was the most ridiculous part of the affair, considering the blunder that Lizzie told me Mrs. Turner made about St. Augustine. What could we have been dreaming of?'

'Midsummer madness,' said Sir Edward.

'But just tell me, Papa,' said Anne, 'do you not think Helen quite the heroine of the story?'

'I think Helen very much improved in appearance and manners,' said Sir Edward; 'and I am quite willing to believe all that I see you have to tell me of her.'

'Do not wait to tell it now, Anne,' said Lady Merton, 'or Mrs. Woodbourne will not think us improved in appearance or manners. It is nearly six o'clock.'

'I will keep it all for the journey home,' said Anne, 'when Papa's ears will be disengaged.'

'And his tongue too, to give you a lecture upon Radicalism, Miss,' said Sir Edward, with a fierce gesture, which drove Anne away laughing.

Elizabeth had finished dressing, a little too rapidly, and had gone to find Mrs. Woodbourne. 'Well, Mamma,' said she, as soon as she came into her room, 'Winifred has lived to say 'the dog is dead'.'

'What do you mean, my dear?' said Mrs. Woodbourne.

'The enemy is dead, Mamma,' said Elizabeth; 'we found him drowned by the green meadow.'

'Poor little fellow! your aunt will be very sorry,' was kind Mrs. Woodbourne's remark.

'But now, Mamma,' said Elizabeth, 'you may be quite easy about Winifred; he could not possibly have been mad.'

'How could he have fallen in, poor little dog?' said Mrs. Woodbourne.

'He must have strayed about upon the bridge while we were at the Mechanics' Institute,' said Elizabeth; 'it was all my fault, and I am afraid it is a very great distress to Lucy. Helen might well say mischief would come of our going.'

'I wish the loss of Fido was all the mischief likely to come of it, my dear,' said Mrs. Woodbourne, with a sigh; 'I am afraid your papa will be very much annoyed by it, with so much as he has on his mind too.'

'Ah! Mamma, that is the worst of it, indeed,' said Elizabeth, covering her face with her hands; 'if I could do anything--'

'My dearest child,' said Mrs. Woodbourne, 'do not go on making yourself unhappy, I am very sorry I said anything about your Papa; you know he cannot be angry with one who grieves so sincerely for what she has done amiss. I am sure you have learnt a useful lesson, and will be wiser in future. Now do put your scarf even, and let me pin this piece of lace straight for you, it is higher on one side than the other, and your band is twisted.'

On her side, Lucy, trembling as she entered her mother's room, but firm in her purpose of preserving her sister from the temptation to prevaricate, by taking all the blame which Mrs. Hazleby chose to ascribe to her, quietly communicated the fatal intelligence to Mrs. Hazleby. Her information was received with a short angry 'H--m,' and no more was said upon the matter, as Mrs. Hazleby was eager to shew Harriet some wonderful bargains which she had met with at Baysmouth.

CHAPTER XI.

As soon as Mrs. Hazleby made her appearance in the drawing-room before dinner, Rupert began repeating,

> 'The wound it seemed both sore and sad
>   To every Christian eye,
> And while they swore the dog was mad,
>   They swore the child would die,
>
> But soon a wonder came to light,
>   That shewed the rogues they lied,
> The child recovered of the bite,
>   It was the dog that died.'

'I beg to offer my congratulations,' continued he, setting a chair for her. Mrs. Hazleby looked surprised.

'On the demonstration we have this day received of your superior judgement, Ma'am,' said Rupert, 'though indeed we could hardly have doubted it before.'

'Pray let me understand you, Mr. Merton,' said Mrs. Hazleby.

'Have you not heard of the circumstance to which I allude?' said Rupert; 'for if you are not already aware of it, I must beg to be excused from relating it; I could not bear to give so great a shock to a lady's feelings.'

'Oh! you mean about Fido,' said Mrs. Hazleby, almost smiling; 'yes, Lucy told me that you had found him. Really, my girls are so careless, I can trust nothing to them.'

'Indeed, Madam,' said Rupert, 'I assure you that nothing could have been more heart-rending than the scene presented to our eyes when the Miss Hazlebys first became aware of the untimely fate of their favourite. Who could behold it with dry eye--or dry foot?' added he, in an under-tone, with a side glance at Anne.

Rupert contrived to talk so much nonsense to Mrs. Hazleby, that he charmed her with his attention, gave her no time to say anything about Fido, and left Anne much surprised that she had never found out that he was laughing at her. At dinner, the grouse he had brought came to their aid; Mrs. Hazleby was delighted to taste a blackcock once more, and was full of reminiscences of Inchlitherock; and by means of these recollections, and Rupert's newly imported histories, Sir Edward and Mr. Woodbourne contrived to make the conversation more entertaining than Elizabeth thought it ever could be in any party in which Mrs. Hazleby was present.

Afterwards in the drawing-room, Dora's bulrushes and the other children's purchases were duly admired, and the little people, being rather fatigued, were early sent to bed, although Edward vehemently insisted, with his eyes half shut, that he was not in the least sleepy. The elder girls then arranged themselves round the table. Helen was working a bunch of roses of different colours; Anne admired it very much, but critics were not wanting to this, as to every other performance of Helen's.

'It is all very pretty except that rose,' said Katherine, 'but I am sure that is an unnatural colour.--Is it not, Anne?'

'I do not think that I ever saw one like it,' said Anne; 'but that is no proof that there is no such flower.'

'What do you think, Lizzie?' said Katherine; 'ought not Helen to alter it?'

Anne was rather alarmed by this appeal; but Elizabeth answered carelessly, without looking up, 'Oh! you know I know nothing about that kind of work.'

'But you can tell what colour a rose is,' persisted Katherine; 'now do not you think Helen will spoil her work with that orange-coloured rose? who ever heard of such a thing?'

Helen was on the point of saying that one of the gable-ends of the house at Dykelands was covered with a single rose of that colour, but she remembered that Dykelands was not a safe subject, and refrained.

'Come, do not have a York and Lancaster war about an orange-coloured rose, Kate,' said Elizabeth, coming up to Helen; 'why, Anne, where are your eyes? did you never see an Austrian briar, just the the colour of Helen's lambs-wools?'

Though this was a mere trifle, Helen was pleased to find that Elizabeth could sometimes be on her side of the question, and worked on in a more cheerful spirit.

'Why, Anne,' said Elizabeth, presently after, 'you are doing that old wreath over again, that you were about last year, when I was at Merton Hall.'

'Yes,' said Anne; 'it is a pattern which I like very much.'

'Do you like working the same thing over again?' said Katherine; 'I always get tired of it.'

'I like it very much,' said Anne; 'going over the same stitches puts me in mind of things that were going on when I was working them before.--Now, Lizzie, the edge of that poppy seems to have written in it all that delightful talk we had together, at home, about growing up, that day when Papa and Mamma dined out, and we had it all to ourselves. And the iris has the whole of Don Quixote folded up in it, because Papa was reading it to us, when I was at work upon it.'

'There certainly seems to be a use and pleasure in never sitting down three minutes without that carpet-work, which I should never have suspected,' said Elizabeth.

'Anne thinks as I do,' said Mrs. Woodbourne; 'I find carpet-work quite a companion to me, but I cannot persuade Lizzie to take any pleasure in it.'

'I have not time for it,' said Elizabeth, 'nor patience if I had time. It is all I can persuade myself to do to keep my clothes from being absolute rags.'

'Yes,' said Katherine; 'you always read with Meg in your lap, when you have no mending to do; you have been six months braiding that frock.'

'Oh! that is company work,' said Elizabeth; 'I began it at Merton Hall for Dora, but I believe Winifred must have it now. But now it is so nearly done, that I shall finish while you are here.'

Elizabeth did not however long continue working, for as soon as tea was over she proposed to play at the game of Conglomeration, as she had talked of doing in the course of the walk. 'I give notice, however,' said she, 'that we are likely to laugh more than will suit the gravity of the elders, therefore I recommend adjourning to the inner drawing-room.--Mamma, may we have candles there?'

Consent was given, and while the candles were being brought, and Elizabeth was looking out some paper, Anne whispered to her brother, 'Rupert, pray say nothing about Fido, or the Mechanics' Institute, or something unpleasant will surely come of it.'

'Oh! Anne,' was the answer, 'you have robbed me of my best couplet--

      Weeping like forsaken Dido,   When she found the slaughtered Fido.

Where is the use of playing if there is to be no fun?'

''Where is the use of fun?' said the cockchafer to the boy who was spinning it,' said Anne.

'Impertinence, impertinence, impertinence,' said Rupert, shaking his head at her.

By this time all was ready, and Elizabeth called the brother and sister to take their places at the table in the inner drawing-room. She then wrote a substantive at the upper end of a long strip of paper, and folding it down, handed it on to Lucy, who also wrote a noun, turned it down, and gave the paper to Helen, who, after writing hers and hiding it, passed it on to Rupert. Thus the paper was handed round till it was filled. It was then unrolled, and each player was required to write a copy of verses in which these words were to be introduced as rhymes in the order in which they stood in the list. Rupert was rather put out by his sister's not allowing him to turn the poem in the way he wished, and he thought proper to find fault with half the words in the list.

'HARROGATE,' said he, 'what is to be done with such a word?'

'You can manage it very well if you choose,' said Elizabeth.

'But who could have thought of such a word?' said he, holding up the list to the candle, and scrutinizing the writing. 'Some one with a watery taste, doubtless.'

'You know those things are never divulged,' said Anne.

'FRANCES, too,' continued Rupert, 'there is another impossible case; I will answer for it, Helen wrote that, a reminiscence of dear Dykelands.'

'No, indeed I did not,' said Helen; 'it is FRANCIS, too, I believe.'

'Oh yes,' said Harriet, 'it is FRANCIS, I wrote it, because--do not you remember, Lucy?--Frank Hollis--'

'Well, never mind,' said Elizabeth, who wished to hear no more of that gentleman; 'you may make it whichever you please. And Rupert, pray do not be so idle; put down the list, no one can see it; write your own verses, and tell me the next word to witch.'

'EYES,' said Rupert, 'and then BOUNCE. I do not believe that word is English.'

'BOUNCE, no,' said Katherine; 'it is BONNET, I wrote it myself.'

'Then why do you make your 't' so short?' said Rupert; 'I must give you a writing lesson, Miss Kitty.'

'I must give you a lesson in silence, Mr. Rupert,' said Elizabeth.

'I obey,' said Rupert, with a funny face of submission, and taking up his paper and pencil; but in a minute or two he started up, exclaiming, 'What are they saying about Oxford?' and walked into the next room, intending to take part in the conversation between his father and uncle. Mr. Woodbourne, however, who was no great admirer of Rupert's forwardness, did not shew so much deference to his nephew's opinion as to make him very unwilling to return to the inner drawing-room, when Anne came to tell him that all the poems were finished, and Elizabeth ready to read them aloud.

'So this is all that you have to shew for yourself,' said Elizabeth, holding up a scrap of paper; 'what is all this?'

'A portrait of Miss Merton,' said Rupert; 'do not you see the poet's eye in a fine frenzy rolling?'

'Is it?' said Elizabeth; 'I took it for Miss Squeers in the agonies of death, as I see that is the subject of the poem--all that there is of it, at least.

> Did ever you see a stupider POEM?
> Pray who is the author? I know him, I know him,
> He went to school to Mr. Squeers,
> Who often made the youth shed TEARS.

Now for the next, which is nearly as short.

> I will write a POEM,
> Clear and flowing,
> It will make you shed TEARS,
> And excite your fears.

'Tis about a witch,
Drowned in a ditch,
Your tears come from your EYES.
If you are wise,
Don't make a BOUNCE,
Or you'll tear your flounce,
And upset the sugar JAR,
Which I cannot spare,
I must give some to FRANCIS,
So well he dances;
Sugar canes packed up in LEAVES,
The canes are tied up like wheat sheaves;
Francis wears a scarlet JACKET,
He made a dreadful racket
At HARROGATE,
Because he had to wait,
In a field of BARLEY,
To hold a parley,
About a bone of marrow;
His heart was transfixed by an ARROW,
By a lady in VELVET,
And he was her pet.'

All laughed heartily at this poem, which perhaps diverted them more than a better would have done; Harriet was highly delighted with what she considered their applause, though she knew that of all the rhymes, scarcely three had been found by herself.

'Why, Mr. Merton, what are you doing?' asked Harriet; 'are you writing any more?'

'Oh! I hope he will tell us about Mr. Squeers,' said Katherine.

No one could doubt that the next which Elizabeth read was her own.

I'm afraid you expect a beautiful POEM,
Though I make a long and tedious proem,
But great and dreadful are my fears,
No poem of mine will put you in TEARS.
My genius suggests neither fairy nor witch,
My tales to adorn with cauldrons of pitch,
Alarm the world with fiery EYES,
And from the hero snatch his prize,
Leap out from her den with a terrible BOUNCE,
And on the trembling damsel pounce,
And bottle her up in a close corked JAR,
Or whirl her away in a flaming car;
Then her knight, the brave Sir FRANCIS,
Upon his noble steed advances,
All his armour off he LEAVES,
Preserves alone his polished greaves,
His defence is a buff JACKET,
Nor sword nor axe nor lance can crack it,
It was made at HARROGATE,
By a tailor whose shop had a narrow gate;
The elves attack with spears of BARLEY,
But he drives them off, oh! rarely,
Then they shoot him with an ARROW,
From bow-strings greased with ear-wigs' marrow,
The feathers, moth-wings downy VELVET,
The bow-strings, of the spider's net:
Thousands come, armed in this PATTERN,
Which proves their mistress is no slattern;
Some wear the legs and hoof of PAN,
And some are in the form of man;
But the knight is armed, for in his POCKET
He has a talismanic locket,
Which once belonged to HERCULES,

Who wore it on his bunch of keys;
The fairy comes, quite old and fat,
Mounted upon a monstrous BAT;
Around the knight a web she weaves,
And holds him fast, and there she LEAVES
Sir Francis weeping for his charmer,
And longing for his knightly ARMOUR.
But his sword was cast in the self-same forge
As that of the great champion GEORGE;
Thus he defies the witch's ARMY,
He breaks his bands; 'Ye elves, beware me,
I fear not your LEVIATHAN,
No spells can stop a desperate man.'
Away in terror flies the REAR-GUARD,
He seizes on the witch abhorred,
Confines her in a COCKLE SHELL,
And breaks all her enchantments fell,
Catches her principal LIEUTENANT,
Makes him of a split pine the tenant;
Carries away the lady, nimble,
As e'er Miss Merton plied her THIMBLE;
Oh! this story would your frowns unbend.
Could I tell it to the END.

'Oh!' said Rupert, glad to seize an opportunity of retaliating upon Elizabeth; 'I give you credit; a very ingenious compound of Thalaba, Pigwiggin, and the Tempest, and the circumstance of the witch whirling away the lady is something new.'

'No, it is not,' said Elizabeth; 'it is the beginning of the story of the Palace of Truth, in the Veillees du Chateau. I only professed to conglomerate the words, not to pass off my story as a regular old traditional legend.'

'Well, well,' said Rupert; 'go on; have you only two more?'

'Only two,' said Elizabeth; 'Kate and Lucy behaved as shabbily as you did. Helen, I believe you must read yours. I can never read your writing readily, and be-

sides, I am growing hoarse.'
  Helen obeyed.

How hard it is to write a POEM,
  Graceful and witty, plain and clear,
Harder than ploughing--'tis, or sowing,
  So hard that I should shed a TEAR.

Did I not know the highest pitch
  Of merit, in the poet's EYES
Is but to laugh, a height to WHICH
  'Tis not so hard for me to rise.

For badness soon is gained, forth BOUNCE
  My rhymes such as they are;
Good critics, on my lines don't pounce,
  Though on the ear they JAR.

I've had a letter from dear FRANCES,
  Who says, through the light plane tree LEAVES,
Upon the lawn the sun-beam glances,
  The wheat is bound up in its sheaves

By Richard, in the fustian JACKET
  His mistress bought at HARROGATE,
And up in lofty ricks they stack it,
  There for the threshing will it wait.

Then will they turn to fields of BARLEY,
  Bearded and barbed with many an ARROW,
Just where the fertile soil is marly,
  And in the spring was used the harrow.

Drawn by the steeds in coats of VELVET,
  Old Steady, Jack, and Slattern,
Their manes well combed, and black as jet,
  Their tails in the same PATTERN.

While Richard's son, with pipe of PAN,
  His hands within his POCKETS,
Walks close beside the old plough-man,
  Dreaming of squibs and rockets.

That youth, he greatly loves his ease,
  He's growing much too fat,
And though as strong as HERCULES,
  He'll only use his BAT.

He won't sweep up the autumn LEAVES,
  The tree's deciduous ARMOUR,
No scolding Dickey's spirit grieves
  Like working like a farmer,

Or labouring like his cousin GEORGE,
  With arms all bare and brawny,
Within the blacksmith's glowing forge;
  He would be in the ARMY.

But no, young Dick, you're not the man
  Our realms to watch and ward,
For worse than a LEVIATHAN
  You'd dread the foe's REAR-GUARD,

And in the storm of shot and SHELL,
  You'd soon desert your pennant,
Care nought for serjeant, corporal,

Or general LIEUTENANT,

But prove yourself quite swift and nimble,
  And thus would meet your END;
No, better take a tailor's THIMBLE
  And learn your ways to mend.

'Capital, Helen!' said Elizabeth.

'How very pretty!' said Lucy.

'And very well described,' said Anne; 'you have brought in those ungainly words most satisfactorily.'

'Now, Helen, here is Anne's,' said Elizabeth; 'it is a choice one, and I have kept it for the last.'

'Let me read Anne's,' said Rupert; 'no one can decypher her writing as well as I can.'

'As was proved by the thorough acquaintance you shewed with the contents of her last letter,' said Elizabeth.

Rupert began as follows:

Now must I write in numbers flowing
Extemporaneously a POEM?

'Why, Rupert,' cried Anne, 'you must be reading Kate's. Mine began with--'

'I declare that I have yours in my hand, Anne,' said Rupert.

'And I did not write one,' said Katherine.

Now must I write in numbers flowing
Extemporaneously a POEM?
One that will fill your eyes with TEARS,
While I relate how our worst fears
Were realized in yonder ditch.
Conveyed there by some water-WITCH,
We found, sad sight for longing EYES!

Fido, much loved, though small in size.
Hard fate, but while our tears bemoan it,
Let us take up the corpse and BONE it,
Then place the mummy in a JAR,
Keep it from sausage-makers far,
Extract his heart to send to FRANCIS;
This gift from HER, his soul entrances,
Within his scarlet gold-laced JACKET
His heart makes a tremendous racket;
Visions of bliss arise, a surrogate,
Ay, and a wedding tour to HARROGATE.

When Rupert came to Fido, Anne uttered one indignant 'Rupert!' but as he proceeded, she was too much confounded to make the slightest demonstration, and yet she was nearly suffocated with laughter in the midst of her vexation, when she thought of the ball at Hull, and 'Frank Hollis.' Elizabeth and Katherine too were excessively diverted, though the former repented of having ever proposed such a game for so incongruous a party. There was a little self-reproach mingled even with Anne's merriment, for she felt that if she had more carefully abstained from criticising the Hazlebys, or from looking amused by what was said of them, Rupert would hardly have attempted this piece of impertinence. Helen, who considered it as a most improper proceeding, sat perfectly still and silent, with a countenance full of demure gravity, which made Elizabeth and Anne fall into fresh convulsions as they looked at her; Lucy only blushed; and as for Harriet, the last two lines could scarcely be heard, for her exclamations of, 'O Mr. Merton, that is too bad! O Mr. Merton, how could you think of such a thing? O Mr. Merton, I can never forgive you! Oh dear! Oh dear! I shall never stop laughing. Oh dear! Mr. Merton, what would Frank Hollis say to you? how ridiculous!'

'Now for Anne's real poem, Rupert,' said Elizabeth, not choosing to make any remarks, lest Rupert should consider them as compliments.

'Have you not heard it?' said Rupert.

'Nonsense,' said Elizabeth.

'Why, I told you I had it in my hand,' said Rupert.

'And you have it still,' said Elizabeth; 'deliver it up, if you please; it is the best of all, I can tell you, I had a cursory view of it.'

'No, no,' said Anne, who saw that her brother meant to teaze her, and not to restore her verses; 'it was a very poor performance, it is much better for my fame that it should never be seen. Only think what a sublime notion the world will have of it, when it is said that even the great Rupert himself is afraid to let it appear.'

Elizabeth made another attempt to regain the poem, but without effect, and Anne recalled the attention of all to Helen's verses.

'What is a pennant?' said Elizabeth; 'I do not like words to be twisted for the sake of the rhyme.'

A flag,' said Helen.

'I never doubted that you intended it for a flag,' said Elizabeth; 'but what I complain of is, that it is a transmogrified pennon.'

'I believe a pennant to be a kind of flag,' said Helen.

'Let us refer the question to Papa,' said Anne, 'as soon as he has finished that interminable conversation with Uncle Woodbourne.'

'Really, in spite of that slight blemish,' said Elizabeth, 'your poem is the best we have heard, Helen.'

'And I can testify,' said Rupert, 'that the description of the cart-horses at Dyke-lands is perfectly correct. But, Helen, is it true that your friend Dicky has been seized with a fit of martial ardour such as you describe?'

'Yes,' said Helen, 'he was very near enlisting, but it made his mother very un-happy, and Mrs. Staunton--'

'Went down upon her knees to beseech him to remain, and let her roast beef be food for him, not himself be food for powder,' said Rupert, 'never considering how glad the parish would be to get rid of him.'

'No,' said Helen, 'her powder became food for him; she made him under-game-keeper.'

'Excellent, Helen, you shine to night,' cried Elizabeth; 'such a bit of wit never was heard from you before.'

'Your poem is a proof that the best way of being original is to describe things as you actually see them,' said Anne.

'Is not mine original? I do not think it was taken from any book,' said Harriet, willing to pick up a little more praise.

'Not perhaps from any book,' said Elizabeth, with a very grave face; 'but I am afraid we must convict you of having borrowed from the mother of books, Oral tradition.'

'Oral tradition!' repeated Harriet, opening her mouth very wide.

'Yes,' said Elizabeth; 'for I cannot help imagining that the former part of your ode is a parody upon

> "I'll tell you a story
> About Jack A'Nory,
>   And now my story's begun;
> I'll tell you another
>   About Jack and his brother,
> And now my story is done."

And that your friend Francis must have been the hero who complains so grievously of Taffy the Welshman, whose house was doubtless situated in a field of barley, while his making a dreadful racket is quite according to the ancient notions of what he did with the marrow-bone.'

'Oh! there is Papa looking in at us,' said Anne; 'now for the question of pennon and pennant.'

'Oh! Anne, it is all nonsense,' cried Helen; 'do not shew it.'

But Anne, with Helen's paper in her hand, had already attacked Sir Edward, who, to the author's great surprise, actually read the poem all through, smiling very kindly, and finished by saying, 'Ah ha! Helen, it is plain enough that your friends are naval. I can see where your pennant came from.'

'But is it not a flag, Uncle Edward?' asked Helen.

'A flag it is,' said Sir Edward, 'and properly called and spelt pendant.'

'There, Helen, you are an antidote to the hydrophobia,' said Rupert; 'everything becomes--'

'Do not let us have any more of that stale joke,' said Elizabeth; 'it is really only a poetical license to use a sea-flag for a land-flag, and Helen had the advantage of us, since we none of us knew that Pennant signified anything but the naturalist.'

'And pray, Helen,' said Sir Edward, 'am I to consider this poem as an equivalent for the music you have cheated us of, this evening?'

'I hope you will consider that it is,' said Elizabeth; 'is it not positively poetical, Uncle Edward?'

Helen was hardly ever in a state of greater surprise and pleasure than at this moment, for though she could not seriously believe that her lines were worthy of all the encomiums bestowed on them, yet she was now convinced that Elizabeth was not absolutely determined to depreciate every performance of hers, and that she really possessed a little kindness for her.

When Mr. Woodbourne rang the bell, Elizabeth gathered up all the papers, and was going to put them into a drawer, when Harriet came up to her, saying in a whisper, evidently designed to attract notice, 'Lizzie, do give me that ridiculous thing, you know, of Mr. Merton's; I could not bear you to have it, you would shew it to everyone.'

'Indeed I should do no such thing,' said Elizabeth; 'I never wish to see it more, you are very welcome to it.'

Harriet received the precious document with great satisfaction, carefully folded it up, and placed it in her bag, very much to Rupert's delight, as he silently watched her proceedings.

When they went up to bed, Anne followed Lady Merton to her room, in order to ask some question about the dress which she was to wear the next day, Sunday, and after remaining with her a few minutes, she returned to Elizabeth. She found her looking full of trouble, quite a contrast to the bright animated creature she had been a few minutes before.

'My dear Lizzie,' exclaimed Anne, 'has anything happened? what has grieved you?'

'Why, Anne,' said Elizabeth, with almost a groan, 'has not enough happened to grieve me? is it not terrible to think of what I have done?'

Anne stood still and silent, much struck by her cousin's sorrow; for she had considered their expedition to the Mechanics' Institute as a foolish girlish frolic, but by no means as serious a matter as it now proved to be.

'I want you to tell me, Anne,' continued Elizabeth; 'was I not quite out of my senses yesterday evening? I can hardly believe it was myself who went to that horrible place, I wish you could prove that it was my double-ganger.'

Anne laughed,

'But does it not seem incredible,' said Elizabeth, 'that I, Elizabeth Woodbourne, should have voluntarily meddled with a radical, levelling affair, should have sought out Mrs. Turner and all the set I most dislike, done perhaps an infinity of mischief, and all because Kate wanted to go out on a party of pleasure with that foolish Willie. Oh! Anne, I wish you would beat me.'

'Would that be any comfort to you?' said Anne, smiling.

'Yes,' said Elizabeth; 'I should feel as if I was suffering a little for my madness. Oh! how I hope Papa will speak to me about it. If he does not, I shall see his displeasure in his eyes, and oh! I could bear anything better than the silent stern way in which he used to look at me, once before, when I had behaved very ill. And then, to-morrow is Sunday, and I shall scarcely see him all day, and he will have no time to speak to me; and how can I get through a Sunday, feeling that he is angry with me? how shall I teach the children, or do anything as usual? Anne, what do you think was the first sound in my ears when I awoke this morning, and has been returning upon me all day?--the words, "It was a tree to be desired to make one wise."'

'Little wisdom we have gained from it,' said Anne.

'Eve's wisdom,' said Elizabeth, 'the knowledge of evil, and the wisdom of vanity and vexation of spirit. But was it not curious, Anne? when first I woke, before I had opened my eyes, those words were sounding in my ears, like a dream of Papa's voice, reading the Lesson at church; I almost fell asleep again, and again those words came back in Papa's voice, and then I woke entirely, and before I had seen what kind of day it was, before I knew whether it was Saturday or Sunday, I was sure there was something wrong, and then there was all this black Mechanics' Institute business before me. And all through this day those words have been ringing in my ears, and coming upon me like the pressure of King James's iron belt.'

'Have they indeed?' said Anne, 'I could hardly have believed it. I have not seen your "look o'ercast and lower," like his.'

'Perhaps not,' said Elizabeth; 'but yet I was like him.'

"Forward he rushed with double glee
Into the tide of revelry."

And I believe that having anything on my mind puts me in wilder spirits, apparently, than usual, but I am sure that my merriment to-day was no proof that I was happy. It was partly, I believe, from a mad spirit, like what drives wicked men to drinking, and partly from folly and levity. It was the same when Mamma's sister, Miss Dorothea Hazleby, died; I am sure I was very sorry for Aunt Dorothy, for she was a most amiable person, and had always been particularly kind to me, and I was very sorry too for Mamma and old Mrs. Hazleby, who were broken-hearted about it; yet would you believe it? the very day that Papa was gone to Hastings, to the funeral, and Mamma was at home, too ill and too wretched to go, even to her mother, I was out in the garden with Horace and Dora, forgot all about her distress, and began a noisy game with them close under her window. She sent Kate to tell them not to make such a noise; and when we came in, and she found that it was my doing, she gave me such a kind, grieved, reproachful look, that I think I shall never forget it. And now it is most strange to think how wildly and merrily I laughed at all Rupert's jokes, when I knew I was in disgrace, and after having behaved so very ill.'

'Indeed, I did not think it would have distressed you so much,' said Anne; 'I never thought it was more than a very foolish affair.'

'It is a very different thing for you,' said Elizabeth; 'you have nothing to do with the town, and you need not have known that it was not a fit place to go to.'

'But you did not know that it was not fit for us,' said Anne.

'I did know that I ought not to go where I had not been told I might go,' said Elizabeth. 'It was relying on my own judgement that led me astray. But, oh! I wish I had been here at the time the Socialist lectures were given; I should as soon have thought of climbing up the kitchen-chimney, as of going to that den, and giving the ragamuffins such a victory over Papa.'

'It was very silly of us not to ask a few more questions,' said Anne.

'Ah! that is the worst part of my behaviour,' said Elizabeth; 'that abominably unfair account which I gave you, at Mr. Turner's door, of Helen's objections. It was in fact almost deceit, and the only thing that can take off from the blackness of it, is that I was sufficiently senseless to believe it myself at the time I spoke.'

'Oh yes, of course you did,' said Anne.

'Yet there must have been a sort of feeling that your hearing her arguments would put a stop to the beautiful scheme,' said Elizabeth; 'you do not know, perhaps, that Kate was nearly convinced by Helen's good sense, and I do believe that the reason I was not, was, what I tremble to think of, that I have been indulging in a frightful spirit of opposing and despising Helen, because I was angry with her for loving Dykelands better than home. I do believe she hardly dares to open her lips. I heard her telling Lucy afterwards that there was a rose at Dykelands of the colour of her pattern, and I dare say she did not say so, when it would have been to the purpose, for fear I should say that damp turns roses orange-coloured; and I could see she did not defend her pendant with Captain Atherley for fear I should tell her he was not infallible. No wonder she pines for Dykelands; a fine sort of sister and home she has found here, poor child.'

'Oh! now you think so--' Anne began, but here she stopped short, checked by her dread of interfering between sisters; she could not bear to add to Elizabeth's bitter feelings of self-reproach, and she could not say that her conduct on the preceding evening had been by any means what it ought to have been, that she had treated Helen kindly, or that Helen had not suffered much from her want of consideration for her. She only kissed her cousin, and wished her good night very affectionately, and nothing more was said that evening.

But Anne's silence was often very expressive to those who could understand it, and of these Elizabeth was one.

The toilette of Katherine and Helen passed in a very different manner that evening; Katherine did nothing but giggle and chatter incessantly, about the game they had been playing at, in order to prevent Helen from saying anything about the result of their excursion the evening before, and to keep herself from thinking of the cowardly part she had been acting all day. Helen only wished to be left in peace, to think over her share in all these transactions, and to consider how she might become a tolerably useful member of society for the future; and on her making no reply to one of Katherine's speeches, the latter suddenly became silent, and she was left to her own reflections.

CHAPTER XII.

Elizabeth was always fully employed on a Sunday, and on that which followed the Consecration she had perhaps more on her hands even than usual, so that she had little opportunity for speaking, or even for thinking, of her troubles.

Mr. Woodbourne was going to assist Mr. Somerville in the services at St. Austin's, leaving Mr. Walker to do the duty at St. Mary's, as the old church was now to be always called.

Mr. Somerville had asked Mrs. Woodbourne to bring all her party to luncheon at his house, and had added a special invitation to the children to be present at the opening of the new Sunday-school, which was to take place between the services. It was however necessary that someone should stay and superintend what the young people called, rather contemptuously, 'the old school;' and this Elizabeth undertook, saying that she did not like to lose one Sunday's teaching of her own class. Anne was about to offer to remain with her and assist her, but on Helen's making the same proposal, she thought it better to give the sisters an opportunity of being alone together, and, as she was more desirous of doing right than of appearing eager to be useful, she said nothing of what she had intended. Elizabeth was much gratified by her sister's voluntary proffer of assistance, for the head and front of Helen's offences on her return from Dykelands, had been, that she had loathed the idea of helping to train the screaming school-girls to sing in church, and had altogether shewn far less interest in parish matters than Elizabeth thought their due.

'I am sure,' said Elizabeth, as they were walking from school to church, 'it is worth while to stay to see the aisle now it is clear of the benches, and there is breathing room left in the dear old church. And listen to the bells! does not it seem as if the two churches were exchanging greetings on St. Austin's first Sunday? Yes,

St. Mary's is our home, our mother church,' added she, as she walked under the heavy stone porch, its groined roof rich with quaint bosses, the support of many a swallow's nest, and came in sight of the huge old square font, standing on one large column and four small ones, where she herself and all her brothers and sisters had been christened.

The three little children were not to go to St. Austin's in the morning, but Katherine had promised to come back to fetch them in time for the luncheon at Mr. Somerville's, and thus Dora had the full advantage of studying the Puddington monument before the service began.

Katherine and Harriet came back whilst Elizabeth and Helen were at luncheon, and after giving them a list of half the people who were at church, they called the children to come to Mr. Somerville's with them.

'Why do not you put on your bonnet, Dora?' said Winifred.

'I am not going,' said Dora.

'Why not?' asked Winifred.

'Because I had rather not,' was the answer.

'Why, you silly little child,' said Katherine; 'are you shy of Mr. Somerville? look there, Edward and Winifred are not shy, and you are quite a great girl. How Horace would laugh!'

'I cannot help it,' said Dora; 'I had rather not go.'

'If you are thinking of your little class, Dora,' said Elizabeth, 'I will hear them for you; you will trust them with me, will you not? and I will remember who is first.'

'Thank you,' said Dora; 'I had rather go to church and school with you.'

'Nonsense, Dora,' said Katherine; 'I wish you would come.'

'Now do,' said Harriet; 'you cannot think what a nice luncheon Mr. Somerville will have for you.'

'There is a very nice luncheon here,' said Dora.

'Oh! but not like a company luncheon,' said Harriet; 'besides, Mr. Somerville will be so disappointed if you do not come. Poor Mr. Somerville, won't you be sorry for him, Dora?'

'Oh no, he does not want me--does he, Lizzie?' said Dora.

'No, I do not suppose he does,' said Elizabeth; 'he only asked you out of good nature.'

'Well, if Dora will not come,' said Katherine, 'there is no use in staying.--Come, Winifred and Edward.'

Elizabeth was sure that Dora had reasons of her own for choosing to remain with her, but she thought it best to ask no questions; and the reasons appeared, when, as they came into the Alms-house Court after evening service, Dora pressed her hand, saying, in a low mysterious tone, 'Lizzie, will you shew me what you promised?'

Elizabeth knew what she meant, and returning through the church into the church-yard, led the way to the east end, where, close beside a projecting buttress, Dora beheld a plain flat white stone, with three small crosses engraven on it, and with a feeling between awe and wonder, read the simple inscription.

KATHERINE,
WIFE OF THE REV. HORATIO WOODBOURNE,
VICAR OF ABBEYCHURCH ST. MARY'S,
MAY 14TH, 1826,
AGED 28.

It was the first time that Elizabeth and Helen had stood together at their mother's grave, for Helen was but three years old at the time she had been deprived of her, and, after their father's second marriage, a kind of delicacy in Elizabeth, young as she was, had prevented her from ever mentioning her to her younger sisters.

After a few minutes, during which no one spoke, the three sisters turned away, and re-entered the church. Helen and Dora had reached the north door, and were leaving the church, when they missed Elizabeth, and looking round, saw her sitting in one of the low pews, in the centre aisle, her face raised towards the flamboyant tracery of the east window. Dora, who seemed to have a sort of perception that her presence was a restraint upon her sisters, whispered, 'I am going to feed the doves,' and hastened across the quadrangle, while Helen came back to Elizabeth's side. Her sister rose, and with her own bright smile, said, 'Helen, I could not help coming here, it was where I sat at the day of the funeral, and I wanted to look at that flame-shaped thing in the top of the window, as I did all through the reading of the Lesson. Do you see? What strange thoughts were in my head, as I sat looking at that deep blue glass, with its shape like an angel's head and meeting wings, and heard of glories celestial! I never hear those words without seeing that form.'

With these words Elizabeth and Helen left the church; Helen put her arm into her sister's, a thing which Elizabeth very seldom liked anyone to do, even Anne, but now the two girls walked slowly arm-in-arm, through the quadrangle, and along the broad gravel path in the Vicarage garden.

'Then you were at her funeral?' was the first thing Helen said.

'Yes,' said Elizabeth; 'Papa wished it, and I am sure I am very glad they let me go.'

No more was spoken till Helen began again. 'When I was at Dykelands, Mrs. Staunton used often to talk to me about our mother, and I began to try to recollect her, but I had only an impression of something kind, some voice I should know again, but I could not remember her in the least.'

'Ah! I wish you could,' said Elizabeth thoughtfully.

'I suppose you remember her quite well,' said Helen, 'and all that happened?'

'Yes,' said Elizabeth, 'I remember some things as well as if they had happened yesterday, and others are all confusion in my mind; I quite remember going to kiss her, the last day, and how strange and silent and sad all the room looked, and Aunt Anne keeping quite calm and composed in the room, but beginning to cry as soon as she had led me out. I shall never forget the awful mysterious feelings I had then.'

'And could she speak to you?' said Helen; 'did she know you?'

'Yes, she gave me one of her own smiles, and said something in a very low voice.'

'Tell me a little more, Lizzie,' said Helen, 'for I have thought very much about her lately. Can you remember her before she was ill?'

'Oh yes,' said Elizabeth, speaking slowly, and pausing now and then; 'I remember her well; I sometimes fancy I can hear her voice and her step at night, when she used to come up to the nursery to see us in bed. I always used to listen for her; and when she began to grow weak, and could not come up so many stairs, I used to lie and cry for half an hour. And now, when I am reading the same books with the children that I read with her, things that she said to me come back upon me.'

'Do you think,' said Helen, 'that you are as like her as Uncle Edward once said you were?'

Elizabeth paused; 'possibly,' said she, 'in eyes, nose, and mouth; but, Helen, I do not think there ever could be anyone really like our mother; I was much too young to know all that she was whilst she was alive, but as I have grown older, and compared what I have seen of other people with what I recollect of her, I have grown certain that she must have been the most excellent, sensible, clever, kind, charming person that ever lived.'

'So Mrs. Staunton says,' replied Helen; 'she used to tell me that I was a good deal like her, and should be more so; but I do not think she would have said so, if she had seen you. I am so slow and so dull, and so unlike to you in your quick active ways.'

'Do you know, Helen,' said Elizabeth, who had been pursuing her own thoughts, rather than listening to her sister's words, 'I do believe that we should all have been more like her if she had lived; at least, I am sure I should.'

Helen did not answer; and Elizabeth continued in her usual rapid manner, 'I do not mean to lay all my faults at Mamma's door, for I should have been much worse without her, and I have spurned away most of the good she would have done me in her kind gentle way; but I do believe no one but my own mother ever knew how to manage me. You never were so wild, Helen, and you will do far far better.'

'O Lizzie, what do you mean?' cried Helen.

'I mean, my dear Helen,' exclaimed Elizabeth, hardly knowing what she was saying, 'that I have been using you shamefully ever since you came home. I have done nothing but contradict you, and snap at you, whether right or wrong; and a pretty spectacle we must have made of ourselves. Now I see that you have twice the sense and understanding that I have, and are so unpretending as to be worth a hundred times more. I wish with all my heart that I had taken your advice, and that the Mechanics' Institute was at the bottom of the sea.'

Before Helen had recovered from her astonishment at this incoherent speech, sufficiently to make any sort of reply, the rest of the party were seen returning from St. Austin's, and Winifred and Edward hastened towards the two sisters, to tell them all the wonders they had seen.

During the remainder of that day, a few words in her mother's feeble voice rung in Elizabeth's ears more painfully even than the text she had mentioned the day before. It was, 'Lizzie, I know you will be a kind sister to Kate and poor little Helen.'

In the course of the evening, Lady Merton found Anne and Helen alone together in the drawing-room. Helen was reclining on the sofa, in a dreamy state, her book half closed in her hand, and Anne was sitting at the window, reading as well as she could by the failing light.

'So you are alone here,' said Lady Merton, as she entered the room.

'Yes,' said Helen, starting up; 'I rather think the Hazlebys are packing up--you know they go by the one o'clock train to-morrow--and I believe Kate is helping them; and Mamma is hearing the little ones say the Catechism.'

'So I thought,' said Lady Merton. 'I was surprised to find you here.'

'Oh!' said Helen, 'we generally say the Catechism to Papa every Sunday evening, and he asks us questions about it; and we are to go on with him till we are confirmed.'

'And when will that be?' said her aunt.

'Next spring,' said Helen; 'we shall all three of us be confirmed at the same time. But if Mrs. Hazleby had not been here, Papa would have heard us all downstairs. I should have liked for you to hear how perfect Edward is now, and how well Dora answers Papa's questions; though perhaps before you she would be too shy.'

'And I should have been glad for Anne to have joined you,' said Lady Merton; 'it is long since your godfather has heard you, Anne.'

'Not since we were here last,' said Anne, 'and that is almost two years ago.'

'And where is Lizzie?' said Lady Merton; 'is she with your Mamma?'

'No,' said Helen, 'her other work is not over yet. On Sunday evening, she always reads with four great girls who have left school, and have no time to learn except on Sunday evenings. I am sure I cannot think how she can; I should have thought morning and afternoon school quite enough for anyone!' And she threw herself back on the sofa, and gave a very long yawn.

Her aunt smiled as she answered, 'You certainly seem to find it so.'

'Indeed I do,' said Helen; 'I think teaching the most tiresome work in the world.'

'O Helen, is it possible?' cried Anne.

'Helen is not much used to it,' said her aunt.

'No,' said Helen, 'there used to be teachers enough without me, but now Lizzie wants me to take a class, I suppose I must, because it is my duty; but really I do not think I can ever like it.'

'If you do it cheerfully because it is your duty, you will soon be surprised to find yourself interested in it,' said her aunt.

'Now, Aunt Anne,' said Helen, sitting up, and looking rather more alive, 'I really did take all the pains I could to-day, but I was never more worried than with the dullness of those children. They could not answer the simplest question.'

'Most poor children seem dull with a new teacher,' said Lady Merton; 'besides which, you perhaps did not use language which they could understand.'

'Possibly,' said Helen languidly; 'but then there is another thing which I dislike--I cannot bear to hear the most beautiful chapters in the Bible stammered over as if the children had not the least perception of their meaning.'

'Their not being able to read the chapter fluently is no proof that they do not enter into it,' said Lady Merton; 'it often happens that the best readers understand less than some awkward blunderers, who read with reverence.'

'Then it is very vexatious,' said Helen.

'You will tell a different story next year,' said Lady Merton, 'when you have learnt a little more of the ways of the poor children.'

'I hope so,' said Helen; 'but what I have seen to-day only makes me wonder how Papa and Lizzie can get the children to make such beautiful answers as they sometimes do in church.'

'And perhaps,' said Lady Merton, smiling, 'the person who taught Miss Helen Woodbourne to repeat Gray's Elegy, would be inclined to wonder how at fourteen she could have become a tolerably well-informed young lady.'

'Oh, Aunt,' said Helen, 'have not you forgotten that day? How dreadfully I must have tormented everybody! I am sure Mamma's patience must have been wonderful.'

'And I am very glad that Lizzie saves her from so much of the labour of teaching now,' said Lady Merton.

'I see what you mean,' said Helen; 'I ought to help too.'

'Indeed, my dear, I had no intention of saying so,' said Lady Merton; 'yourself and your mamma can be the only judges in such a matter.'

'I believe Mamma does think that Lizzie has almost too much to do,' said Helen; 'but there has been less since Horace has been at school.'

'But Edward is fast growing up to take his place,' said her aunt.

'Edward will never take Horace's place,' said Helen; 'he will be five times the trouble. Horace could learn whatever he pleased in an instant, and the only draw-back with him was inattention; but Edward is so slow and so dawdling, that his lessons are the plague of the school-room. His reading is tiresome enough, and what Lizzie will do with his Latin I cannot think; but that can be only her concern. And Winifred is sharp enough, but she never pays attention three minutes together; I could not undertake her, I should do her harm and myself too.'

'I am rather of your opinion, so far,' said Lady Merton; 'but you have said nothing against Dora.'

'Dora!' said Helen; 'yes, she has always been tolerably good, but she knows nearly as much as I do. Lizzie says she knows the reasons of a multiplication sum, and I am sure I do not.'

'Perhaps you might learn by studying with her,' aaid Lady Merton.

'Yes, Lizzie says she has learnt a great deal from teaching the children,' said Helen; 'but then she had a better foundation than most people. You know she used to do her lessons with Papa, and he always made her learn everything quite perfect, and took care she should really understand each step she took, so that she knows more about grammar and arithmetic, and all the latitude and longitude puzzling part of geography than I do--a great deal more.'

'I am sorry to find there is some objection to all the lessons of all the children,' said Lady Merton.

'I suppose I might help in some,' said Helen; 'but then I have very little time; I have to draw, and to practise, and to read French and Italian and history to Mamma, and to write exercises; but then Mamma has not always leisure to hear me, and it is very unsatisfactory to go on learning all alone. At Dykelands there were Fanny and Jane.'

'I should not have thought a person with four sisters need complain of having to learn alone,' said her aunt.

'No more should I,' said Helen; 'but if you were here always, you would see how it is; Lizzie is always busy with the children, and learns her German and Latin no one knows when or how, by getting up early, and reading while she is dressing, or while the children are learning. She picks up knowledge as nobody else can; and Kate will only practise or read to Mamma, and she is so desultory and unsettled, that I cannot go on with her as I used before I went to Dykelands; and Dora--I see I ought to take to her, but I am afraid to do so--I do not like it.'

'So it appears,' said Lady Merton.

'I should think it the most delightful thing!' cried Anne.

'You two are instances of the way in which people wish for the advantages they have not, and undervalue those they have,' said Lady Merton, smiling.

'Advantages!' repeated Helen.

'Why, do not you think it an advantage to have sisters?' said Anne; 'I wish you would give some of them to me if you do not.'

'Indeed,' said Helen warmly, 'I do value my sisters very much; I am sure I am very fond of them.'

'As long as they give you no trouble,' said Lady Merton.

'Well,' said Helen, 'I see you may well think me a very poor selfish creature, but I really do mean to try to improve. I will offer to undertake Dora's music; Lizzie does not understand that, and it is often troublesome to Mamma to find time to hear her practise, and I think I should pay more attention to it than Kate does sometimes. I think Dora will play very well, and I should like her to play duets with me.'

'I am glad you can endure one of your sisters,' said Anne, laughing rather maliciously.

'Pray say no more of that, Anne,' said Helen; 'it was only my foolish indolence that made me make such a speech.'

As Helen finished speaking, Elizabeth came into the room, looking rather weary, but very blithe. 'I have been having a most delightful talk about the Consecration with the girls,' said she, 'hearing what they saw, and what they thought of it. Mary Watson took her master's children up the hill to see the church-yard consecrated, and the eldest little boy--that fine black-eyed fellow, you know, Helen--said he never could play at ball there again, now the Bishop had read the prayers there. I do really hope that girl will be of great use to those little things; her mistress says no girl ever kept them in such good order before.'

'I was going to compliment you on the good behaviour of your children at St.

Austin's, Lizzie,' said Lady Merton; 'I thought I never saw a more well conducted party.'

'Ah! some of our best children are gone to St. Austin's,' said Elizabeth; 'I quite grudge them to Mr. Somerville; I hate the girls to get out of my sight.'

'So do I,' said Anne, 'I am quite angry when our girls go out to service, they **will** get such horrid places--public houses, or at best farm houses, where they have a whole train of babies to look after, and never go to church.'

'And very few of the most respectable fathers and mothers care where their children go to service,' said Elizabeth; 'I am sure I often wish the children had no parents.'

'In order that they may learn a child's first duty?' said Lady Merton.

'Well, but is it not vexatious, Aunt Anne,' said Elizabeth, 'when there is a nice little girl learning very well in school, but forgetting as soon as she is out of it, her mother will not put herself one inch out of the way to keep her there regularly; when the child goes to church continually, the mother never comes at all, or never kneels down when she is there. If you miss her at school on the Sunday morning, her mother has sent her to the shop, and perhaps told her to tell a falsehood about it; if her hand is clammy with lollipops, or there is a perfume of peppermint all round her, or down clatters a halfpenny in the middle of church, it is all her father's fault.'

'Oh! except the clatter, that last disaster never happens with us,' said Anne; 'the shop is not open on Sunday.'

'Ah! that is because Uncle Edward is happily the king of the parish,' said Elizabeth; 'it has the proper Church and State government, like Dante's notion of the Empire. But you cannot help the rest; and we are still worse off, and how can we expect the children to turn out well with such home treatment?'

'No, Lizzie,' said Lady Merton; 'you must not expect them to turn out well.'

'O Mamma! Mamma!' cried Anne.

'What do you teach them for?' exclaimed Helen.

'I see what you mean,' said Elizabeth; 'we can only cast our bread upon the waters; we must look to the work, and not to the present appearance. But, Aunt Anne, the worst is, if they go wrong, I must be afraid it is my fault; that it is from some slip in my teaching, some want of accordance between my example and my precept, and no one can say that it is not so.'

'No one on earth,' said her aunt solemnly; 'and far better it is for you, that you should teach in fear.'

'I sometimes fancy,' said Elizabeth, 'that the girls would do better if we had the whole government of them, but I know that is but fancy; they are each in the place and among the temptations which will do them most good. But oh! it is a melancholy thing to remember that of the girls whom I myself have watched through the school and out into the world, there are but two on whom I can think with perfect satisfaction.'

'Taking a high standard, of course?' said Lady Merton.

'Oh yes, and not reckoning many who I hope will do well, like this one of whom I was talking, but who have had no trial,' said Elizabeth; 'there are many very good ones now, if they will but keep so. One of these girls that I was telling you of, has shewn that she had right principle and firmness, by her behaviour towards a bad fellow-servant; she is at Miss Maynard's.'

'And where is the other?' asked Anne.

'In her grave,' said Elizabeth.

'Ah!' said Helen, 'I missed her to-day, in the midst of her little class, bending over them as she used to do, and looking in their faces, as if she saw the words come out of their mouths.'

'Do you mean the deaf girl with the speaking eyes?' said Anne; 'you wrote to tell me you had lost her.'

'Yes,' said Elizabeth; 'she it was whose example shewed me that an infirmity may be a blessing. Her ear was shut to the noises of the world, the strife of tongues, and as her mother said, "she did not know what a bad word was," only it was tuned to holy things. She always knew what was going on in church, and by her eager attention learnt to do everything in school; and when her deafness was increased by her fever, and she could not hear her mother's and sisters' voices, she could follow the prayers Papa read, the delirium fled away from them. Oh! it is a blessing and a privilege to have been near such a girl; but then--though the last thing she said was to desire her sisters to be good girls and keep to their church and school--she would have been the same, have had the same mind, without our teaching--our mere school-keeping, I mean. Aunt Anne, you say you have kept school in your village for thirty years; you were just in my situation, the clergyman's daughter; so do tell me what effect your teaching has had as regards the children of your first set of girls. Are they better managed at home than their mothers?'

'More civilized and better kept at school, otherwise much the same,' said Lady Merton. 'Yes, my experience is much the same as yours; comparatively few of those I have watched from their childhood have done thoroughly well, and their good conduct has been chiefly owing to their parents. Some have improved and returned to do right, perhaps partly in consequence of their early teaching.'

'Sad work, sad work, after all!' said Elizabeth, as she left the room to finish hearing the little ones, and release Mrs. Woodbourne.

'And yet,' said Helen, as the door closed, 'no one is so happy at school as Lizzie, or delights more in the children, or in devising pleasure for them.'

'I never shall understand Lizzie,' said Anne, with a kind of sigh; 'who would have suspected her of such desponding feelings? and I cannot believe it is so bad an affair. How can it be, taking those dear little things fresh from their baptism, training them with holy things almost always before them, their minds not dissipated by all kinds of other learning, like ours.'

'I do not know that that is quite the best thing, though in a degree it is unavoidable,' said her mother.

'So I was thinking,' said Helen; 'I think it must make religious knowledge like a mere lesson; I know that is what Lizzie dreads, and they begin the Bible before they can read it well.'

'But can it, can it really be so melancholy? will all those bright-faced creatures, who look so earnest and learn so well, will they turn their backs upon all that is right, all they know so well?' said poor Anne, almost ready to cry. 'O Mamma, do not tell me to think so.'

'No, no, you need not, my dear,' said Lady Merton; 'it would be grievous and sinful indeed to say any such things of baptized Christians, trained up by the Church. The more you love them, and the more you hope for them, the better. You will learn how to hope and how to fear as you grow older.'

'But I have had as much experience as Lizzie,' said Anne; 'I am but a month younger, and school has been my Sunday delight ever since I can remember; Mamma, I think the Abbeychurch people must be very bad--you see they keep shop on

Sunday; but then you spoke of our own people. It must have been my own careless levity that has prevented me from feeling like Lizzie; but I cannot believe--'

'You have not been the director of the school for the last few years, as Lizzie has,' said Lady Merton; 'the girls under your own protection are younger, their trial is hardly begun.'

'I am afraid I shall be disheartened whenever I think of them,' said Anne; 'I wish you had not said all this--and yet--perhaps--if disappointment is really to come, I had better be prepared for it.'

'Yes, you may find this conversation useful, Anne,' said Lady Merton; 'if it is only to shew you why I have always tried to teach you self-control in your love of the school.'

'I know I want self-control when I let myself be so engrossed in it as to neglect other things,' said Anne; 'and I hope I do manage now not to shew more favour to the girls I like best, than to the others; but in what other way do you mean, Mamma?'

'I mean that you must learn not to set your heart upon individual girls, or plans which seem satisfactory at first,' said Lady Merton; 'disappointment will surely be sent in some form or other, to try your faith and love; and if you do not learn to fear now that your hopes are high, you will hardly have spirit enough left to persevere cheerfully when failure has taught you to mistrust yourself.'

'I know that I must be disappointed if I build upon schemes or exertions of my own,' said Anne; 'but I should be very conceited--very presumptuous, I mean--to do so, and I hope I never shall.'

'I cannot think how you, or anybody who thinks like you, can ever undertake to keep school,' said Helen; 'I never saw how awful a thing it is, before; not merely hearing lessons, and punishing naughty children, I am sure I dread it now; I would have nothing to do with it if Papa did not wish it, and so make it my duty.'

'Nobody would teach the children at all if they thought like you, Helen,' said Anne; 'and then what would become of them?'

'People who are not fit often do teach them, and is not that worse than nothing?' said Helen; 'I should think irreverence and false doctrine worse than ignorance.'

'Certainly,' said Lady Merton; 'and happy it is, that, as in your case, Helen, the duty of obedience, or some other equally plain, teaches us when to take responsibility upon ourselves and when to shrink from it.'

'I must say,' said Anne, 'I cannot recover from hearing Mamma and Lizzie talk of their "little victims," just in Gray's tone.'

'No,' said Lady Merton; 'I only say,

"If thou wouldst reap in love,
First sow in holy fear."'

CHAPTER XIII.

On Monday morning, as soon as breakfast was over, Elizabeth and Katherine went to the school to receive the penny-club money, and to change the lending library books. They were occupied in this manner for about half an hour; and on their return, Elizabeth went to Mrs. Woodbourne's dressing-room, to put away the money, and to give her an account of her transactions. While she was so employed, her father came into the room with a newspaper in his hand.

'Look here, Mildred,' said he, laying it down on the table before his wife, 'this is what Walker has just brought me.'

Mrs. Woodbourne glanced at the paragraph he pointed out, and exclaimed, 'O Lizzie! this is a sad thing!'

Elizabeth advanced, she grew giddy with dismay as she read as follows:

'On Friday last, a most interesting and instructive lecture on the Rise and Progress of the Institution of Chivalry was delivered at the Mechanics' Institute, in this city, by Augustus Mills, Esq. This young gentleman, from whose elegant talents and uncommon eloquence we should augur no ordinary career in whatever profession may be honoured with his attention, enlarged upon the barbarous manners of the wild untutored hordes among whom the proud pageantry of pretended faith, false honour, and affected punctilio, had its rise. He traced it through its gilded course of blood and carnage, stripped of the fantastic and delusive mantle which romance delights to fling over its native deformity, to the present time, when the general civilization and protection enjoyed in this enlightened age, has left nought but the grim shadow of the destructive form which harassed and menaced our trembling ancestors. We are happy to observe that increasing attendance at the Mechanics' Institute of Abbeychurch, seems to prove that the benefits of education are becom-

ing more fully appreciated by all classes. We observed last Friday, at the able lecture of Mr. Mills, among a numerous assemblage of the distinguished inhabitants
and visitors of Abbeychurch, Miss Merton, daughter of Sir Edward Merton, of Merton Hall, Baronet, together with the fair and accomplished daughters of the Rev. H.
Woodbourne, our respected Vicar.'

'I shall certainly contradict it,' continued Mr. Woodbourne, while Elizabeth
was becoming sensible of the contents of the paragraph; 'I did not care what Higgins chose to any of my principles, but this is a plain fact, which may be believed if
it is not contradicted.'

'O Mamma, have not you told him?' said Elizabeth faintly.

'What, do you mean to say that this is true?' exclaimed Mr. Woodbourne, in a
voice which sounded to Elizabeth like a clap of thunder.

'Indeed, Papa,' said she, once looking up in his face, and then bending her eyes
on the ground, while the colour in her checks grew deeper and deeper; 'I am sorry
to say that it is quite true, that we did so very wrong and foolishly as to go. Helen
and Lucy alone were sensible and strong-minded enough to refuse to go.'

Mr. Woodbourne paced rapidly up and down the room, and Elizabeth plainly
saw that his displeasure was great.

'But, Mr. Woodbourne,' said her mamma, 'she did not know that it was wrong.
Do you not remember that she was not at home at the time that Socialist was here?
and I never told her of all that passed then. You see it was entirely my fault.'

'Oh! no, no, Mamma, do not say so!' said Elizabeth; 'it was entirely mine. I was
led away by my foolish eagerness and self-will, I was bent on my own way, and
cast aside all warnings, and now I see what mischief I have done. Cannot you do
anything to repair it, Papa? cannot you say that it was all my doing, my wilfulness,
my carelessness of warning, my perverseness?'

'I wish I had known it before,' said Mr. Woodbourne, 'I could at least have
spoken to Mr. Turner on Saturday, and prevented the Mertons' name from appearing.'

'I did not tell you because I had no opportunity,' said Mrs. Woodbourne; 'Lizzie
came and told me all, the instant she knew that she had done wrong; but I thought
it would harass you, and you were so much occupied that I had better wait till all
this bustle was over, but she told me everything most candidly, and would have

come to you, but that Mr. Roberts was with you at the time.--My dear Lizzie, do not distress yourself so much, I am sure you have suffered a great deal.'

'O Mamma,' said Elizabeth, 'how can I ever suffer enough for such a tissue of ill-conduct? you never will see how wrong it was in me.'

'Yet, Lizzie,' said her father kindly, 'we may yet rejoice over the remembrance of this unpleasant affair, if it has made you reflect upon the faults that have led to it.'

'But what is any small advantage to my own character compared with the injury I have done?' said Elizabeth; 'I have made it appear as if you had granted the very last thing you would ever have thought of; I have led Kate and Anne into disobedience. Oh! I have done more wrongly than I ever thought I could.'

At this moment Katherine came into the room with some message for Mrs. Woodbourne.

'Come here, Kate,' said her father; 'read this.'

Katherine cast a frightened glance upon Elizabeth, who turned away from her. She read on, and presently exclaimed, 'Fair and accomplished daughters! dear me! that is ourselves.' Then catching Elizabeth by the arm, she whispered, 'Does he know it?'

'Yes, Katherine,' said Mr. Woodbourne sternly; 'your sister has shewn a full conviction that she has done wrong, a feeling of which I am sorry to see that you do not partake.'

'Indeed, indeed, Papa,' cried Katherine, bursting into tears, 'I am very sorry; I should never have gone if it had not been for the others.'

'No excuses, if you please, Katherine,' said Mr. Woodbourne; 'I wish to hear exactly how it happened.'

'First, Papa,' said Elizabeth, 'let me beg one thing of you, do not tell Mrs. Hazleby that Harriet went with us, for she could not know that it was wrong of us to go, and she is very much afraid of her mother's anger.'

Mr. Woodbourne made a sign of assent; and Elizabeth proceeded to give a full account of the indiscreet expedition, taking the blame so entirely upon herself, that although Katherine was on the watch to contradict anything that might tell unfavourably for her, she could not find a word to gainsay--speaking very highly of Helen, not attempting to make the slightest excuse, or to plead her sorrow for what had happened as a means of averting her father's displeasure, and ending by asking permission to go to Mrs. Turner the instant the Hazlebys had left Abbeychurch, to tell her that the excursion had been entirely without Mr. Woodbourne's knowledge or consent. 'For,' said she, 'that is the least I can do towards repairing what can never be repaired.'

'I am not sure that that would be quite a wise measure, my dear Lizzie,' said Mrs. Woodbourne.

'Certainly not,' said Mr. Woodbourne; 'it would put Lizzie in a very unsuitable situation, and in great danger of being impertinent.'

'Yes,' said Elizabeth; 'I see that I do wrong whichever way I turn.'

'Come, Lizzie,' said her father, 'I see that I cannot be as much displeased with you as you are with yourself. I believe you are sincerely sorry for what has passed, and now we will do our best to make it useful to you, and prevent it from having any of the bad consequences to my character which distress you so much.'

Elizabeth was quite overcome by Mr. Woodbourne's kindness, she sprung up, threw her arms round his neck, kissed him, and taking one more look to see that his eyes no longer wore the expression which she dreaded, she darted off to her own room, to give a free course to the tears with which she had long been struggling.

Katherine, who had been studying the newspaper all this time, seeing Elizabeth's case so easily dismissed, and not considering herself as nearly so much to blame, now giggled out, 'Mamma, did you ever see anyone so impertinent as this man? "Fair and accomplished daughters," indeed! was there ever anything so impertinent?'

'Yes, Katherine,' said Mr. Woodbourne, 'there is something far more impertinent in a young lady who thinks proper to defy my anger, and to laugh at the consequences of her giddy disobedience.'

'Indeed, Papa,' said Katherine, 'I am very sorry, but I am sure it was not disobedience. I did not know we were not to go.'

'Not when you had heard all that was said on the subject last year?' said Mr. Woodbourne; 'I am ashamed to see you resort to such a foolish subterfuge.'

'I did not remember it,' said Katherine; 'I am sure I should never have gone if I had, but Lizzie was so bent upon it.'

'Again throwing the blame upon others,' said Mr. Woodbourne; 'your sister has set you a far better example. She forbore from saying what I believe she might have said with perfect truth, that had you not chosen to forget my commands when they interfered with your fancies, she would not have thought of going; and this is the return which you make to her kindness.'

'Well,' sobbed Katherine, 'I never heard you say we should not go, I do not remember it. You know Mamma says I have a very bad memory.'

'Your memory is good enough for what pleases yourself,' said Mr. Woodbourne; 'you have been for some time past filling your head with vanity and gossiping, without making the slightest attempt to improve yourself or strengthen your mind, and this is the consequence. However, this you will remember if you please, that it is my desire that you associate no more with that silly chattering girl, Miss Turner, than your sisters do. You know that I never approved of your making a friend of her, but you did not choose to listen to any warnings.'

Katherine well knew that her father had often objected to her frequently going to drink tea with the Turners, and had checked her for talking continually of her friend; and anyone not bent on her own way would have thought these hints enough, but as they were not given with a stern countenance, or in a peremptory manner, she had paid no attention to them. Now, she could not be brought to perceive what her fault really had been, but only sobbed out something about its being very hard that she should have all the scolding, when it was Lizzie's scheme, not hers. Again forgetting that she had been the original proposer of the expedition.

'Pray, my dear, do not go on defending yourself,' said Mrs. Woodbourne, 'you see it does no good.'

'But, Mamma,' whined Katherine, in such a tone that Mr. Woodbourne could bear it no longer, and ordered her instantly to leave the room, and not to appear again till she could shew a little more submission. She obeyed, after a little more sobbing and entreating; and as she closed the door behind her, Harriet came out of the opposite room.

'What is the matter?' whispered she; 'has it all come out?'

'Yes, it is in the paper, and Papa is very angry,' sighed Katherine.

'Is there anything about me?' asked Harriet eagerly, paying no regard to poor Katherine's woful appearance and streaming eyes.

'Oh no, nothing,' said Katherine, hastening away, as Mrs. Hazleby and Lucy came into the passage.

'Hey-day! what is all this about?' exclaimed the former, encountering Mr. Wood-bourne, as he came out of his wife's dressing-room; 'what is the matter now?'

'I believe your daughter can explain it better than I can,' answered Mr. Wood-bourne, giving her the paper, and walking away to his study as soon as he came to the bottom of the stairs.

As soon as Mrs. Hazleby found herself in the drawing-room she called upon her eldest daughter to explain to her the meaning of what she saw in the newspaper.

'Why, Mamma,' Harriet began, 'you know Miss Merton and Lizzie Wood-bourne care for nothing but history and all that stuff, and do not mind what they do, as long as they can talk, talk, talk of nothing else all day long. So they were at it the day you dined out, and they had some question or other, whether King Arthur's Round Table were knights or not, till at last Kate said something about the Institute, and they were all set upon going, though Helen told them they had better not, so out we went, we walked all together to Mrs. Turner's, and she took them. I suppose Fido must have fallen into the river while they were at the Institute.'

'Poor dear little fellow, I dare say that was the way he was lost,' said Mrs. Ha-zleby; 'when once young people take that kind of nonsense into their head, there is an end of anything else. Well, and how was it we never heard of it all this time?'

'I think no one would wish to tell of it,' said Harriet; 'you would not have heard of it now, if it had not been in the paper.'

'Well, I hope Miss Lizzie will have enough of it,' said Mrs. Hazleby; 'it will open her papa's eyes to all her conceit, if anything will.'

'I am sure it is time,' said Harriet; 'she thinks herself wiser than all the world, one cannot speak a word for her.'

'O Harriet!' said Lucy, looking up from her work with some indignation in her eyes.

'I believe you think it all very grand, Lucy,' said her mother; 'you care for nothing as long as you can dawdle about with Helen. Pray did you go to this fine place?'

'No, Mamma,' said Lucy.

'H--m,' said Mrs. Hazleby, rather disappointed at losing an opportunity of scolding her.

Anne had gone to write a letter in her mother's room, whilst Elizabeth was busy. She had just finished it, and was thinking of going to see whether anyone was ready to read in the school-room, when Rupert came in, and making a low bow, addressed her thus: 'So, Miss Nancy, I congratulate you.'

'What is the matter now?' said Anne.

'Pray, Anne,' said he, 'did you ever experience the satisfaction of feeling how pleasant it is to see one's name in print?'

'You were very near having something like that pleasure yourself,' said Anne; 'it was only your arrival on Friday that saved the expense of an advertisement at the head of a column in the Times--

"R. M., return, return, return to your sorrowing friends."'

'Pray be more speedy next time,' said Rupert, 'for then I shall be even with you.'

'I am sure you have some wickedness in your head, or all your speeches would not begin with "Pray,"' said Anne; 'what do you mean?'

'What I say,' answered Rupert; 'I have just read Miss Merton's name in the paper.'

'Some other Miss Merton, you foolish boy!' said Anne.

'No, no, yourself, Anne Katherine Merton, daughter of Sir Edward,' said Rupert.

'My dear Rupert, you do not mean it!' said Anne, somewhat alarmed.

'I saw it with my eyes,' said Rupert.

'But where?'

'In the Abbeychurch Reporter, or whatever you call it.'

'Oh!' said Anne, looking relieved, 'we are probably all there, as having been at the Consecration.'

'The company there present, are, I believe, honoured with due mention of Sir Edward Merton and family,' said Rupert; 'but I am speaking of another part of the paper where Miss Merton is especially noted, alone in her glory.'

'In what paper did you say, Rupert?' said Lady Merton.

'The Abbeychurch Reporter,' said he.

'Mr. Higgins's paper!' said Anne. 'O Mamma, I see it all--that horrible Mechanics' Institute!'

'Why, Anne,' said her brother, 'I thought you would be charmed with your celebrity.'

'But where have you seen it, Rupert?' said Anne; 'poor Lizzie, has she heard it?'

'Mr. Walker came in just now in great dismay, to shew it to Mr. Woodbourne,' said Rupert; 'and they had a very long discussion on the best means of contradicting it, to which I listened with gravity, quite heroic, I assure you, considering all things. Then my uncle carried it off to shew it to his wife, and I came up to congratulate you.'

'I am sure it is no subject of congratulation,' said Anne; 'where was Papa all the time?'

'Gone to call on Mr. Somerville,' said Rupert.

'But I thought Lizzie had told her father,' said Lady Merton.

'She told Mrs. Woodbourne directly,' said Anne; 'but she could not get at my uncle, and I suppose Mrs. Woodbourne had not told him. What an annoyance for them all! I hope Mr. Woodbourne is not very much displeased.'

'He was more inclined to laugh than to be angry, said Rupert; 'and it is indeed a choice morceau, worthy of Augustus Mills, Esquire, himself. I hope Mr. Woodbourne will bring it down-stairs, that you may explain to me the rare part which describes the decrepid old Giant Chivalry, sitting in his den, unable to do any mischief, only biting his nails at the passers by, like the Giant Pope in the Pilgrim's Progress.'

Anne could not help laughing. 'But, Rupert,' said she, 'pray do not say too much about it in the evening. I am not at all sure that Papa will not be very much displeased to see his name figuring in the paper as if he was a supporter of this horrid place. I wish, as Lizzie says, that I had cut my head off before I went, for it has really come to be something serious. Papa's name will seem to sanction their proceedings.'

'My dear,' said Lady Merton, 'you may comfort yourself by remembering that your Papa's character is too well known to be affected by such an assertion as this; most people will not believe it, and those who do, can only think that his daughter is turning radical, not himself.'

'Ay, this is the first public decisive act of Miss Merton's life,' said Rupert; 'no wonder so much is made of it.'

'But, Rupert,' said Anne, 'I only beg of you not to say anything about it to Lizzie.'

'You cut me off from everything diverting,' said Rupert; 'you are growing quite impertinent, but I will punish you some day when you do not expect it.'

'I do not care what you do when we are at home,' said Anne; 'I defy you to do your worst then; only spare Lizzie and me while we are here.'

'Spare Lizzie, indeed!' said Rupert; 'she does not want your protection, she is able enough to take care of herself.'

'I believe Rupert's five wits generally go off halting, from the sharp encounter of hers,' said Lady Merton.

'And therefore he wants to gain a shabby advantage over a wounded enemy,' said Anne; 'I give you up, you recreant; your name should have been Oliver, instead of Rupert.'

'There is an exemplification of the lecture,' said Rupert; 'impotent chivalry biting its nails with disdain and despite.'

'Well, Mamma,' said Anne, 'since chivalry is impotent, I shall leave you to tame that foul monster with something else; I will have no more to do with him.'

She went to fetch her work out of her bed-room, but on seeing Elizabeth there, her pocket-handkerchief in her hand, and traces of tears on her face, was hastily retreating, when her cousin said, 'Come in,' and added, 'So, Anne, you have heard, the murder is out.'

'The Mechanics' Institute, you mean,' said Anne, 'not Fido.'

'Not Fido,' said Elizabeth; 'but the rest of the story is out; I mean, it is not known who killed Cock Robin, and I do not suppose it ever will be; but the Mechanics' Institute affair is in the newspaper, and it is off my mind, for I have had it all out with Papa. And, Anne, he was so very kind, that I do not know how to think of it. He made light of the annoyance to himself on purpose to console me, and but,' added she, smiling, while the tears came into her eyes again, 'I must not talk of him, or I shall go off into another cry, and not be fit for the reading those unfortunate children have been waiting for so long. Tell me, are my eyes very unfit to be seen?'

'Not so very bad,' said Anne.

'Well, I cannot help it if they are,' said Elizabeth; 'come down and let us read.'

They found Helen alone in the school-room, where she had been sitting ever since breakfast-time, thinking that the penny club was occupying Elizabeth most unusually long this morning.

'Helen,' said Elizabeth, as she came into the room, 'Papa knows the whole story, and I can see that he is as much pleased with your conduct as I am sure you deserve.'

All was explained in a few words. Helen was now by no means inclined to triumph in her better judgement, for, while she had been waiting, alone with her drawing, she had been thinking over all that had passed since the unfortunate Friday evening, wondering that she could ever have believed that Elizabeth was not overflowing with affection, and feeling very sorry for the little expression of triumph which she had allowed to escape her in her ill-temper on Saturday. 'Lizzie,' said she, 'will you forgive me for that very unkind thing I said to you?'

Elizabeth did not at first recollect what it was, and when she did, she only said, 'Nonsense, Helen, I never consider what people say when they are cross, any more than when they are drunk.'

Anne was very much diverted by the idea of Elizabeth's experience of what drunken people said, or of drunkenness and ill-temper being allied, and her merriment restored the spirits of her cousins, and took off from what Elizabeth called the 'awfulness of a grand pardoning scene.' Helen was then sent to summon the children to their lessons, which were happily always supposed to begin later on a Monday than on any other day of the week.

The study door was open, and as she passed by, her father called her into the room. 'Helen,' said he, 'Elizabeth tells me that you acted the part of a sensible and obedient girl the other evening, and I am much pleased to hear it.'

Helen stood for a few moments, too much overcome with delight and surprise to be able to speak. Mr. Woodbourne went on writing, and she bounded upstairs with something more of a hop, skip, and jump, than those steps had known from her foot since she had been an inhabitant of the nursery herself, thinking 'What would he say if he knew that I only refused to go, out of a spirit of opposition?' yet feeling the truth of what Anne had said, that her father's praise, rarely given, and only when well earned, was worth all the Stauntons' admiration fifty times over.

When Mrs. Woodbourne came down, she advised Helen not to call Katherine, saying that she thought it would be better for her to be left to herself, so that she was seen no more till just before the Hazlebys departed, when she came down to take leave of them, looking very pale, her eyes very red, and her voice nearly choking, but still there was no appearance of submission about her.

'Helen,' said Lucy, as they were standing in the window of the inner drawing-room, 'I should like you to tell Aunt Mildred how very much I have enjoyed this visit.'

'I wish you would tell her so yourself,' said Helen; 'I am sure you cannot be afraid of her, Lucy.'

'Oh no, I am not afraid of her,' said Lucy, 'only I do not like to say this to her. It is putting myself too forward almost, to say it to you even, Helen; but I have been wishing all the time I have been here, to thank her for having been so very kind as to mention me especially, in her letter to Papa.'

'But have you really enjoyed your visit here?' said Helen, thinking how much she had felt for Lucy on several occasions.

'Oh! indeed I have, Helen,' answered she; 'to say nothing of the Consecration, such a sight as I may never see again in all my life, and which must make everyone very happy who has anything to do with your Papa, and Aunt Mildred; it has been a great treat to be with you all again, and to see your uncle and aunt, and Miss Merton. I hardly ever saw such a delightful person as Miss Merton, so clever and so sensible, and now I shall like to hear all you have to say about her in your letters.'

'Yes, I suppose Anne is clever and sensible,' said Helen musingly.

'Do not you think her so?' said Lucy, with some surprise.

'Why, yes, I do not know,' said Helen, hesitating; 'but then, she does laugh so very much.'

Lucy could not make any answer, for at this moment her mother called her to make some arrangement about the luggage; but she pondered a little on the proverb which declares that it is well to be merry and wise.

Mrs. Hazleby had been condoling with Mr. Woodbourne upon his daughter's misbehaviour, and declaring that her dear girls would never dream of taking a single step without her permission, but that learning was the ruin of young ladies.

Mr. Woodbourne listened to all this discourse very quietly, without attempting any remark, but as soon as the Hazlebys had gone up-stairs to put on their bonnets, he said, 'Well, I wish Miss Harriet joy of her conscience.'

'I wish Barbara had been more gentle with those girls,' replied Mrs. Wood-bourne, with a sigh. And this was all that passed between the elders on the subject of the behaviour of Miss Harriet Hazleby.

Mr. Woodbourne and Rupert accompanied Mrs. Hazleby and her daughters to the railroad station, Rupert shewing himself remarkably polite to Mrs. Hazleby's pet baskets, and saving Lucy from carrying the largest and heaviest of them, which generally fell to her share.

CHAPTER XIV.

Well,' said Elizabeth, drawing a long breath, as she went out to walk with Anne and Helen, 'there is the even-handed justice of this world. Of the four delinquents of last Friday, there goes one with flying colours, in all the glory of a successful deceit; you, Anne, who, to say the best of you, acted like a very great goose, are considered as wise as ever; I, who led you all into the scrape with my eyes wilfully blinded, am only pitied and comforted; poor Kitty, who had less idea of what she was doing than any of us, has had more crying and scolding than anybody else; and Lucy, who behaved so well--oh! I cannot bear to think of her.'

'It is a puzzle indeed,' said Helen; 'I mean as far as regards Harriet and Lucy.'

'Not really, Helen,' said Elizabeth; 'it is only a failure in story book justice. Lucy is too noble a creature to be rewarded in a story-book fashion; and as for Harriet, impunity like hers is in reality a greater punishment than all the reproof in the world.'

'How could she sit by and listen to all that Papa and Mrs. Hazleby were saying?' said Helen.

'How could she bear the glance of Papa's eye?' said Elizabeth; 'did you watch it? I thought I never saw it look so stern, and yet that contemptible creature sat under it as contentedly as possible. Oh! it made me quite sick to watch her.'

Are you quite sure that she knew whether my uncle was aware of her share in the matter?' said Anne.

'She must have seen it in that glance, or have been the most insensible creature upon earth,' said Elizabeth.

'Ah!' said Anne, 'I have some notion what that eye of your Papa's can be.'

'You, Anne?' said Elizabeth; 'you do not mean that you could ever have done anything to make him look at you in that way?'

'Indeed I have,' said Anne; 'do not you remember?'

'No, indeed,' said Elizabeth.

'However, it was not quite so bad as this,' said Anne.

'But do tell us what it was,' said Elizabeth, 'or I shall think it something uncommonly shocking.'

'I never spoke of it since, because I was too much ashamed,' said Anne; 'and it was very silly of me to do so now.'

'But when was it?' said Elizabeth.

'Two years ago,' said Anne, 'when you were all staying at Merton Hall, just before that nice nursery-maid of yours, Susan, married our man Evans.'

'Yes, I remember,' said Elizabeth; 'but what has that to do with your crime, whatever it may be?'

'A great deal,' said Anne; 'do not you recollect our hunting all over the garden one day for Winifred and Dora, and at last our asking old Ambrose whether he had seen them?'

'Oh yes, I think I do,' said Elizabeth; 'and he said that he had seen Susan and the children go down the blind walk. Then I said Dora had talked of seeing a blackbird's nest there, and he answered, with a most comical look, 'Ah! ha! Miss Woodbourne, I fancy they be two-legged blackbirds as Susan is gone to see.''

'Why, blackbirds have but two legs,' said Helen, looking mystified; 'what did he mean'?'

'That is exactly what Kate said,' said Elizabeth; 'but really I thought you were sharper, Helen. Cannot you guess?'

'Not in the least,' said Helen.

'That Evans was clipping the hedges,' said Anne.

Elizabeth and Anne indulged in a good laugh at Helen, as much as at Ambrose, and presently Elizabeth said, 'Well, but, Anne, where is your crime?'

'Oh! I thought you had remembered, and would spare me,' said Anne.

'But we have not,' said Elizabeth; 'so now for it.'

'Then if I am to tell,' said Anne, 'do not you recollect that I began to tell Rupert the story in the middle of dinner, when all the servants were there?'

'O Anne, I never fancied you such a goose!' said Elizabeth.

'My delinquencies made very little impression on you, then,' said Anne; 'I went on very fluently with the story till just as I had pronounced the words, "two-legged blackbirds," I saw Uncle Woodbourne's eye upon me, as he sat just opposite, with all its cold heavy sternness of expression, and at the same moment I heard a strange suppressed snort behind my chair.'

'Poor creature!' said Elizabeth; 'but you certainly deserved it.'

'I was ready to sink under the table,' said Anne; 'I did not dare to look up to Papa or Mamma, and I have been very much obliged to Mamma ever since for never alluding to that terrible dinner.'

'It is a regular proof that Fun is one of the most runaway horses in existence,' said Elizabeth; 'very charming when well curbed, but if you give him the rein--'

'Yes, I have been learning that by sad experience all my life,' said Anne, with a sigh.

'You will never be silly enough to give him up, though,' said Elizabeth.

'Silly, do you call it?' said Helen.

'People think so differently on those matters,' said Anne.

'Yes, but a "spirit full of glee" is what I think the most delightful thing in the world,' said Elizabeth, 'and so do you.'

'Yes, in old age, when its blitheness has been proved to be something beyond animal spirits,' said Anne.

'And it is right that people should have animal spirits in their youth,' said Elizabeth, 'not grey heads on green shoulders, like some people of my acquaintance.--Do not be affronted, Helen; I dare say your head will grow greener all your life, it is better to-day than it was on Saturday morning.'

'But the worst of it is,' said Anne, 'that I believe it is very silly of me, but I am afraid Uncle Woodbourne has always thought me a most foolish girl ever since, and I do not like the idea of it.'

'Who would?' said Elizabeth; 'I am afraid I cannot tell you what he thinks of your sense, but of this I am sure, that he must think you the choicest damsel of his acquaintance, and wish his daughters were more like you.'

'And there could not have been the same meaning in his eye when he looked at you, as when he looked at Harriet,' said Helen.

'Oh no, I hope not,' said Anne.

'And you understood it a little better than one who can only feel personal inconvenience,' said Elizabeth; 'but how can I blame Harriet when I was the occasion of her fault? it is a thing I can never bear to think of.'

As Elizabeth said this, they came to a shop where Anne wished to buy some little presents for some children in the village at home, who, she said, would value them all the more for not being the production of the town nearest them. They pursued their search for gay remnants of coloured prints, little shawls, and pictured pocket-handkerchiefs, into the new town, and passed by Mr. Higgins's shop, the window of which was adorned with all the worst caricatures which had found their way to Abbeychurch, the portraits of sundry radical leaders, embossed within a halo of steel-pens, and a notice of a lecture on 'Personal Respectability,' to be given on the ensuing Friday at the Mechanics' Institute, by the Rev. W. Pierce, the Dissenting preacher.

Mr. Higgins appeared at the shop door, for the express purpose, as it seemed, of honouring Miss Merton and Miss Woodbourne each with a very low bow.

'There, Helen, is my punishment,' said Elizabeth; 'since you are desirous of poetical justice upon me.'

'Not upon you,' said Helen, 'only upon Harriet.'

'Harriet has lost Fido,' said Elizabeth.

Here Rupert came to meet them, and no more was said on the subject.

Rupert obeyed his sister tolerably well during most of the day, though he was sorely tempted to ask Elizabeth to send Anne an abstract, in short-hand, of the lecture on Personal Respectability; but he refrained, for he was really fond of his cousin, and very good-natured, excepting when his vanity was offended.

Anne however was in a continual fright, for he delighted in tormenting her by going as near the dangerous subject as he dared; and often, when no one else thought there was any danger, she knew by the expression of his eye that he had some spiteful allusion on his lips. Besides, he thought some of the speeches he had made in the morning too clever to be wasted on his mother and sister, when his cousins were there to hear them, and Anne could not trust to his forbearance to keep them to himself all day, so that she kept a strict watch upon him.

In the evening, however, Mr. Woodbourne called her and Helen to play some Psalm tunes from which he wanted to choose some for the Church. He spoke to her in a way which made her hope that he did not think her quite foolish, but she would have been glad to stay and keep Rupert in order. However, she was rejoiced to hear Elizabeth propose to him to play at chess, and she saw them sit down very amicably.

This proposal, however, proved rather unfortunate, for Elizabeth was victorious in the first battle, the second was a drawn game, and Rupert lost the third, just as he thought he was winning it, from forgetting to move out the castle's pawn after castling his king. He could not bear to be conquered, and pushed away the chessboard rather pettishly.

'Good morning to you, Prince Rupert,' said Elizabeth triumphantly; 'do you wish for any more?'

Rupert made no answer, but pulled the inkstand across the table, opened the paper-case, and took up a pen.

'Oh!' said Elizabeth, 'I suppose we may expect a treatise on the art of fortification, salient angles, and covered ways, not forgetting the surrender of Bristol.'

No reply, but Rupert scratched away very diligently with his pen, the inkstand preventing Elizabeth from seeing what he was about.

'Anne,' said Elizabeth, leaning back, and turning round, 'I am thinking of making a collection of the heroes who could not bear to be beaten at chess, beginning with Charlemagne's Paladins, who regularly beat out each other's brains with the silver chess-board, then the Black Prince, and Philippe of Burgundy. Can you help me to any more?'

Anne did not hear, and Rupert remained silent as ever; and Elizabeth, determining to let him make himself as silly as he pleased, took up her work and sewed on her braid very composedly. Katherine had come down again at dinner-time, and was working in silence. She had been standing by the piano, but finding that no one asked her to play, or took any notice of her, she had come back to the table.

'Dear me, Prince Rupert,' said she, looking over his shoulder, 'what strange thing are you doing there?'

'A slight sketch,' said he, 'to be placed in Lizzie's album as a companion to a certain paragraph which I believe she has studied.'

Rupert threw his pen-and-ink drawing down before Elizabeth. It was really not badly done, and she saw in a moment, by the help of the names which he had scribbled below in his worst of all bad writing, that it represented the Giants, Pope and Pagan, as described in the Pilgrim's Progress, while, close to Pope, was placed a delineation very like Don Quixote, purporting to be the superannuated Giant Chivalry, biting his nails at a dapper little personification of 'Civil and Religious Liberty.' A figure whose pointed head, lame foot, and stout walking-stick, shewed him to be intended for Sir Walter Scott, was throwing over him an embroidered surcoat, which a most striking and ludicrous likeness of Mr. Augustus Mills was pulling off at the other end; and the scene was embellished by a ruined castle in the distance, and a quantity of skulls and cross-bones in the fore-ground. Elizabeth could not but think it unkind of him to jest on this matter, while her eye-lids were still burning and heavy from the tears it had caused her to shed; but she knew Rupert well enough to be certain that it was only a sign that he was out of temper, and had not yet conquered his old boyish love of teazing. She put the paper into her basket, saying, in a low tone, 'Thank you, Rupert; I shall keep it as a memorial of several things, some of which may do me good; but I fear it will always put me in mind that cavaliers of the present day would have little objection to such battles as I was speaking of, even with women, if this poor old gentleman did not retain a small degree of vitality.'

Rupert was vexed, both at being set down in a way he did not expect, and because he was really sorry that his wounded self-conceit had led him to do what he saw had mortified Elizabeth more than he had intended.

'What is it? what is it?' asked Katherine.

'Never mind, Kate,' said Rupert.

'Well, but what fun is it?' persisted Katherine.

'Only downright nonsense,' said Rupert, looking down, and unconsciously drawing very strange devices on the blotting paper, 'unworthy the attention of so wise a lady.'

'Only the dry bones of an ill-natured joke,' said Lady Merton, who had seen all that passed, from the other end of the table. She spoke so low as only to be heard by her son; but Elizabeth saw his colour deepen, and, as he rose and went to the piano, she felt sorry for him, and soon found an opportunity of reminding him that he had promised to draw something for Edward's scrap-book, and asked him if he would do so now.

'Willingly,' said Rupert, 'but only on one condition, Lizzie.'

'What?' said Elizabeth.

'That you give me back that foolish thing,' said Rupert, fixing his eyes intently on the coach and horses which he was drawing.

'There it is,' said Elizabeth, restoring it to him. 'No, no, Rupert, do not tear it up, it is the cleverest thing you ever drew, Sir Walter is excellent.'

Yet, in spite of this commendation, Rupert had torn his performance into the smallest scraps, before his sister came back to the table.

Anne had been in some anxiety ever since the conclusion of the games; but Sir Edward and Mr. Woodbourne were standing between her and the table, so that she could neither see nor hear, and when at length she had finished playing, and was released, she found Rupert and Elizabeth so quiet, and so busy with their several employments, that she greatly dreaded that all had not gone right. She bethought herself of the sketches Rupert had made in Scotland, asked him to fetch them, and by their help, she contrived to restore the usual tone of conversation between the cousins, so that the remainder of the evening passed away very pleasantly.

When Anne and Elizabeth awoke the following morning, Anne said that she had remembered, the evening before, just when it was too late to do anything, that the last Sunday Rupert had left his Prayer-book behind him at St. Austin's; and as they were to set off on their journey homewards immediately after breakfast, she asked Elizabeth whether there would be time to walk to the new church and fetch it before breakfast.

'I think it would be a very pleasant walk in the freshness of the morning, if you like to go,' said she.

'Oh yes,' said Elizabeth, 'there is plenty of time, and I should like the walk very much; but really, Anne, you spoil that idle boy in a terrible way.'

'Ah! Rupert is an only son,' said Anne; 'he has a right to be spoilt.'

'Then I hope that Horace and Edward will save each other from the same fate,' said Elizabeth; 'I do not like to see a sister made such a slave as you have been all your life.'

'Wait till Horace and Edward are at home in the holidays before you talk of slavery,' said Anne; 'there will be five slaves and two masters, that will be all the difference.'

'Well are the male kind called barons in heraldry,' said Elizabeth; 'there is no denying that they are a lordly race; but I think I would have sent Mr. Rupert up the hill himself, rather than go before breakfast, with a day's journey before me.'

'Suppose he would not go?' said Anne.

'Let him lose his Prayer-book, then,' said Elizabeth.

'But if I had rather fetch it for him?' said Anne.

'I can only answer that there are no slaves as willing as sisters,' said Elizabeth.

The two cousins had a pleasant morning walk up the hill, enjoying the freshness of the morning air, and watching the various symptoms of wakening in the town. They carried the keys of the church with them, as no clerk had as yet been appointed, and they were still in Mr. Woodbourne's possession, so that it was not necessary to call anyone to open the doors for them.

Whilst Anne was searching for the Prayer-book, Elizabeth stood in the aisle, her eyes fixed on the bright red cross in the centre window over the Altar. The sun-beams were lighting it up gloriously, and from it, her gaze fell upon the Table of Commandments, between it and the Altar. Presently, Anne came and stood by her side in silence. 'Anne,' said Elizabeth, after a few minutes, 'I will tell you what I have been thinking of. On the day when Horace laid the first stone of this church, two years ago, something put me, I am sorry to say, into one of my old fits of ill temper. It was the last violent passion I ever was in; I either learnt to control them, or outgrew them. And now, may this affair at the Consecration be the last of my self-will and self-conceit; for indeed there is much that is fearfully wrong in me to be corrected, before I can dare to think of the Confirmation.'

Perhaps we cannot take leave of Elizabeth Woodbourne at a better moment, therefore we will say no more of her, or of the other inhabitants of the Vicarage, but make a sudden transition to the conversation, which Anne had hoped to enjoy on the journey back to Merton Hall.

She had told her father of nearly all her adventures, had given Fido's history more fully, informed Rupert of all that he had missed, and was proceeding with an account of Helen. 'Really,' said she, 'I have much more hope of her being happy at home, than I had at first.'

'I will answer for it that she will be happy enough,' said Rupert; 'she has been living on flummery for the last half-year, and you cannot expect her to be contented with mutton-chops just at first.'

'Helen does not find so much fault with the mutton-chops as with the pepper Lizzie adds to them,' said Anne.

'I should be sorry to live without pepper,' said Rupert.

'I am not so sure of that,' said Lady Merton.

'At least you do not wish to have enough to choke you,' said Anne; 'you must have it in moderation.'

'I think Lizzie is learning moderation,' said Lady Merton; 'she is acquiring more command of impulse, and Helen more command of feeling, so that I think there is little danger of their not agreeing.'

'Is it not curious, Mamma,' said Anne, 'that we should have been talking of the necessity of self-control, just before we set out on this visit, when I told you that line of Burns was your motto; and now we find that the want of it is the reason of all that was wrong between those two sisters. I wonder whether we could make out that any more of the follies we saw in this visit were caused by the same deficiency in anyone else.'

'Beginning at home?' said Sir Edward.

'Of course, Papa,' said Anne; 'I know that my failure in self-control has done mischief, though I cannot tell how much. I laughed at the Hazlebys continually, in spite of Mamma's warning, and encouraged Lizzie to talk of them when I had better not have done so; and I allowed myself to be led away by eagerness to hear that foolish lecture. I suppose I want control of spirits.'

'And now having finished our own confession, how merrily we begin upon our neighbours!' said Rupert; 'whom shall we dissect first?'

'Indeed, Rupert,' said Anne, 'I do not want to make the most of their faults, I only wish to study their characters, because I think it is a useful thing to do. Now I do not see that Kate's faults are occasioned by want of self-control; do you think they are, Mamma?'

'Do you think that piece of thistle-down possesses any self-control?' said Rupert.

'You mean that Kate does not control her own conduct at all, but is drifted about by every wind that blows,' said Anne; 'yes, it was Miss Hazleby's influence that made her talk so much more of dress than usual, and really seem sillier than I ever saw her before.'

'And what do you say of the fair Harriet herself?' said Rupert.

'Nothing,' said Anne.

'And Mrs. Hazleby is her daughter in a magnifying glass,' said Rupert; 'a glorious specimen of what you all may come to. And Mrs. Woodbourne?'

'Oh! I have nothing to do with the elders,' said Anne; 'but if you want me to find you a fault in her, I shall say that she ought to control her unwillingness to correct people. And now we have discussed almost everyone.'

'From which discussion,' said Rupert, 'it appears that of all the company at Abbeychurch, the sole possessor of that most estimable quality, the root of all other excellencies, is--your humble servant.'

On this unfortunate speech of poor Rupert's, father, mother, and sister, all set up a shout of laughter, which lasted till Rupert began to feel somewhat enraged.

'Oh! I did not say that I had done with everybody,' said Anne; 'but, perhaps, whatever I might think, I might not have presumed--'

'O Rupert!' said Lady Merton,

       'Could some fay the giftie gie us   To see oursels as others see us--'

'Mamma's beloved Burn's Justice again,' interrupted Rupert.

'No, no, we do not mean to let our mouths be stopped,' said Lady Merton; 'such a challenge must be answered.'

'Shew him no mercy, Anne,' said Sir Edward; 'he likes pepper.'

'Pray, Rupert,' said Anne, 'what would you have been without self-control, if, possessing such a quantity of it, you still allowed so much spirit of mischief to domineer over you, that you frightened Dora out of her wits about Winifred, and tormented Helen all the way to Whistlefar, and worst of all, that you could not help writing that wicked poem, and then pretending that it was mine; why, it was an outrage upon us all, it would have been bad enough if the name had belonged to no one, but when you knew that he was a real man--'

'And that Miss Hazleby wrote his name on purpose that something of the kind might be done,' said Rupert; 'I gratified her beyond measure, and then was so kind and disinterested as to give you the credit of it, if you would have accepted it. You may be sure that she will shew the poem to her hero, and tell him what a charming fellow that young Rupert Merton is.'

'Now just listen, Mamma,' said Anne; 'I begged of Mr. Rupert not to write anything about Fido in the Conglomeration on Saturday evening; and because I did so, he would write nothing on his own account, but pretending to read my verses, he brings out a horrible composition about a certain Mr. Francis Hollis, who, Miss Hazelby had been telling us, had been the means of her going to an officers' ball, at Hull, and whom she had danced with--'

'Capital, capital!' cried Rupert; 'I never heard all this; I did not know how good my poem was, I knew the truth by intuition.'

'But having heard this made it all the worse for me,' said Anne; 'and Mamma, this dreadful doggerel--'

'Anne, I declare--' cried Rupert.

'And, Mamma, this dreadful doggerel,' proceeded Anne, 'proposed to send Fido's heart to this Mr. Hollis, and so put him in raptures with a gift from Miss Hazleby, and fill his mind with visions of a surrogate, and a wedding tour to Harrogate. Now was it not the most impertinent ungentlemanlike thing you ever heard of?'

'How can you talk such nonsense, Anne?' said Rupert; 'do you think I should have written it, if I had not known it would please her?'

'I believe you would not have dared to behave in such a manner to Lizzie, or to anyone else who knew what was due to her,' said Anne; 'if Miss Hazleby is vain and vulgar, she is still a woman, and ought to be respected as such.'

Rupert laughed rather provokingly. 'It is just as I say,' said Anne; 'now is it not, Mamma?'

'Oh yes, Anne,' said Rupert, 'perfectly right, you have caught Helen's sententious wisdom exactly; I have no doubt that such were the thoughts which passed through her mind, while she sat like propriety personified, wondering how you could have so little sense of decorum as to laugh at anything so impudent.'

'I know I ought not to have laughed,' said Anne; 'that was one of the occasions when I did not exert sufficient self-control. But there was really very little to laugh at, it was quite an old joke. Rupert had disposed of Fido's heart long before, but he is so fond of his own wit, that he never knows when we have had enough of a joke.'

'I could tell you of something much worse, Anne,' said Lady Merton, 'which quite proves the truth of what you say.'

Rupert coloured, made an exclamation about something in the road, and seemed so much discomposed by this hint, that Anne forbore to ask any questions.

'Rupert fitted himself to a T, that we must say for him,' said Sir Edward.

'What do you mean, Papa?' said Anne.

'There is another word which begins with self-con--' said Lady Merton,' which suits him remarkably well.'

'Ah! ha!' cried Anne.

'At any rate,' cried Rupert vigorously, 'do not make it appear as if I were the only individual with a tolerable opinion of my own advantages--when Helen looks like the picture of offended dignity if you presume to say a syllable contrary to some of her opinions, or in disparagement of dear Dykelands; and Kate thinks herself the most lovely creature upon earth, and the only useful person in the house; and Harriet believes no one her equal in the art of fascination; and Mrs. Woodbourne thinks no children come within a mile of hers in beauty and excellence; and Lizzie--'

'I am sure few people are more humble-minded than Lizzie,' interrupted Anne indignantly.

'What, when she would take no one's advice but her own, if it were to save her life?' said Rupert.

'But she thinks everyone better than herself, and makes no parade either of her talents or of her usefulness,' said Anne.

'Still she has a pretty high opinion of her own judgement,' said Rupert.

'Well she may,' said Anne.

'When it leads her to go to Mechanics' Institutes,' said Rupert; 'that is the reason Anne respects her so much.'

'I advise you to throw no stones at her, Sir,' said Sir Edward; 'it would be well if some people of my acquaintance were as upright in acknowledging deficiencies in themselves, as she is.'

'Besides, I cannot see that Helen is conceited,' said Anne; 'if she was, she would not be made unhappy by other people's criticisms.'

'Helen wants a just estimate of herself,' said Lady Merton; 'she cares more for what people say of what she does, than whether it is good in itself.'

'But, Anne,' said Sir Edward, 'why do not you claim to be the only person in the world devoid of conceit?'

'Because I am conceited in all the ways which Rupert has mentioned,' said Anne; 'I believe myself witty, and wise, and amiable, and useful, and agreeable, and I do not like taking advice, and I am very angry when my friends are abused, and I do believe I think I have the most exquisite brother in the world; and besides, if I said I was not conceited it would be the best possible proof of the contrary.--But, Mamma, there is a person whom we have not mentioned, who has no conceit and plenty of self-control.'

'Do you mean little Dora?' said Lady Merton.

'No, not Dora, though I am pretty much of Mrs. Woodbourne's opinion respecting her,' said Anne; 'I meant one who is always overlooked, Miss Lucy Hazleby.'

'She may have every virtue upon earth for aught I know,' said Rupert; 'I can only testify that she has un grand talent pour le silence.'

'I only know her from what my cousins told me,' said Anne; 'they seem to have a great respect for her, though Helen is the only person she ever seems to talk to. I never could make her speak three words to me.'

'She has a fine countenance and very sweet expression, certainly,' said Lady Merton.

'Poor girl,' said Sir Edward; 'she blushes so much, that it was almost painful to look at her.'

'You seem to be utterly deficient in proofs of her excellence,' said Rupert; 'you will leave her a blank page at last.'

'Pages are not always blank when you see nothing on them,' said Lady Merton; 'characters may be brought out by the fire.'

'Yes, Mamma, the fire of temptation,' said Anne; 'and I have heard Lucy tried by her mother's violence, and she never concealed any part of the truth as far as only regarded herself, even to avoid those terrible unjust reproofs, and put herself forward to bear her sister's share of blame; and she was firm in turning back from the Mechanics' Institute when her sister scolded her.'

'Firmness, which, in so timid a person, proved that she had more self-control than any of you,' said Sir Edward.

'Then let us wind up the history of our visit in a moral style,' said Anne, 'and call it a lesson on Self-control and Self-conceit.'

'Nonsense,' said Rupert; 'do you think that if anyone read its history, they would learn any such lesson unless you told them beforehand?'

'Perhaps not,' said Sir Edward, 'as you have not learnt it from your whole life.'

'No,' said Lady Merton; 'that lesson is not to be learnt by anyone who is not on the watch for it.'

'So we conclude with Mamma's wisdom,' said Rupert.

'And Rupert's folly,' said Anne.

The Codes Of Hammurabi And Moses
W. W. Davies

QTY

The discovery of the Hammurabi Code is one of the greatest achievements of archaeology, and is of paramount interest, not only to the student of the Bible, but also to all those interested in ancient history...

Religion   **ISBN: *1-59462-338-4***   **Pages:132**

MSRP $12.95

The Theory of Moral Sentiments
Adam Smith

QTY

This work from 1749. contains original theories of conscience amd moral judgment and it is the foundation for systemof morals.

Philosophy **ISBN: *1-59462-777-0***   **Pages:536**

MSRP $19.95

Jessica's First Prayer
Hesba Stretton

QTY

In a screened and secluded corner of one of the many railway-bridges which span the streets of London there could be seen a few years ago, from five o'clock every morning until half past eight, a tidily set-out coffee-stall, consisting of a trestle and board, upon which stood two large tin cans, with a small fire of charcoal burning under each so as to keep the coffee boiling during the early hours of the morning when the work-people were thronging into the city on their way to their daily toil...

Childrens   **ISBN: *1-59462-373-2***

Pages:84

MSRP $9.95

My Life and Work
Henry Ford

QTY

Henry Ford revolutionized the world with his implementation of mass production for the Model T automoblle. Gain valuable business insight into his life and work with his own auto-biography... "We have only started on our development of our country we have not as yet, with all our talk of wonderful progress, done more than scratch the surface. The progress has been wonderful enough but..."

Pages:300

Biographies/   **ISBN: *1-59462-198-5***   *MSRP $21.95*

The Art of Cross-Examination
Francis Wellman

QTY

I presume it is the experience of every author, after his first book is published upon an important subject, to be almost overwhelmed with a wealth of ideas and illustrations which could readily have been included in his book, and which to his own mind, at least, seem to make a second edition inevitable. Such certainly was the case with me; and when the first edition had reached its sixth impression in five months, I rejoiced to learn that it seemed to my publishers that the book had met with a sufficiently favorable reception to justify a second and considerably enlarged edition. ...

Pages:412

Reference   ISBN: *1-59462-647-2*   *MSRP $19.95*

On the Duty of Civil Disobedience
Henry David Thoreau

QTY

Thoreau wrote his famous essay, On the Duty of Civil Disobedience, as a protest against an unjust but popular war and the immoral but popular institution of slave-owning. He did more than write—he declined to pay his taxes, and was hauled off to gaol in consequence. Who can say how much this refusal of his hastened the end of the war and of slavery ?

Law   ISBN: *1-59462-747-9*   **Pages:48**

MSRP $7.45

Dream Psychology Psychoanalysis for Beginners
Sigmund Freud

QTY

Sigmund Freud, born Sigismund Schlomo Freud (May 6, 1856 - September 23, 1939), was a Jewish-Austrian neurologist and psychiatrist who co-founded the psychoanalytic school of psychology. Freud is best known for his theories of the unconscious mind, especially involving the mechanism of repression; his redefinition of sexual desire as mobile and directed towards a wide variety of objects; and his therapeutic techniques, especially his understanding of transference in the therapeutic relationship and the presumed value of dreams as sources of insight into unconscious desires.

Dream Psychology
Psychoanalysis for Beginners

Sigmund Freud

Pages:196

Psychology   ISBN: *1-59462-905-6*   *MSRP $15.45*

The Miracle of Right Thought
Orison Swett Marden

QTY

Believe with all of your heart that you will do what you were made to do. When the mind has once formed the habit of holding cheerful, happy, prosperous pictures, it will not be easy to form the opposite habit. It does not matter how improbable or how far away this realization may see, or how dark the prospects may be, if we visualize them as best we can, as vividly as possible, hold tenaciously to them and vigorously struggle to attain them, they will gradually become actualized, realized in the life. But a desire, a longing without endeavor, a yearning abandoned or held indifferently will vanish without realization.

Pages:360

Self Help   ISBN: *1-59462-644-8*   *MSRP $25.45*

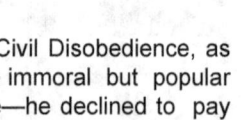

www.bookjungle.com *email: sales@bookjungle.com fax: 630-214-0564 mail: Book Jungle PO Box 2226 Champaign, IL 61825*

QTY

The Rosicrucian Cosmo-Conception Mystic Christianity *by Max Heindel* ISBN: *1-59462-188-8* **$38.95**
The Rosicrucian Cosmo-conception is not dogmatic, neither does it appeal to any other authority than the reason of the student. It is: not controversial, but is: sent forth in the, hope that it may help to clear... New Age/Religion Pages 646

Abandonment To Divine Providence *by Jean-Pierre de Caussade* ISBN: *1-59462-228-0* **$25.95**
"The Rev. Jean Pierre de Caussade was one of the most remarkable spiritual writers of the Society of Jesus in France in the 18th Century. His death took place at Toulouse in 1751. His works have gone through many editions and have been republished... Inspirational/Religion Pages 400

Mental Chemistry *by Charles Haanel* ISBN: *1-59462-192-6* **$23.95**
Mental Chemistry allows the change of material conditions by combining and appropriately utilizing the power of the mind. Much like applied chemistry creates something new and unique out of careful combinations of chemicals the mastery of mental chemistry... New Age Pages 354

The Letters of Robert Browning and Elizabeth Barret Barrett 1845-1846 vol II ISBN: *1-59462-193-4* **$35.95**
by Robert Browning and Elizabeth Barrett Biographies Pages 596

Gleanings In Genesis (volume I) *by Arthur W. Pink* ISBN: *1-59462-130-6* **$27.45**
Appropriately has Genesis been termed "the seed plot of the Bible" for in it we have, in germ form, almost all of the great doctrines which are afterwards fully developed in the books of Scripture which follow... Religion/Inspirational Pages 420

The Master Key *by L. W. de Laurence* ISBN: *1-59462-001-6* **$30.95**
In no branch of human knowledge has there been a more lively increase of the spirit of research during the past few years than in the study of Psychology, Concentration and Mental Discipline. The requests for authentic lessons in Thought Control, Mental Discipline and... New Age/Business Pages 422

The Lesser Key Of Solomon Goetia *by L. W. de Laurence* ISBN: *1-59462-092-X* **$9.95**
This translation of the first book of the "Lernegton" which is now for the first time made accessible to students of Talismanic Magic was done, after careful collation and edition, from numerous Ancient Manuscripts in Hebrew, Latin, and French... New Age/Occult Pages 92

Rubaiyat Of Omar Khayyam *by Edward Fitzgerald* ISBN: *1-59462-332-5* **$13.95**
Edward Fitzgerald, whom the world has already learned, in spite of his own efforts to remain within the shadow of anonymity, to look upon as one of the rarest poets of the century, was born at Bredfield, in Suffolk, on the 31st of March, 1809. He was the third son of John Purcell... Music Pages 172

Ancient Law *by Henry Maine* ISBN: *1-59462-128-4* **$29.95**
The chief object of the following pages is to indicate some of the earliest ideas of mankind, as they are reflected in Ancient Law, and to point out the relation of those ideas to modern thought. Religion/History Pages 452

Far-Away Stories *by William J. Locke* ISBN: *1-59462-129-2* **$19.45**
"Good wine needs no bush, but a collection of mixed vintages does. And this book is just such a collection. Some of the stories I do not want to remain buried for ever in the museum files of dead magazine-numbers an author's not unpardonable vanity..." Fiction Pages 272

Life of David Crockett *by David Crockett* ISBN: *1-59462-250-7* **$27.45**
"Colonel David Crockett was one of the most remarkable men of the times in which he lived. Born in humble life, but gifted with a strong will, an indomitable courage, and unremitting perseverance... Biographies/New Age Pages 424

Lip-Reading *by Edward Nitchie* ISBN: *1-59462-206-X* **$25.95**
Edward B. Nitchie, founder of the New York School for the Hard of Hearing, now the Nitchie School of Lip-Reading, Inc, wrote "LIP-READING Principles and Practice". The development and perfecting of this meritorious work on lip-reading was an undertaking... How-to Pages 400

A Handbook of Suggestive Therapeutics, Applied Hypnotism, Psychic Science ISBN: *1-59462-214-0* **$24.95**
by Henry Munro Health/New Age/Health/Self-help Pages 376

A Doll's House: and Two Other Plays *by Henrik Ibsen* ISBN: *1-59462-112-8* **$19.95**
Henrik Ibsen created this classic when in revolutionary 1848 Rome. Introducing some striking concepts in playwriting for the realist genre, this play has been studied the world over. Fiction/Classics/Plays 308

The Light of Asia *by sir Edwin Arnold* ISBN: *1-59462-204-3* **$13.95**
In this poetic masterpiece, Edwin Arnold describes the life and teachings of Buddha. The man who was to become known as Buddha to the world was born as Prince Gautama of India but he rejected the worldly riches and abandoned the reigns of power when... Religion/History/Biographies Pages 170

The Complete Works of Guy de Maupassant *by Guy de Maupassant* ISBN: *1-59462-157-8* **$16.95**
"For days and days, nights and nights, I had dreamed of that first kiss which was to consecrate our engagement, and I knew not on what spot I should put my lips..." Fiction/Classics Pages 240

The Art of Cross-Examination *by Francis L. Wellman* ISBN: *1-59462-309-0* **$26.95**
Written by a renowned trial lawyer, Wellman imparts his experience and uses case studies to explain how to use psychology to extract desired information through questioning. How-to/Science/Reference Pages 408

Answered or Unanswered? *by Louisa Vaughan* ISBN: *1-59462-248-5* **$10.95**
Miracles of Faith in China Religion Pages 112

The Edinburgh Lectures on Mental Science (1909) *by Thomas* ISBN: *1-59462-008-3* **$11.95**
This book contains the substance of a course of lectures recently given by the writer in the Queen Street Hall, Edinburgh. Its purpose is to indicate the Natural Principles governing the relation between Mental Action and Material Conditions... New Age/Psychology Pages 148

Ayesha *by H. Rider Haggard* ISBN: *1-59462-301-5* **$24.95**
Verily and indeed it is the unexpected that happens! Probably if there was one person upon the earth from whom the Editor of this, and of a certain previous history, did not expect to hear again... Classics Pages 380

Ayala's Angel *by Anthony Trollope* ISBN: *1-59462-352-X* **$29.95**
The two girls were both pretty, but Lucy who was twenty-one who supposed to be simple and comparatively unattractive, whereas Ayala was credited, as her Bombwhat romantic name might show, with poetic charm and a taste for romance. Ayala when her father died was nineteen... Fiction Pages 484

The American Commonwealth *by James Bryce* ISBN: *1-59462-286-8* **$34.45**
An interpretation of American democratic political theory. It examines political mechanics and society from the perspective of Scotsman James Bryce Politics Pages 572

Stories of the Pilgrims *by Margaret P. Pumphrey* ISBN: *1-59462-116-0* **$17.95**
This book explores pilgrims religious oppression in England as well as their escape to Holland and eventual crossing to America on the Mayflower, and their early days in New England... History Pages 268

QTY

The Fasting Cure *by Sinclair Upton* ISBN: *1-59462-222-1* **$13.95**
In the Cosmopolitan Magazine for May, 1910, and in the Contemporary Review (London) for April, 1910, I published an article dealing with my experiences in fasting. I have written a great many magazine articles, but never one which attracted so much attention... New Age/Self Help/Health Pages 164

Hebrew Astrology *by Sepharial* ISBN: *1-59462-308-2* **$13.45**
In these days of advanced thinking it is a matter of common observation that we have left many of the old landmarks behind and that we are now pressing forward to greater heights and to a wider horizon than that which represented the mind-content of our progenitors... Astrology Pages 144

Thought Vibration or The Law of Attraction in the Thought World ISBN: *1-59462-127-6* **$12.95**
by William Walker Atkinson Psychology/Religion Pages 144

Optimism *by Helen Keller* ISBN: *1-59462-108-X* **$15.95**
Helen Keller was blind, deaf, and mute since 19 months old, yet famously learned how to overcome these handicaps, communicate with the world, and spread her lectures promoting optimism. An inspiring read for everyone... Biographies/Inspirational Pages 84

Sara Crewe *by Frances Burnett* ISBN: *1-59462-360-0* **$9.45**
In the first place, Miss Minchin lived in London. Her home was a large, dull, tall one, in a large, dull square, where all the houses were alike, and all the sparrows were alike, and where all the door-knockers made the same heavy sound... Childrens/Classic Pages 88

The Autobiography of Benjamin Franklin *by Benjamin Franklin* ISBN: *1-59462-135-7* **$24.95**
The Autobiography of Benjamin Franklin has probably been more extensively read than any other American historical work, and no other book of its kind has had such ups and downs of fortune. Franklin lived for many years in England, where he was agent... Biographies/History Pages 332

Name	
Email	
Telephone	
Address	
City, State ZIP	

☐ **Credit Card**   ☐ **Check / Money Order**

Credit Card Number	
Expiration Date	
Signature	

Please Mail to: Book Jungle
PO Box 2226
Champaign, IL 61825
or Fax to: 630-214-0564